My Weird School graphic Novel

SchooL

Ella MeNtRY SchooL
"Learn...or else"

Get a Grip! We're on a Trip!

New York Times Bestselling Author
Dan Gutman

Pictures by
Jim Paillot

HARPER alley

An Imprint of HarperCollinsPublishers

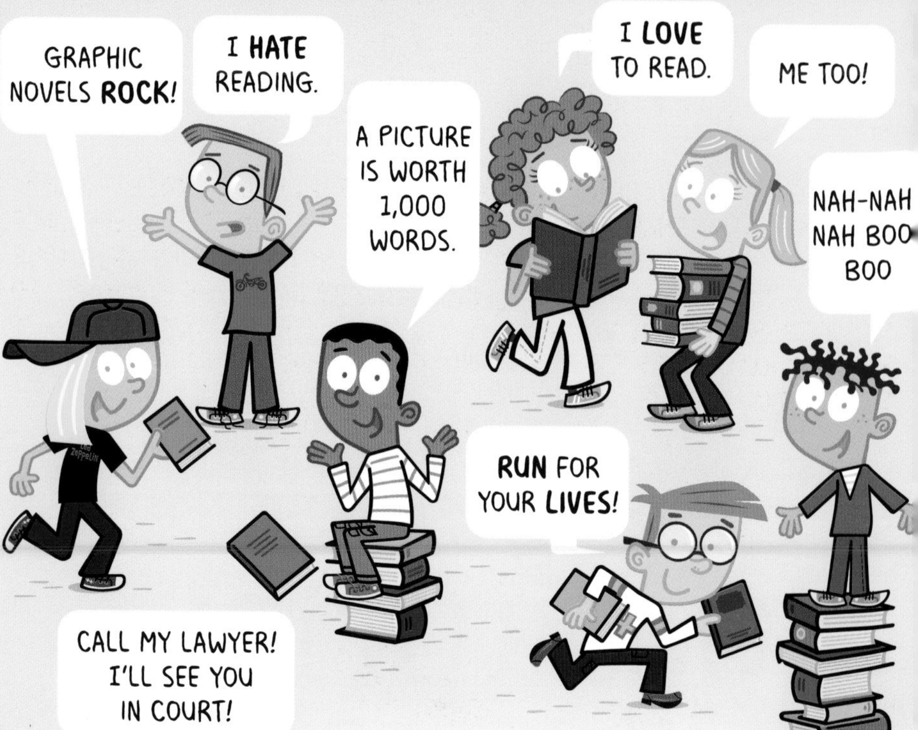

GRAPHIC NOVELS ROCK!
I HATE READING.
A PICTURE IS WORTH 1,000 WORDS.
I LOVE TO READ.
ME TOO!
NAH-NAH NAH BOO BOO
RUN FOR YOUR LIVES!

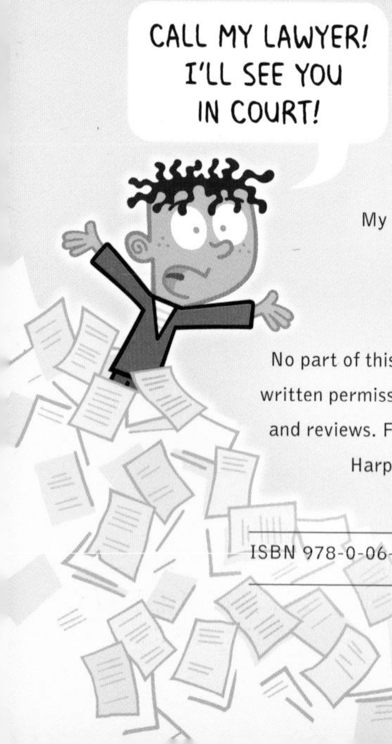

CALL MY LAWYER! I'LL SEE YOU IN COURT!

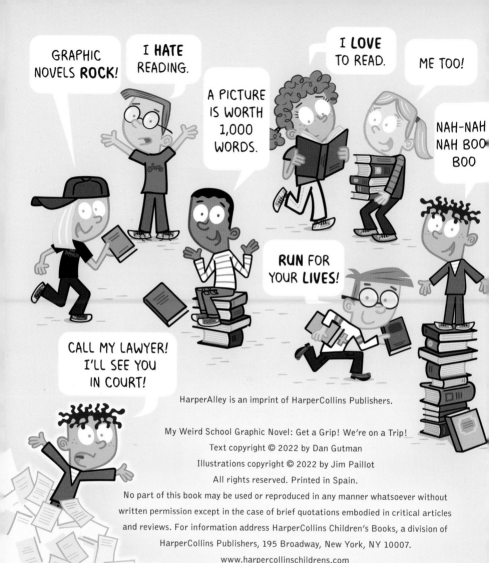

HarperAlley is an imprint of HarperCollins Publishers.

ISBN 978-0-06-305448-6 (pbk. bdg.) — ISBN 978-0-06-305452-3 (hardcover bdg.)

Typography by Martha Maynard
22 23 24 25 EP 10 9 8 7 6 5 4 3 2
❖
First Edition

Warning!

THIS BOOK CONTAINS SCENES OF GRAPHIC VIOLINS, AS WELL AS OTHER MUSICAL INSTRUMENTS. ALL CHARACTERS IN THIS BOOK ARE FICTIONAL. ANY RESEMBLANCE TO ACTUAL PERSONS, LIVING OR DEAD, IS ENTIRELY INTENTIONAL. ENTER AT YOUR OWN RISK. NO LIFEGUARD ON DUTY. HA-HA! HE SAID DUTY. YOU'RE ALLOWED TO SAY DUTY, BUT YOU'RE NOT SUPPOSED TO SAY DOODY. NOBODY KNOWS WHY. THEY SHOULD DEFINITELY HAVE NEW WORDS FOR DUTY AND DOODY THAT DON'T SOUND SO MUCH ALIKE.

OH, IT DOESN'T MATTER. YOU'RE PROBABLY NOT EVEN READING THIS ANYWAY. WHO WANTS TO READ A BUNCH OF WORDS SCRUNCHED TOGETHER THAT ARE ALL CAPITAL LETTERS? WORDS ARE FOR NERDS. BRING ON THE PICTURES.

To all the weird kids (and grown-ups) out there who are creative, original, and brave enough to be themselves

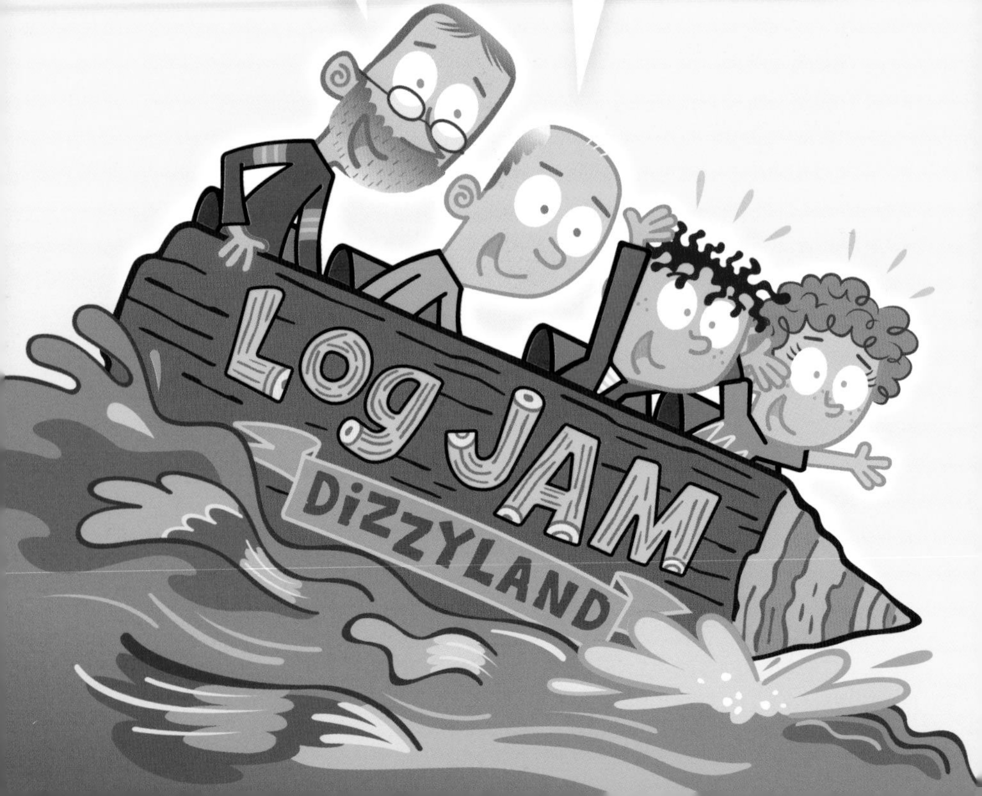
Log JAM
DiZZYLAND

Table of Contents*

Chapter 1: Stuff   1

Chapter 2: More Stuff   15

Chapter 3: Even More Stuff   27

Chapter 4: A Ridorkulous Amount of Stuff   45

Chapter 5: Too Much Stuff   61

Chapter 6: We Should Really Get Rid   91

of Some of This Stuff!

*I'M **CONTENT** TO SIT ON A **TABLE**.

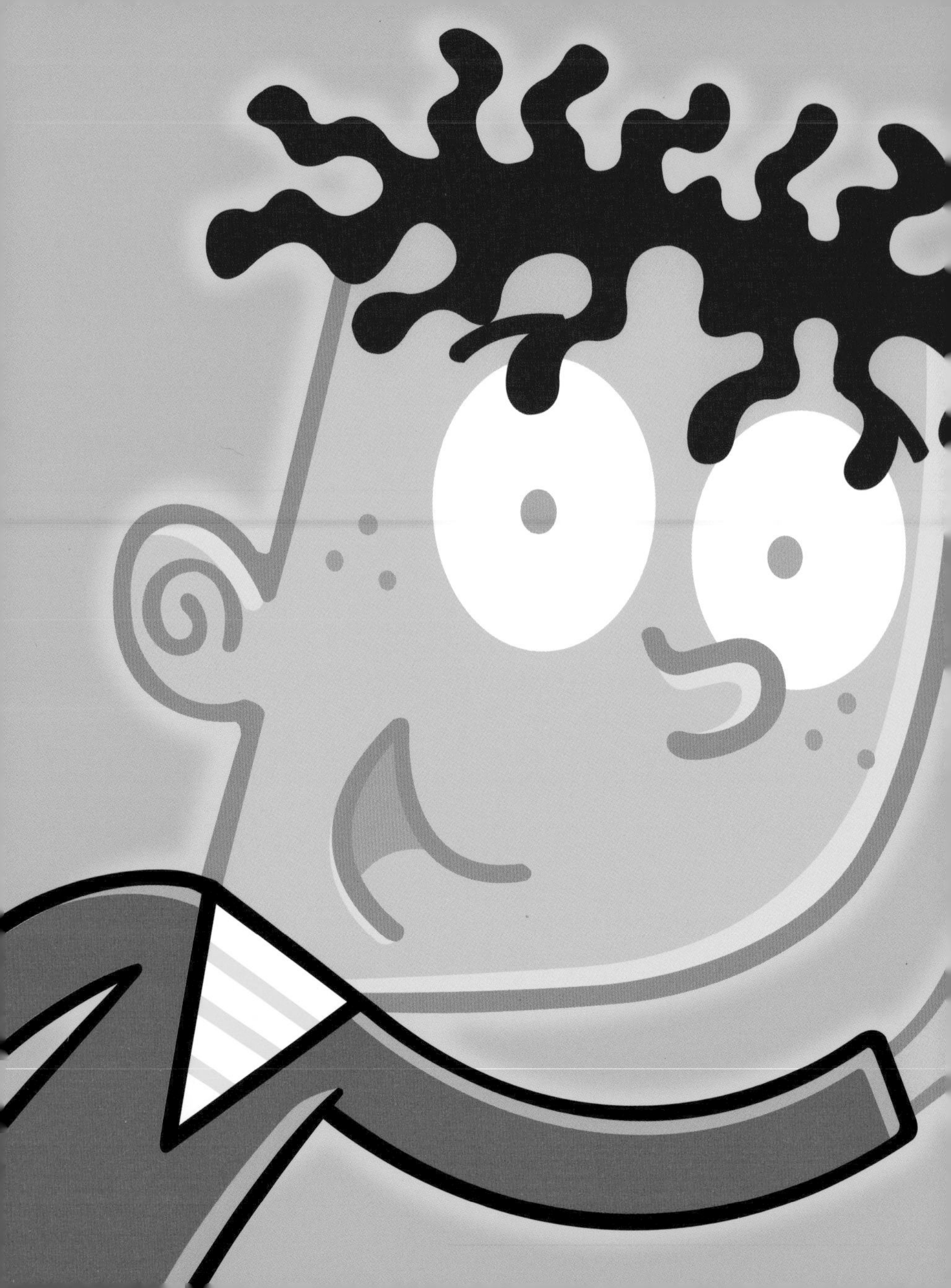

CHAPTER 1

Stuff

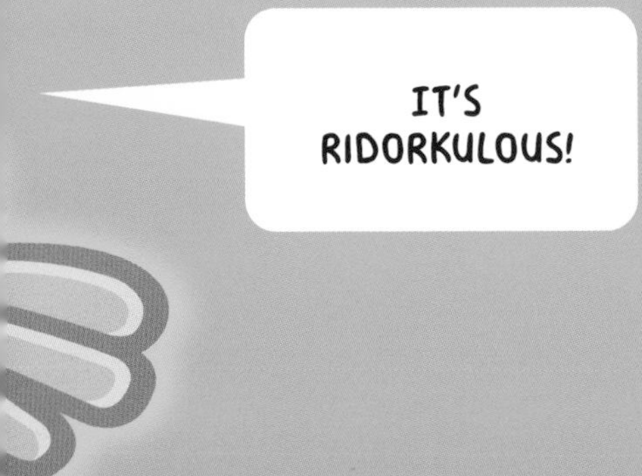
IT'S RIDORKULOUS!

A short time ago in a school system not far away . . .

Episode I
The Big Jerk

IT IS A DARK TIME. SINISTER FORCES HAVE CAUSED UNREST IN THE UNIVERSE. UNDER THE LEADERSHIP OF THE EVIL AND EXTREMELY ANNOYING DR. CARBLES—THE PRESIDENT OF THE BOARD OF EDUCATION—TURMOIL* HAS ENGULFED* ELLA MENTRY SCHOOL. CARBLES AND HIS MERCILESS LEGIONS HAVE TRAVELED A MILLION HUNDRED LIGHT-YEARS TO ONCE AND FOR ALL CONFRONT MR. KLUTZ, HIS LONG-TIME ADVERSARY* AND BENEVOLENT PRINCIPAL. KLUTZ AND THE BRAVE RESISTANCE TEACHERS HAVE STRUGGLED TO MAINTAIN PEACE AND ORDER IN THE SCHOOL. BUT EVIL IS EVERYWHERE, AND TOILETS HAVE OVERFLOWED. MR. KLUTZ HAS MOUNTED A DESPERATE MISSION TO RESCUE THE BESIEGED SCHOOL, SAVE THE STUDENTS AND TEACHERS, AND RESTORE PEACE AND EDUCATION TO THE THIRD GRADE. LITTLE DOES HE KNOW THAT THE DIABOLICAL DR. CARBLES HAS DEVISED A PLAN THAT WILL SPELL CERTAIN DOOM FOR THE SMALL BAND OF TEACHERS AND STAFF STRUGGLING TO STAND AGAINST TYRANNY* AND RESTORE READING, WRITING, AND ARITHMETIC TO THE SCHOOL SYSTEM. IN AN ALARMING CHAIN OF EVENTS, DR. CARBLES HAS DEVISED A SECRET WEAPON THAT WILL HAVE THE CAPABILITY TO DESTROY AN ENTIRE ELEMENTARY SCHOOL. HE IS RUTHLESS AND DETERMINED TO VANQUISH ANY THREAT TO HIS POWER. HE WILL NOT REST UNTIL MR. KLUTZ AND ELLA MENTRY SCHOOL ARE NO MORE.

(*Oooh, big words! You must be a real smarty-pants.)

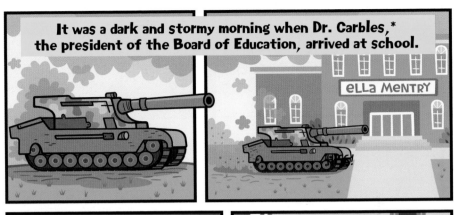

It was a dark and stormy morning when Dr. Carbles,*
the president of the Board of Education, arrived at school.
eLLa MeNTRY
Boo! HiSS!
(*Designated bad guy.)
GASP!

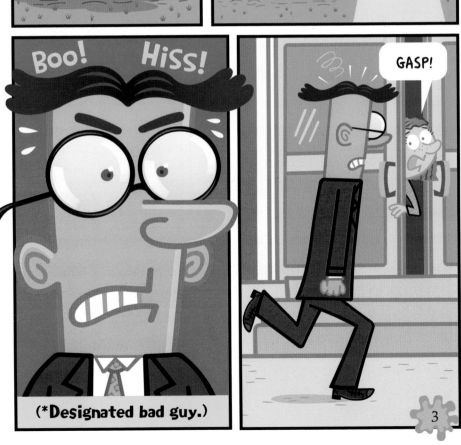

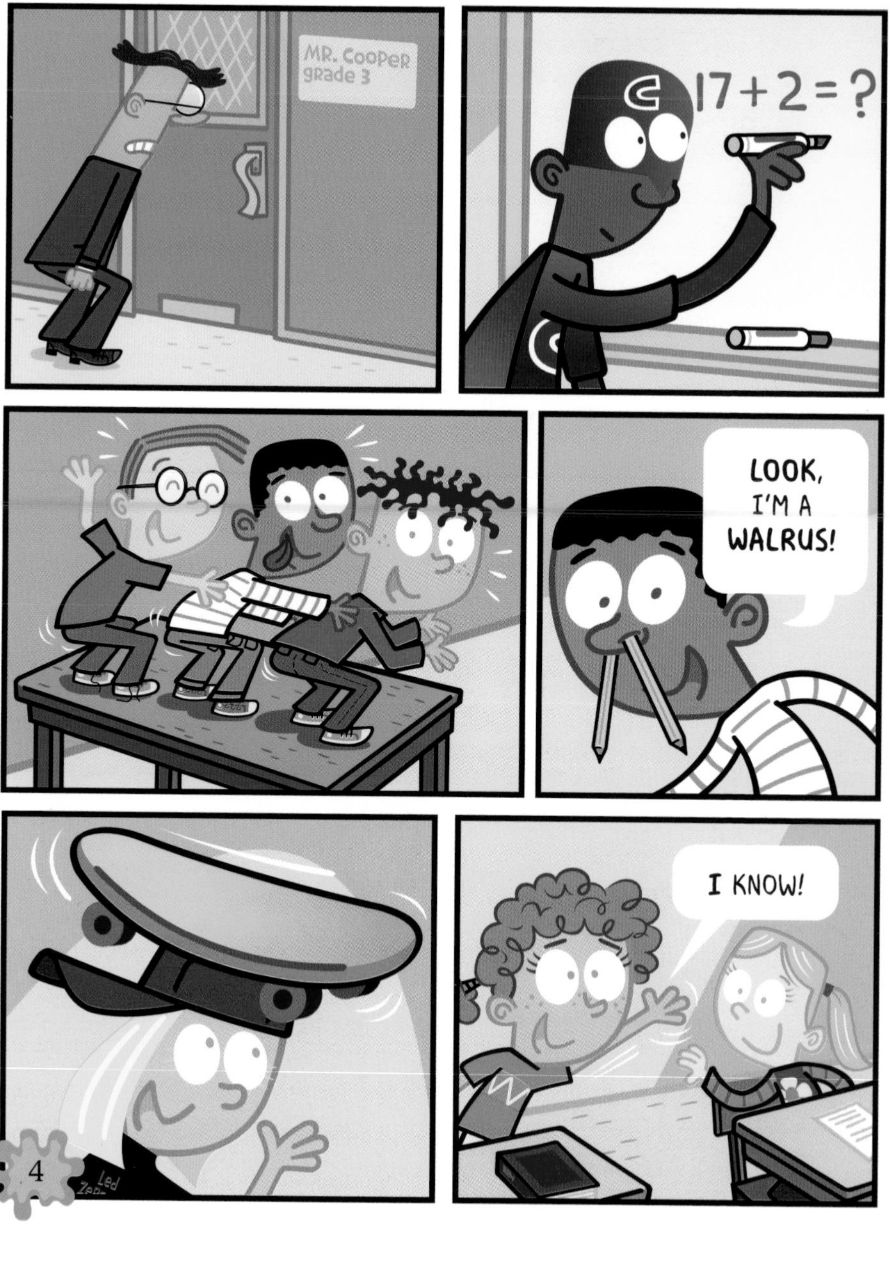
MR. COOPER
grade 3
17 + 2 = ?
LOOK, I'M A WALRUS!
I KNOW!

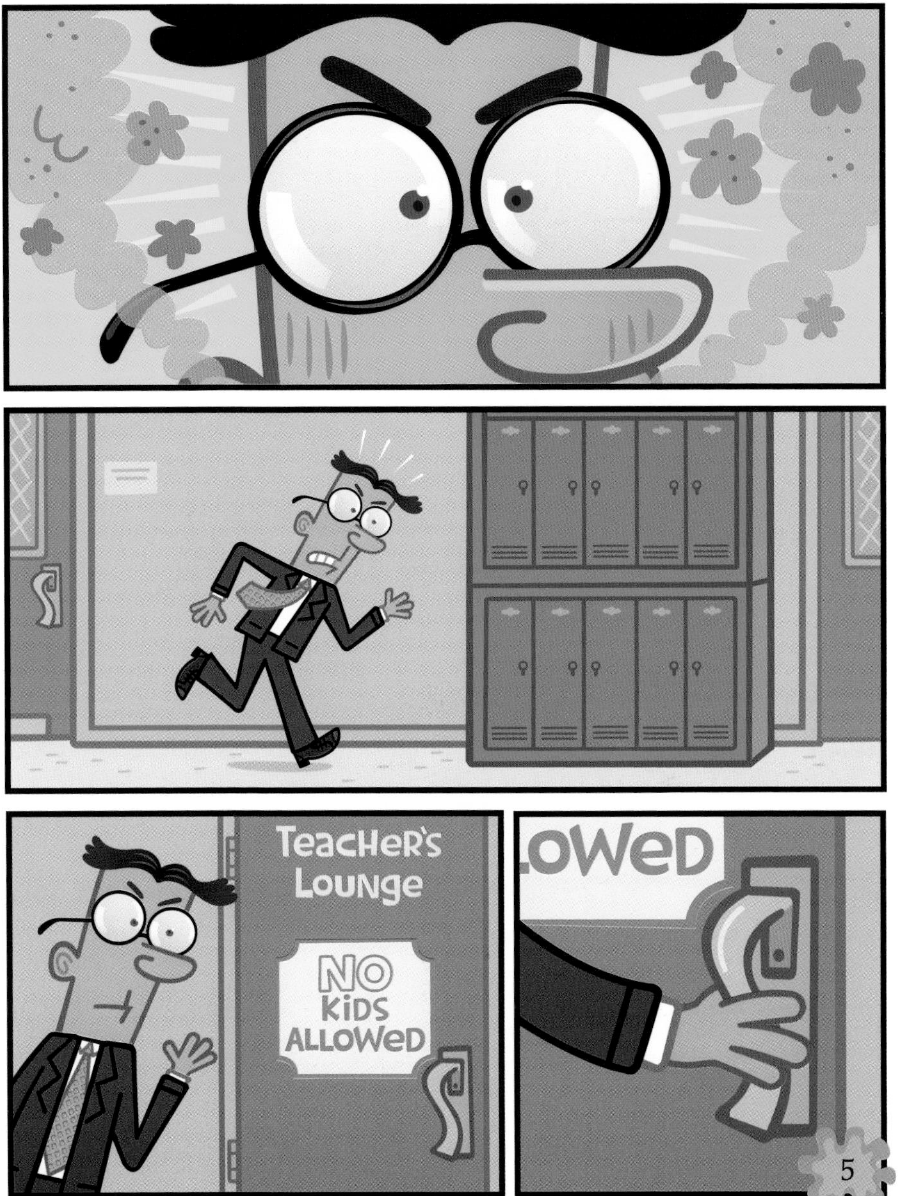

TEACHER'S LOUNGE
NO KIDS ALLOWED
LOWED

Inside the Teachers' Lounge

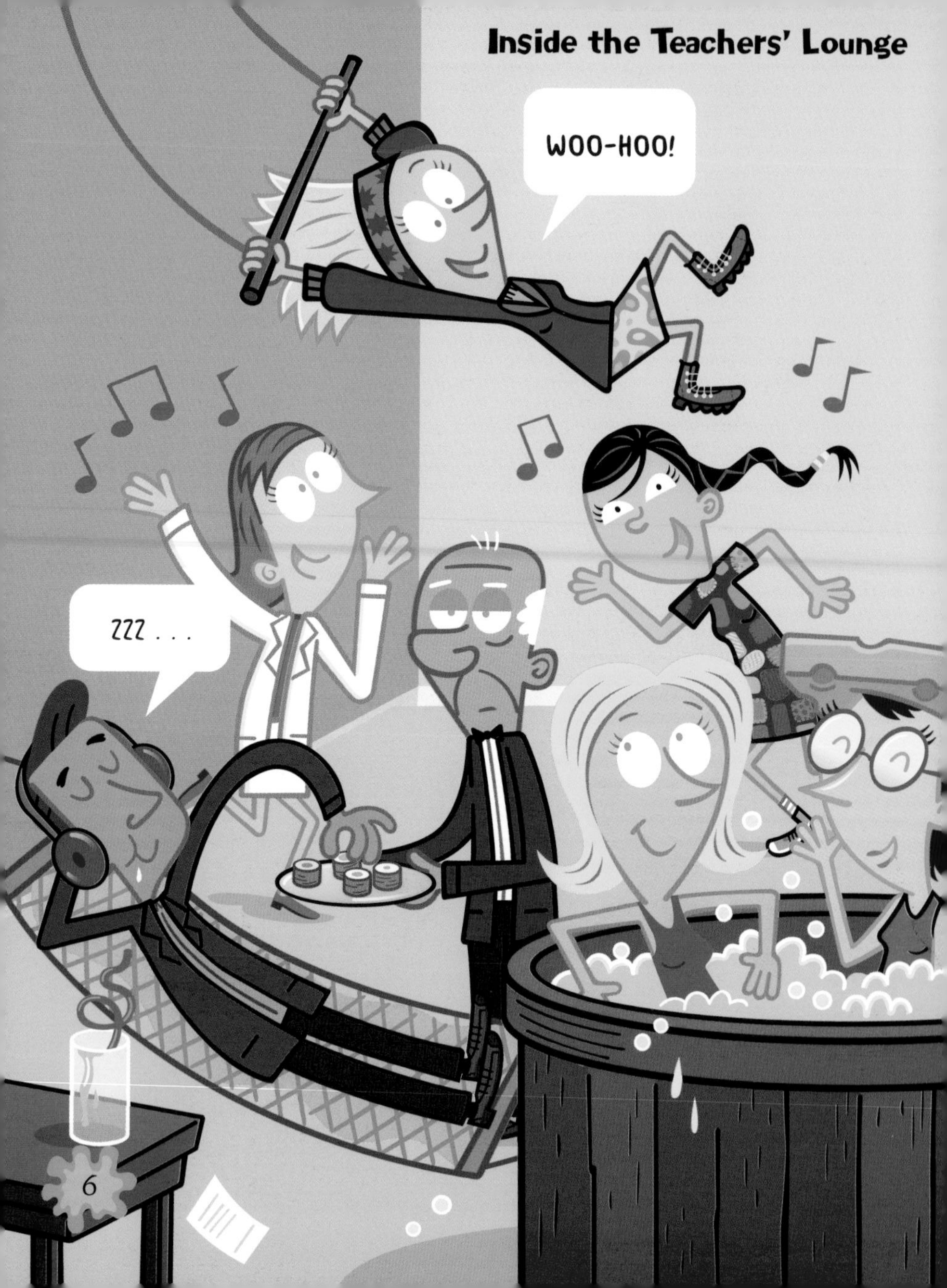
WOO-HOO!
ZZZ . . .

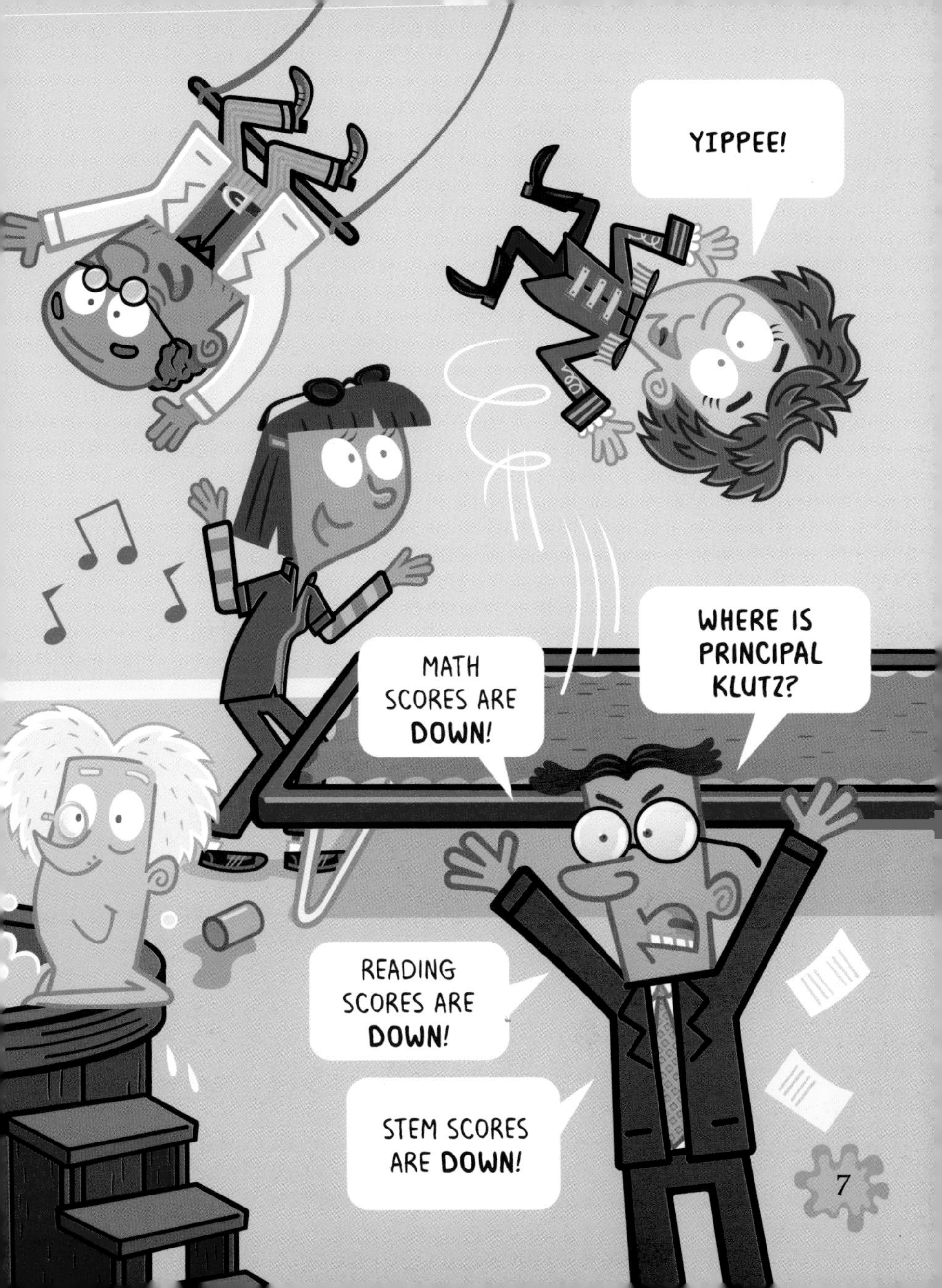
YIPPEE!
WHERE IS PRINCIPAL KLUTZ?
MATH SCORES ARE DOWN!
READING SCORES ARE DOWN!
STEM SCORES ARE DOWN!

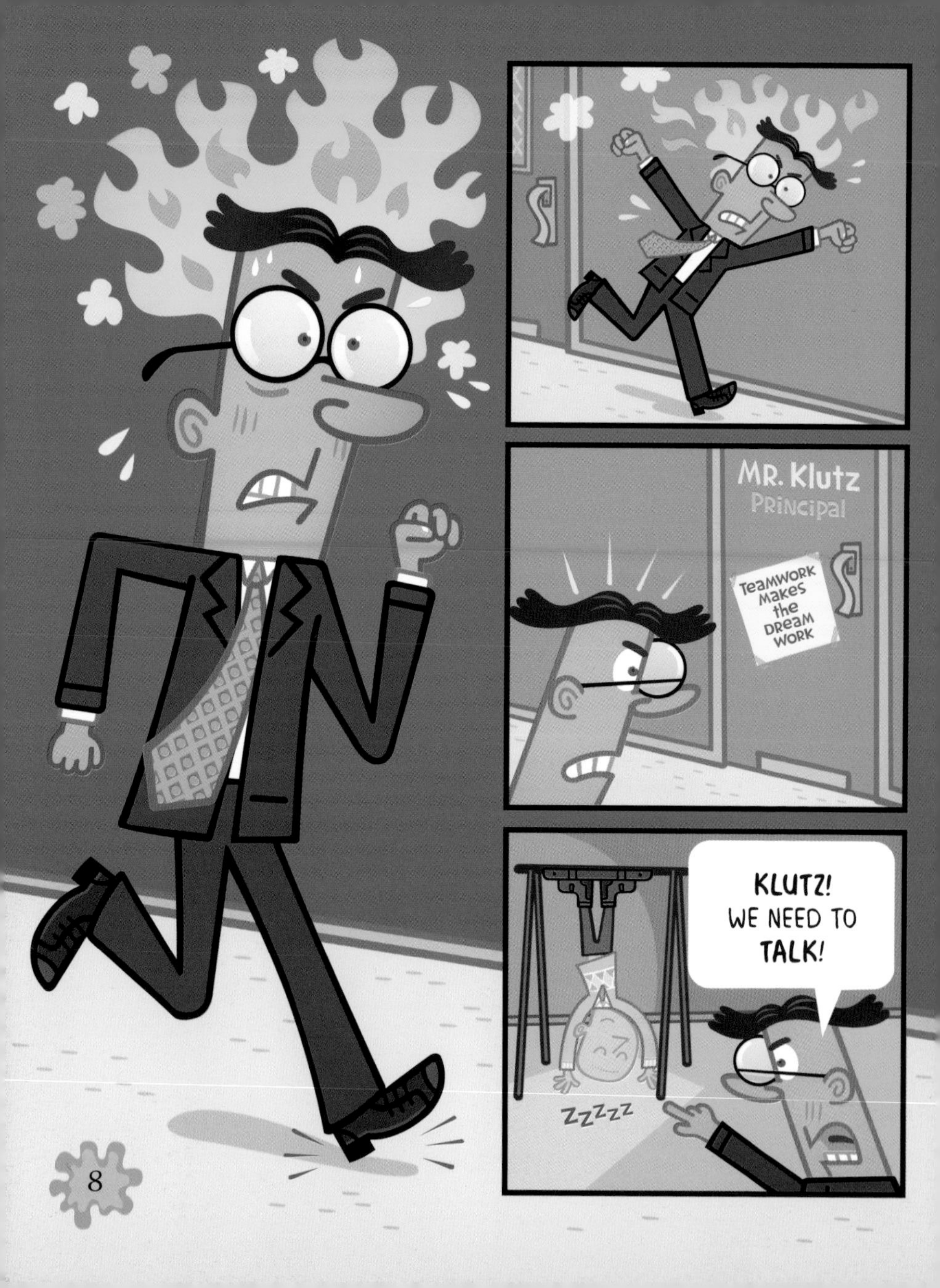
MR. Klutz
PRINCIPAL
TEAMWORK MAKES THE DREAM WORK
KLUTZ! WE NEED TO TALK!
ZZZZZ

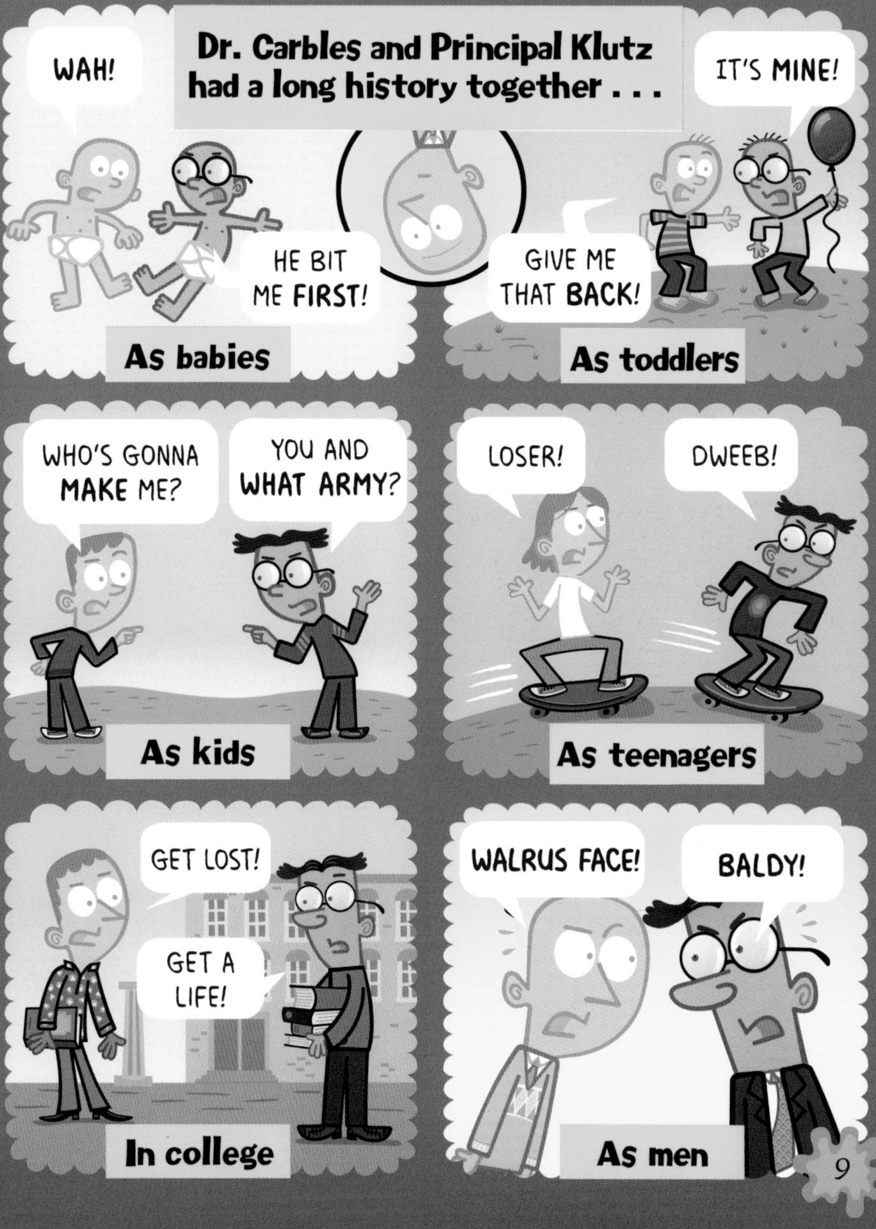
Dr. Carbles and Principal Klutz had a long history together . . .
WAH!
HE BIT ME FIRST!
As babies
IT'S MINE!
GIVE ME THAT BACK!
As toddlers
WHO'S GONNA MAKE ME?
YOU AND WHAT ARMY?
As kids
LOSER!
DWEEB!
As teenagers
GET LOST!
GET A LIFE!
In college
WALRUS FACE!
BALDY!
As men

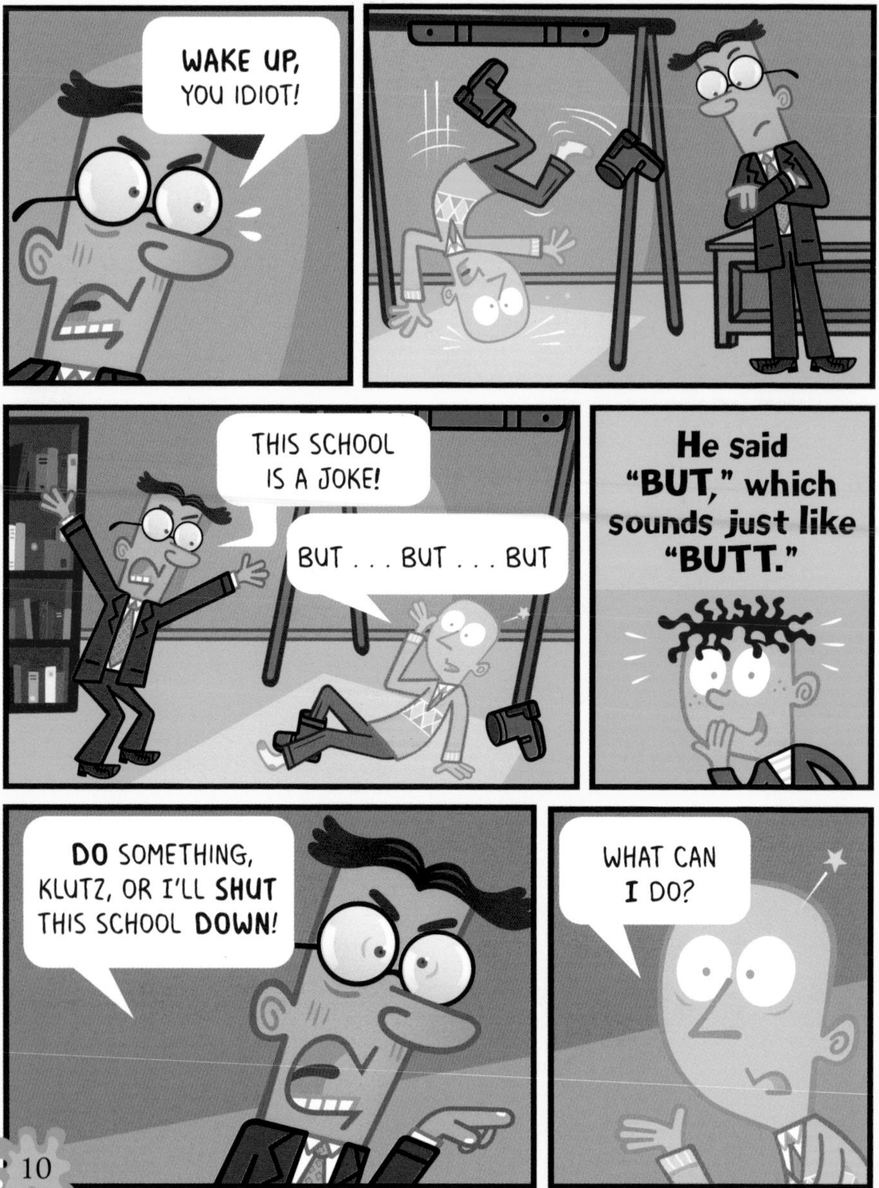
WAKE UP,
YOU IDIOT!
THIS SCHOOL
IS A JOKE!
BUT . . . BUT . . . BUT
He said
"BUT," which
sounds just like
"BUTT."
DO SOMETHING,
KLUTZ, OR I'LL SHUT
THIS SCHOOL DOWN!
WHAT CAN
I DO?

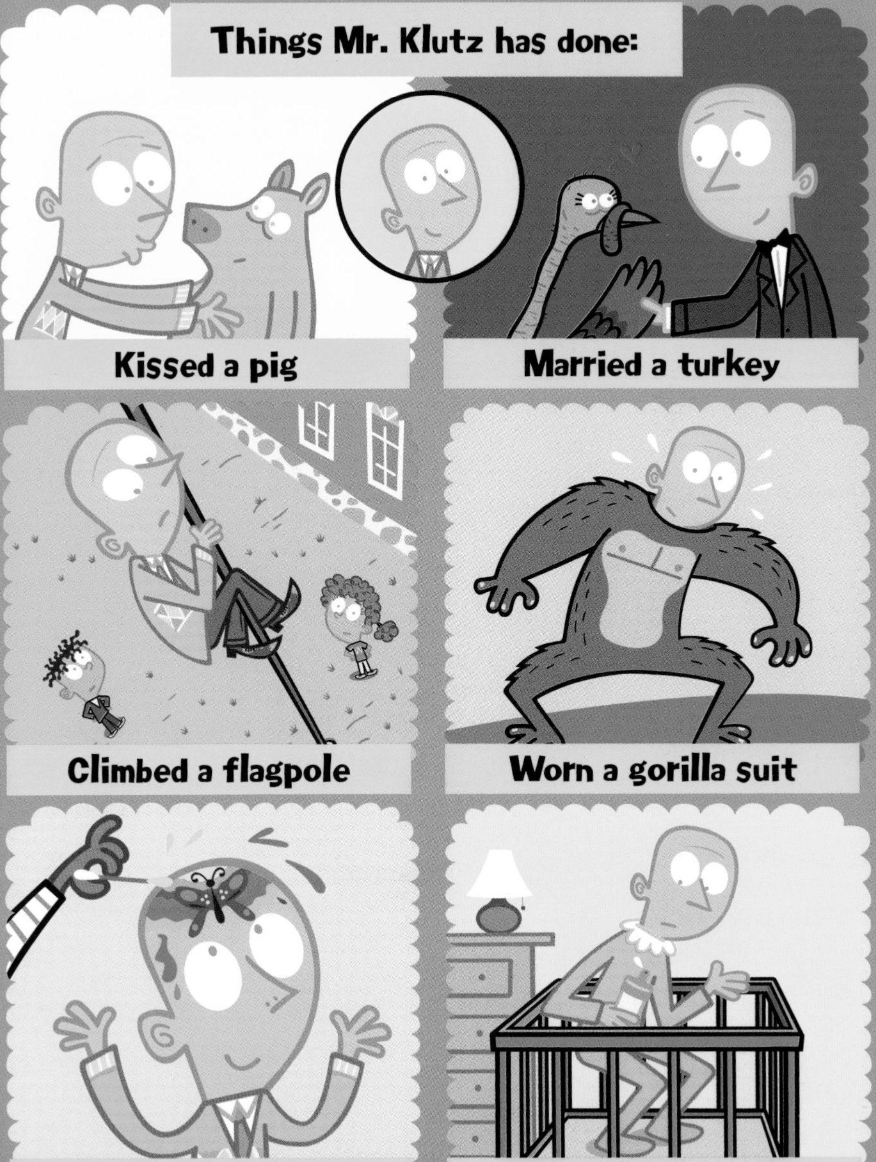
Things Mr. Klutz has done:
Kissed a pig
Married a turkey
Climbed a flagpole
Worn a gorilla suit
Gotten his head painted
Dressed like a baby

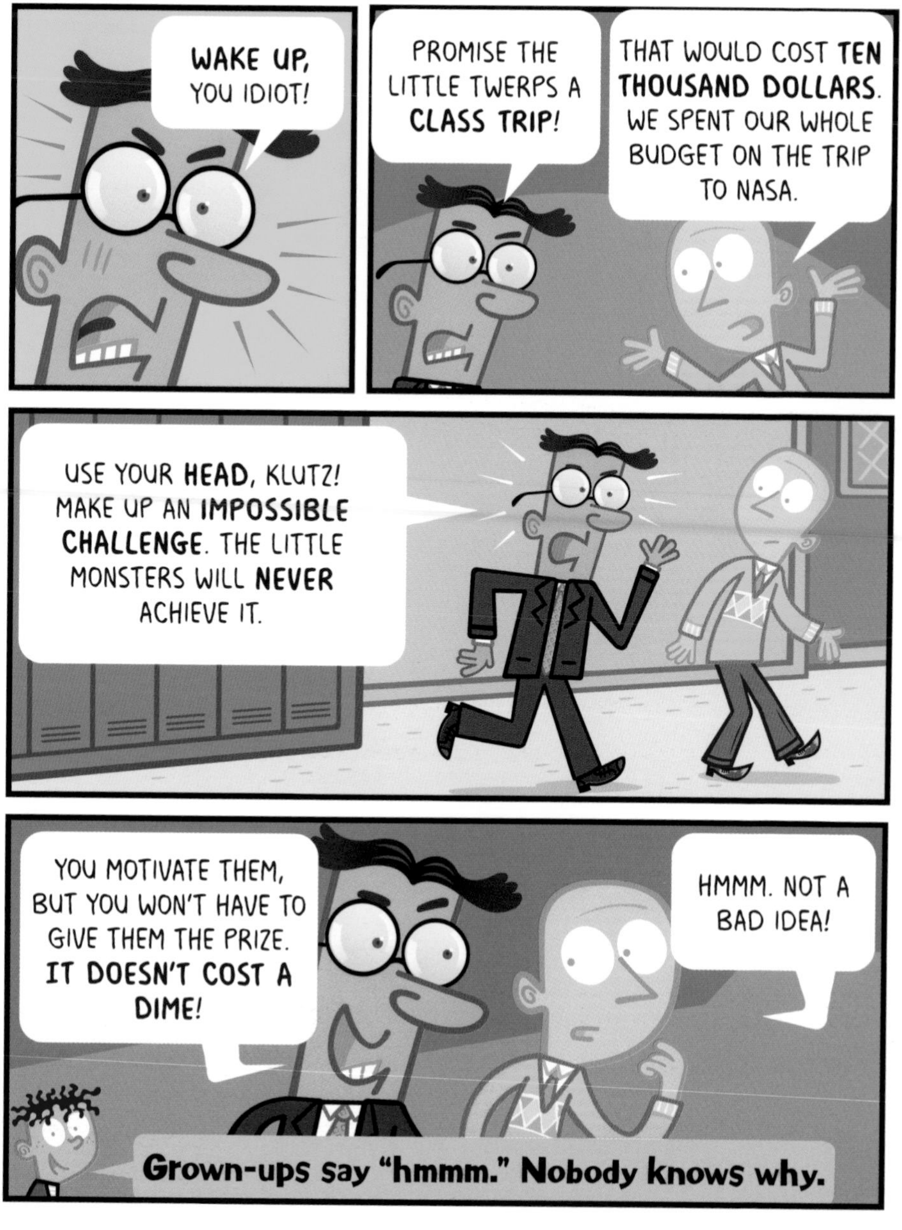

WAKE UP, YOU IDIOT!
PROMISE THE LITTLE TWERPS A CLASS TRIP!
THAT WOULD COST TEN THOUSAND DOLLARS. WE SPENT OUR WHOLE BUDGET ON THE TRIP TO NASA.
USE YOUR HEAD, KLUTZ! MAKE UP AN IMPOSSIBLE CHALLENGE. THE LITTLE MONSTERS WILL NEVER ACHIEVE IT.
YOU MOTIVATE THEM, BUT YOU WON'T HAVE TO GIVE THEM THE PRIZE. IT DOESN'T COST A DIME!
HMMM. NOT A BAD IDEA!
Grown-ups say “hmmm.” Nobody knows why.

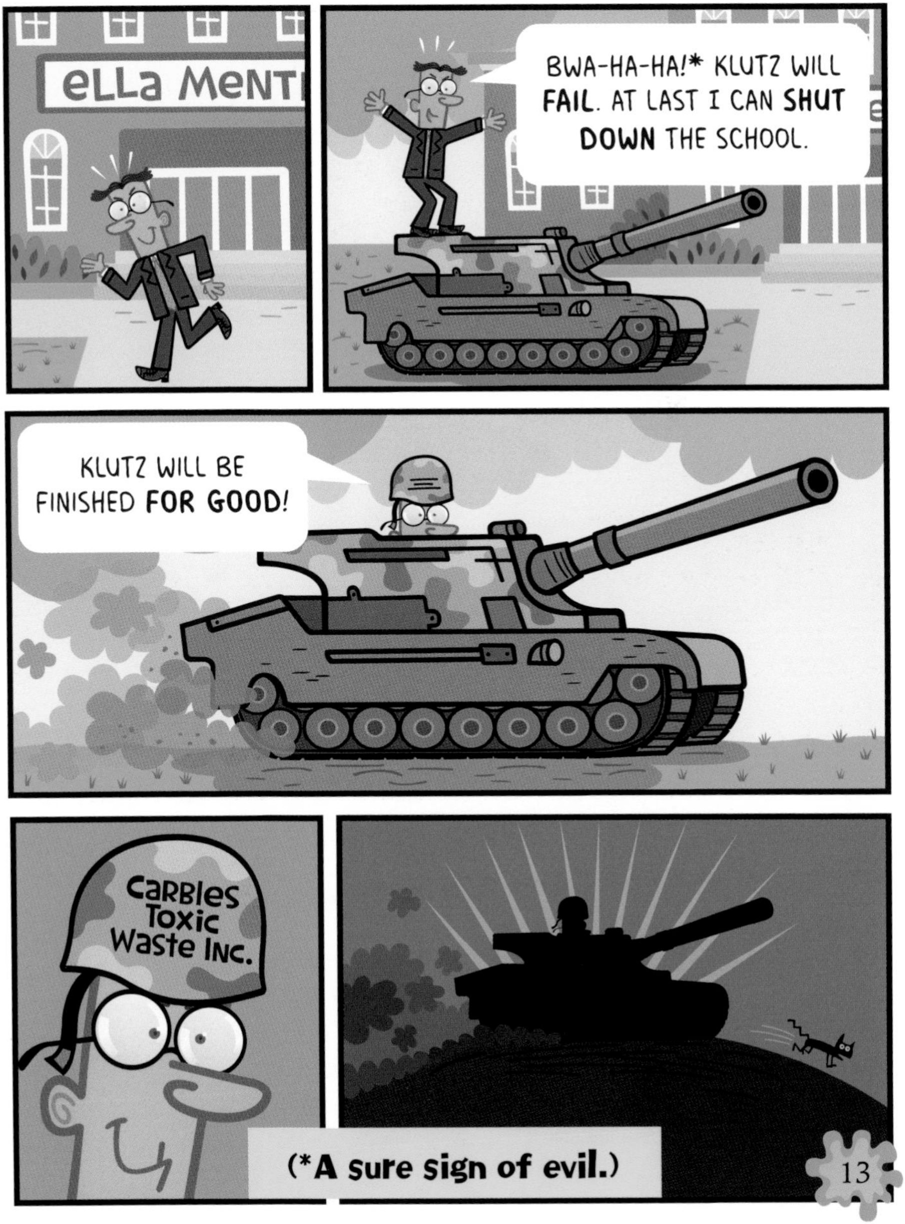
eLLa MENT
BWA-HA-HA!* KLUTZ WILL FAIL. AT LAST I CAN SHUT DOWN THE SCHOOL.
KLUTZ WILL BE FINISHED FOR GOOD!
CaRBles Toxic Waste Inc.
(*A sure sign of evil.)

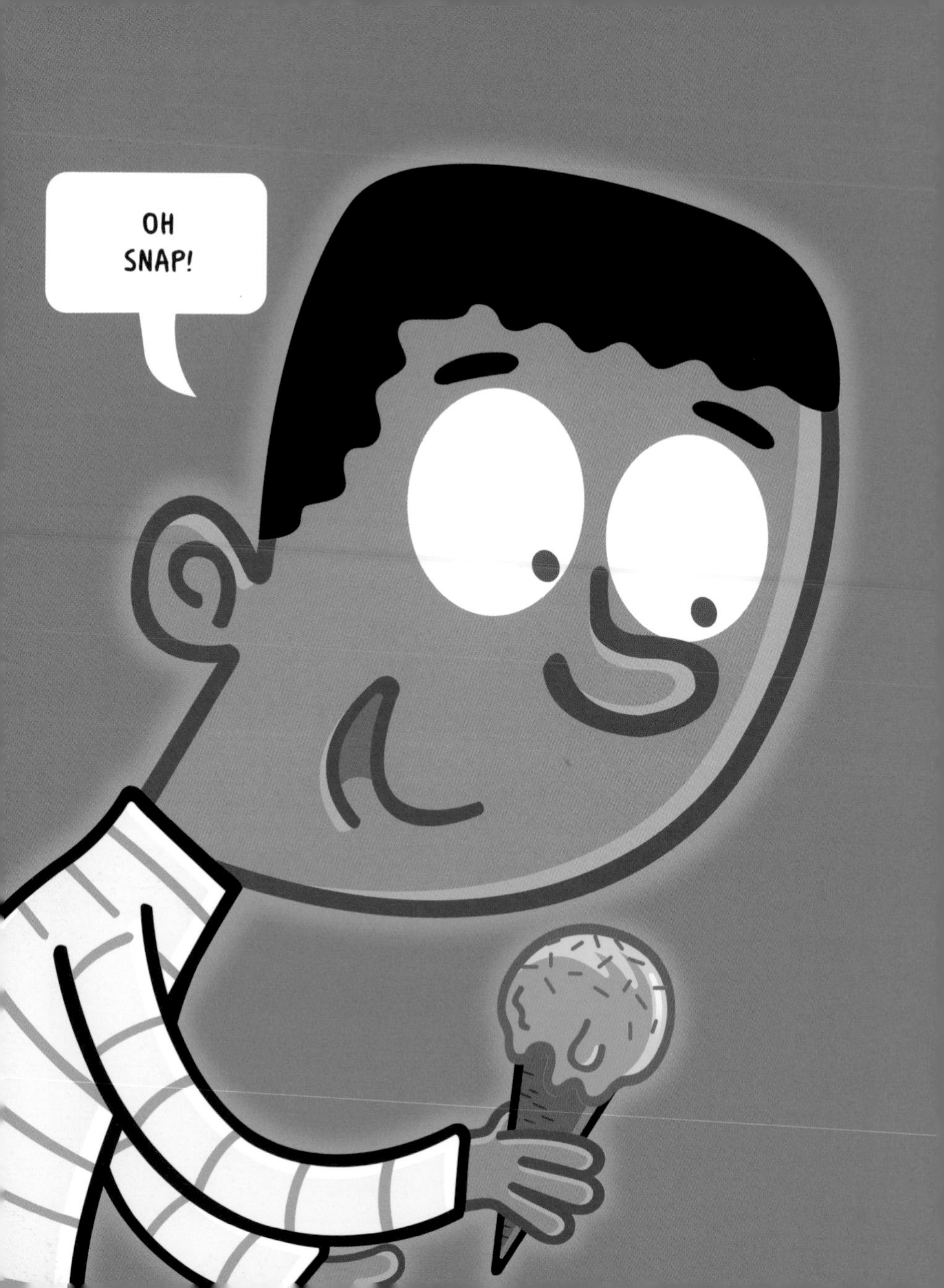
OH SNAP!

CHAPTER 2

More Stuff

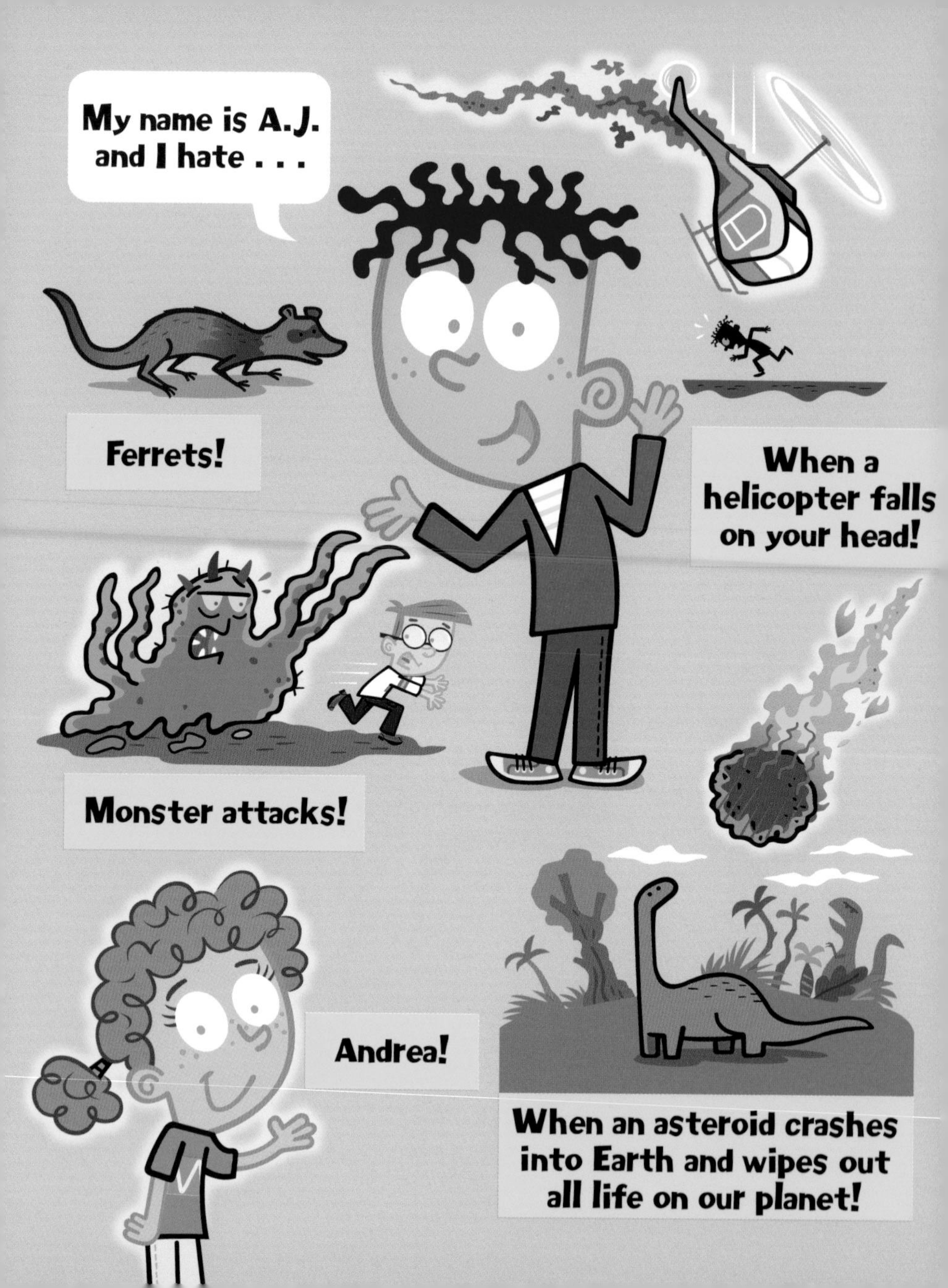
My name is A.J. and I hate . . .
Ferrets!
When a helicopter falls on your head!
Monster attacks!
Andrea!
When an asteroid crashes into Earth and wipes out all life on our planet!

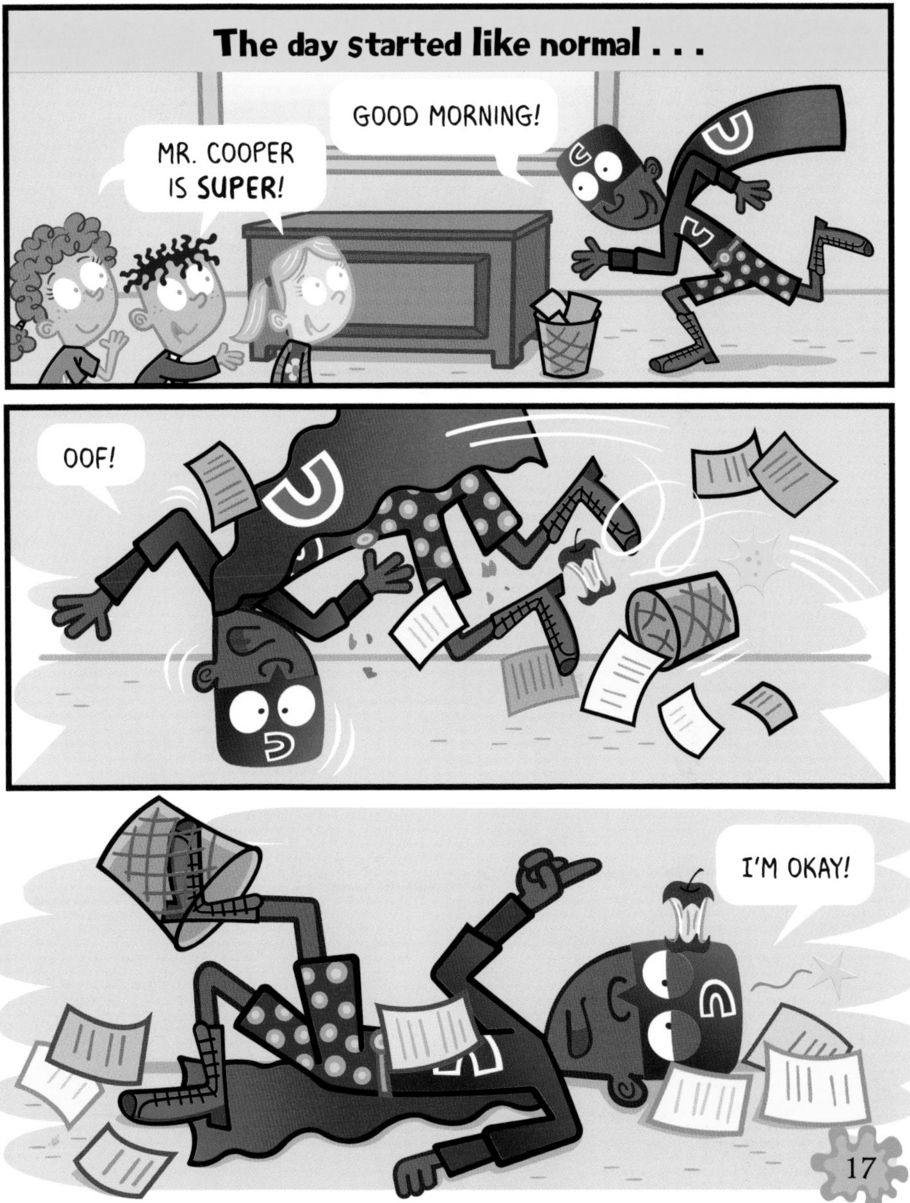
The day started like normal . . .
MR. COOPER IS SUPER!
GOOD MORNING!
OOF!
I'M OKAY!

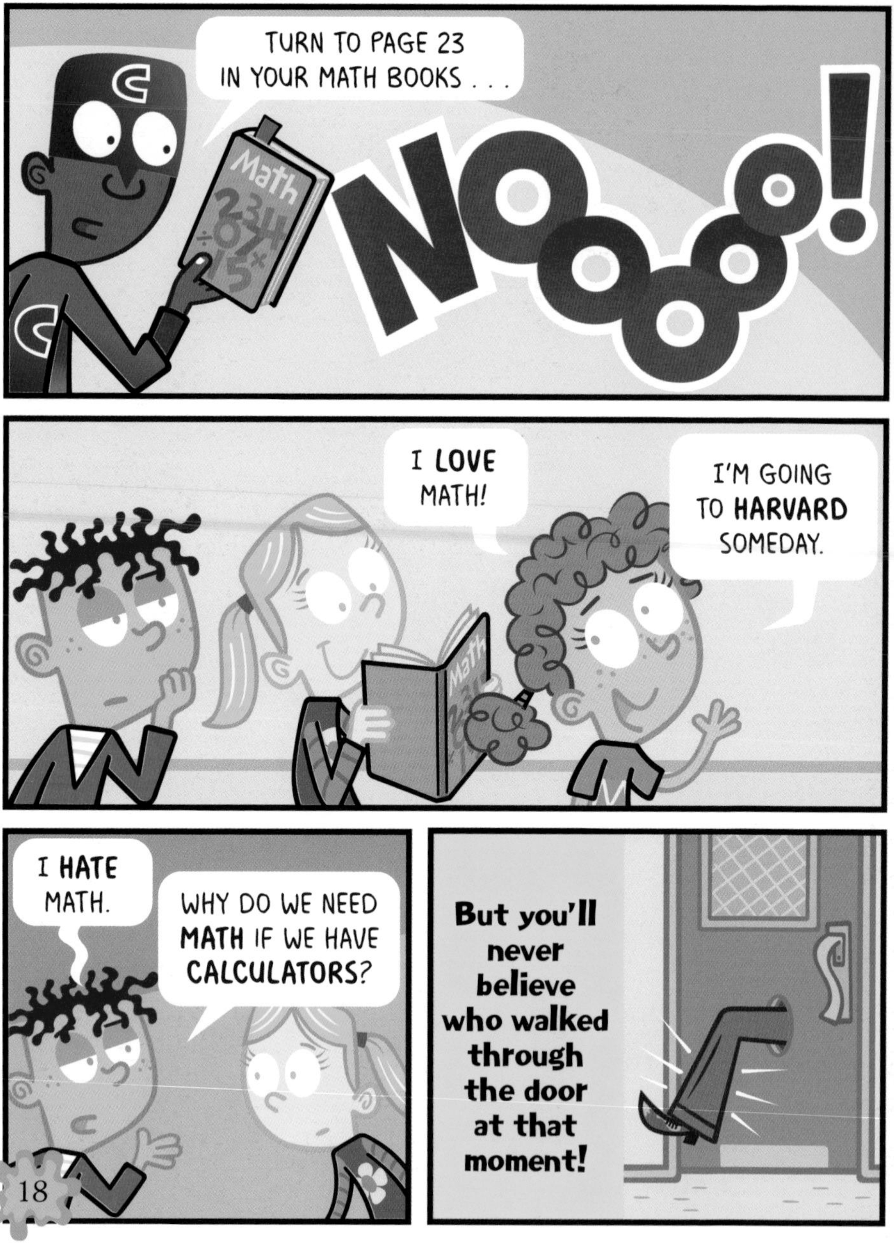
TURN TO PAGE 23 IN YOUR MATH BOOKS . . .
Math
NOOOOOO!
I **LOVE** MATH!
I'M GOING TO **HARVARD** SOMEDAY.
Math
I **HATE** MATH.
WHY DO WE NEED **MATH** IF WE HAVE **CALCULATORS**?
But you'll never believe who walked through the door at that moment!

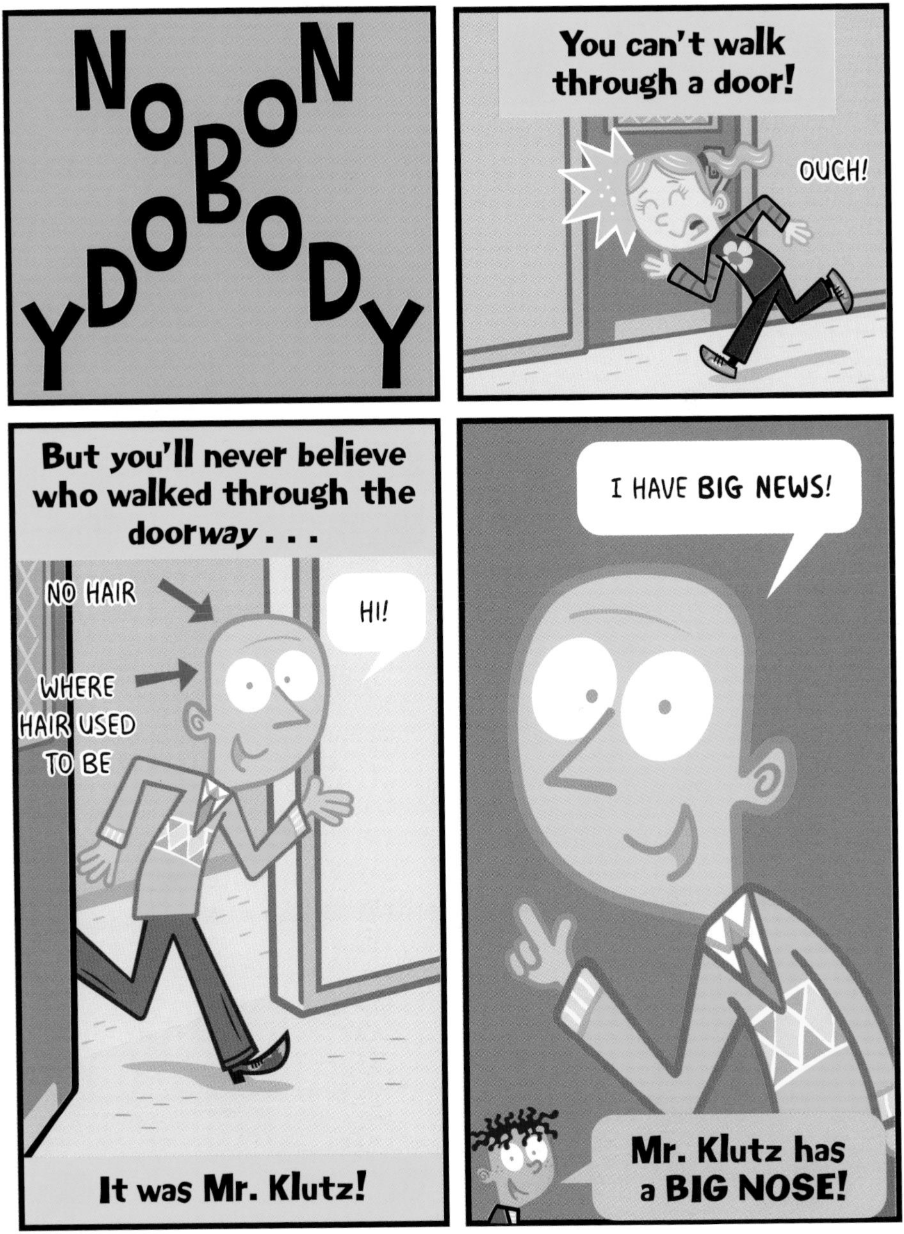
NOBODY
YDOBODY
You can't walk through a door!
OUCH!
But you'll never believe who walked through the doorway . . .
NO HAIR
WHERE HAIR USED TO BE
HI!
It was Mr. Klutz!
I HAVE BIG NEWS!
Mr. Klutz has a BIG NOSE!

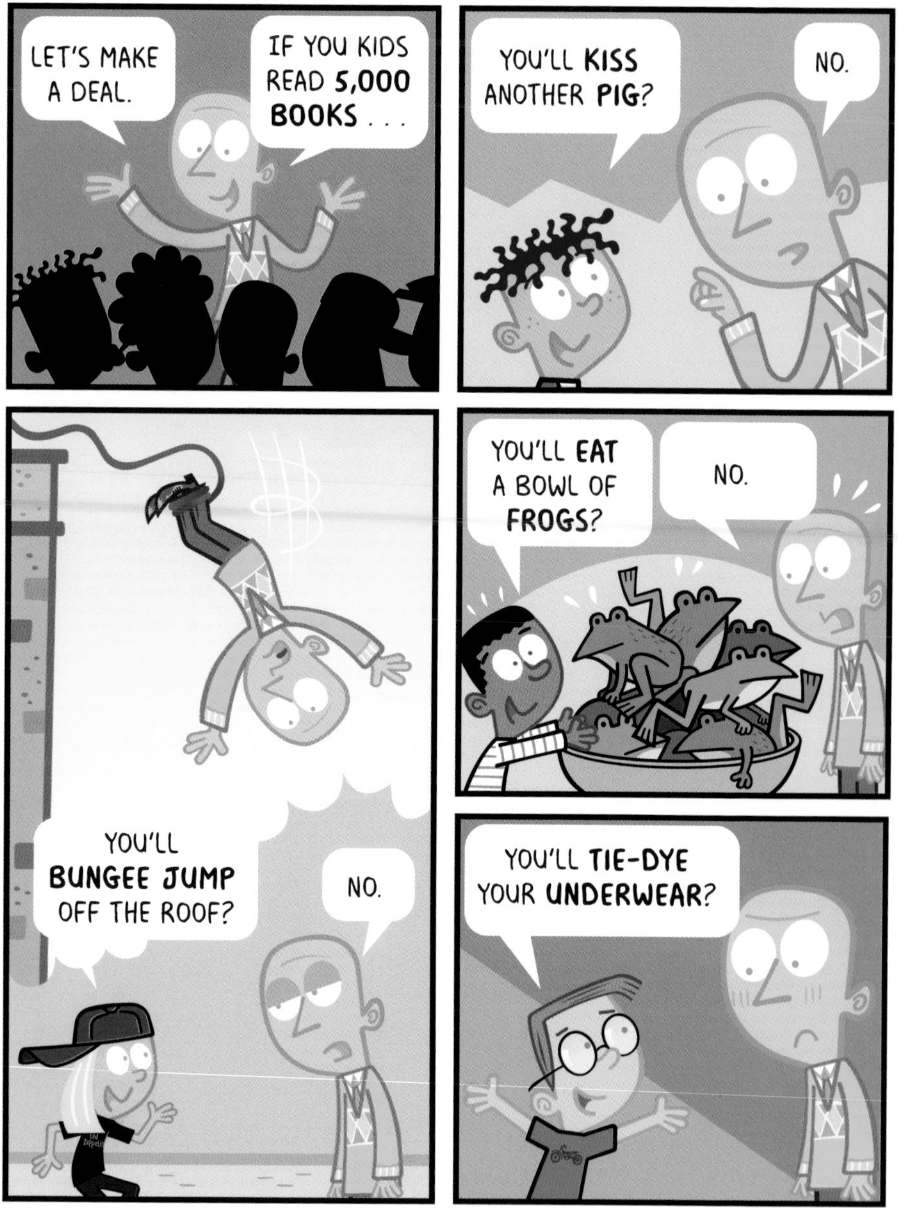
LET'S MAKE A DEAL.
IF YOU KIDS READ 5,000 BOOKS . . .
YOU'LL KISS ANOTHER PIG?
NO.
YOU'LL BUNGEE JUMP OFF THE ROOF?
NO.
YOU'LL EAT A BOWL OF FROGS?
NO.
YOU'LL TIE-DYE YOUR UNDERWEAR?

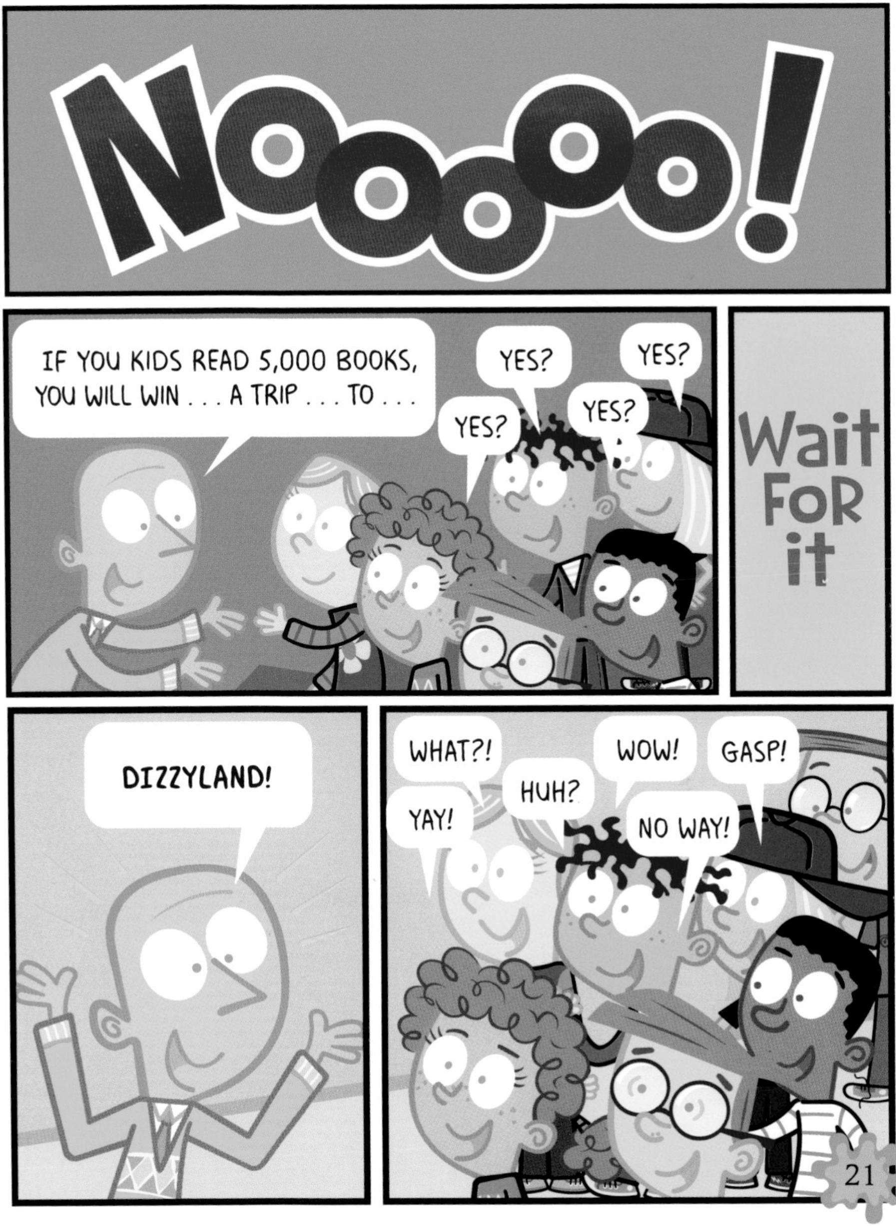
NOOOOO!
IF YOU KIDS READ 5,000 BOOKS, YOU WILL WIN . . . A TRIP . . . TO . . .
YES?
YES?
YES?
YES?
Wait For it
DIZZYLAND!
WHAT?!
YAY!
HUH?
WOW!
NO WAY!
GASP!

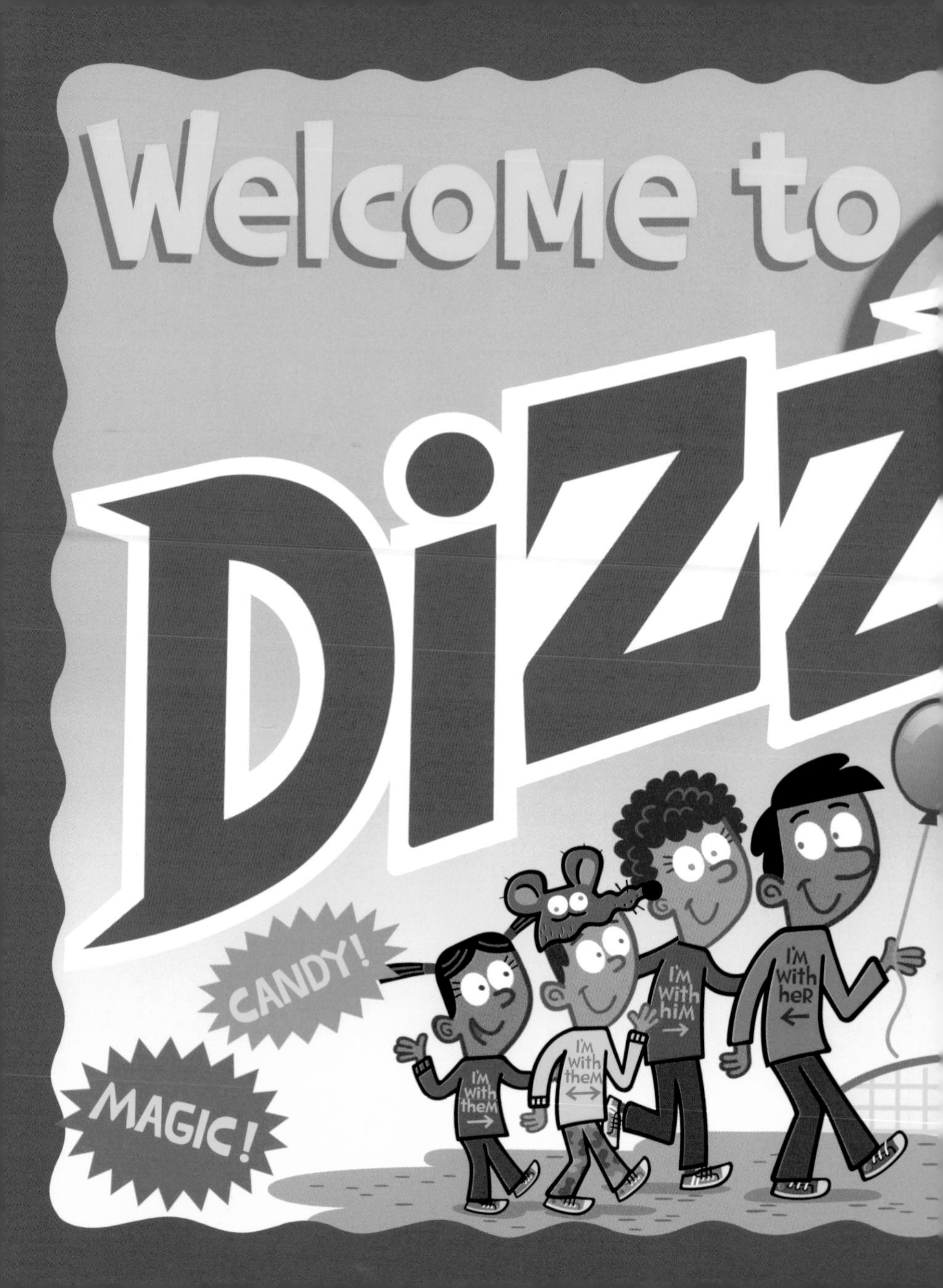
Welcome to
DiZZ
CANDY!
MAGIC!
I'M with them →
I'M with them ↔
I'M with him →
I'M with her ←

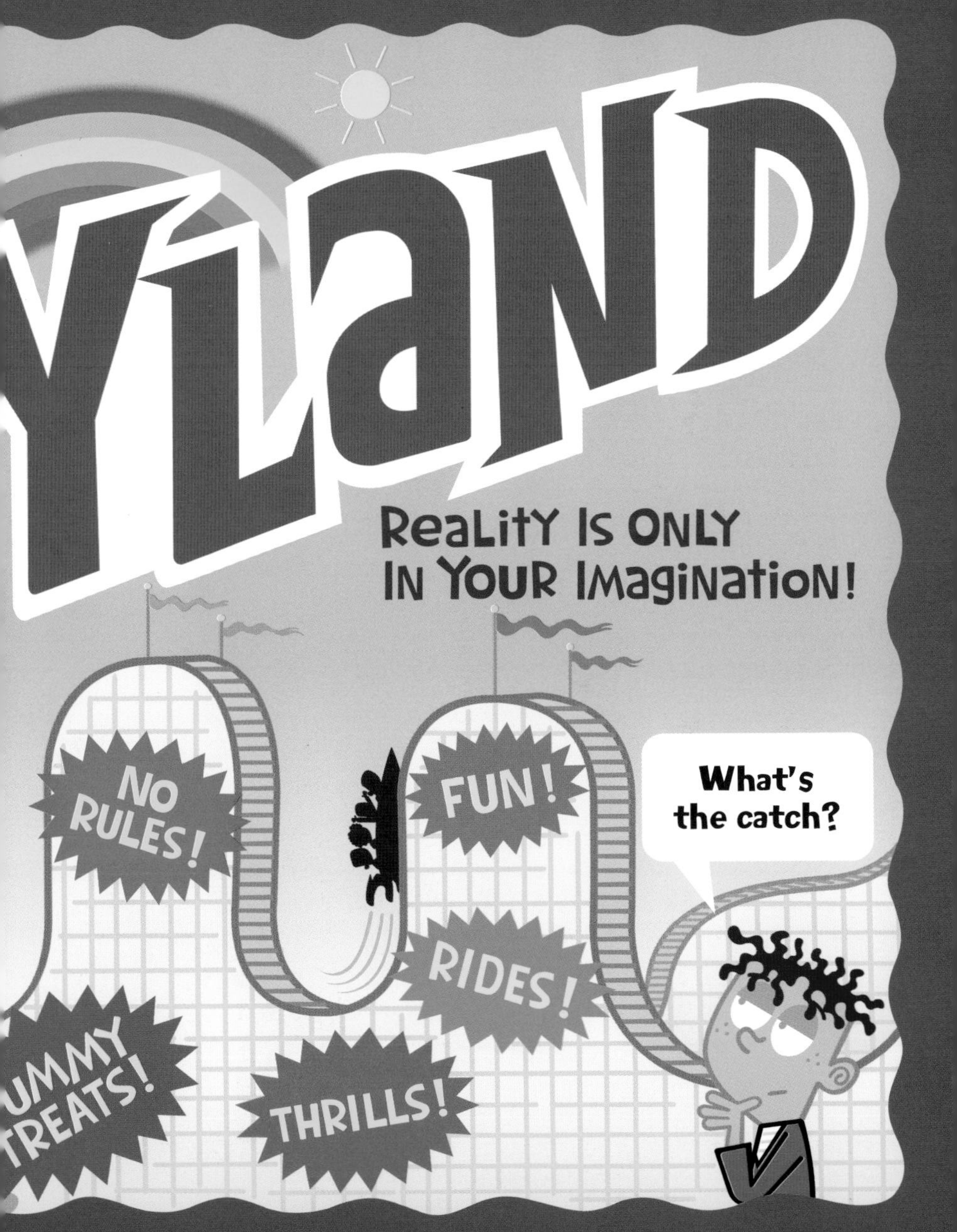
YLAND
Reality Is Only
In Your Imagination!
No Rules!
Fun!
What's the catch?
Rides!
UMMY TREATS!
THRILLS!

READER SURVEY

YOUR AGE:
- 0-5
- 6-7
- 9-12
- 13-99
- OVER 100

HOW TALL DO YOU WEIGH?
- 103 FOOT POUNDS
- I'M AS HIGH AS AN ELEPHANT'S EYE
- TALL ENOUGH FOR MY FEET TO REACH THE GROUND
- BOB

HOW MANY MY WEIRD SCHOOL BOOKS HAVE YOU READ?
- NONE. I'M NOT EVEN READING THIS ONE.
- 1-5
- 5-10
- ALL OF THEM
- MY WEIRD WHAT?

HOW DO YOU THINK THIS STORY WILL END?
- THE KIDS WILL READ 5,000 BOOKS AND GO TO DIZZYLAND
- MR. KLUTZ WILL APPEAR IN A SHAMPOO COMMERCIAL
- A.J. AND ANDREA WILL GET MARRIED
- EVERYBODY WILL LIVE HAPPILY EVER AFTER
- EVERYBODY WILL DIE IN A MINE SHAFT EXPLOSION

THINGS YOU COULD DO INSTEAD OF READING THIS BOOK . . .

- CURE CANCER
- SOLVE THE CLIMATE CRISIS
- END ALL WARS
- THE DISHES

WHY DON'T BASKETBALL PLAYERS GO ON VACATIONS?

- HOW SHOULD I KNOW?
- NONE OF YOUR BUSINESS
- WHAT DOES THAT HAVE TO DO WITH ANYTHING?
- I THOUGHT THEY DID
- THEY WOULD BE CALLED FOR TRAVELING

WHAT IS YOUR PET PEEVE?

- PETS
- PEOPLE WHO TALK TOO LOUDLY
- PEOPLE WHO TALK TOO SOFTLY
- PEOPLE WHO ASK ME WHAT MY PET PEEVE IS

TWO TRAINS ARE GOING 100 MPH. TRAIN *A* IS 50 MILES AWAY, AND TRAIN *B* IS 75 MILES AWAY. HOW MUCH SOONER WILL TRAIN *A* ARRIVE?

- WHO CARES?
- I PREFER TO DRIVE
- THOSE ARE DUMB NAMES FOR TRAINS
- BOB

TEAR OUT THIS PAGE AND MAKE IT INTO A PAPER AIRPLANE. THROW IT OUT THE WINDOW. THEN BUY A NEW BOOK TO REPLACE THE ONE YOU RUINED. NEXT, TEAR OUT THE SAME PAGE IN THE SECOND BOOK AND FILL OUT THE SURVEY. APPLY TO WET HAIR AND LATHER WITH A GENTLE MASSAGING MOTION. RINSE AND REPEAT.

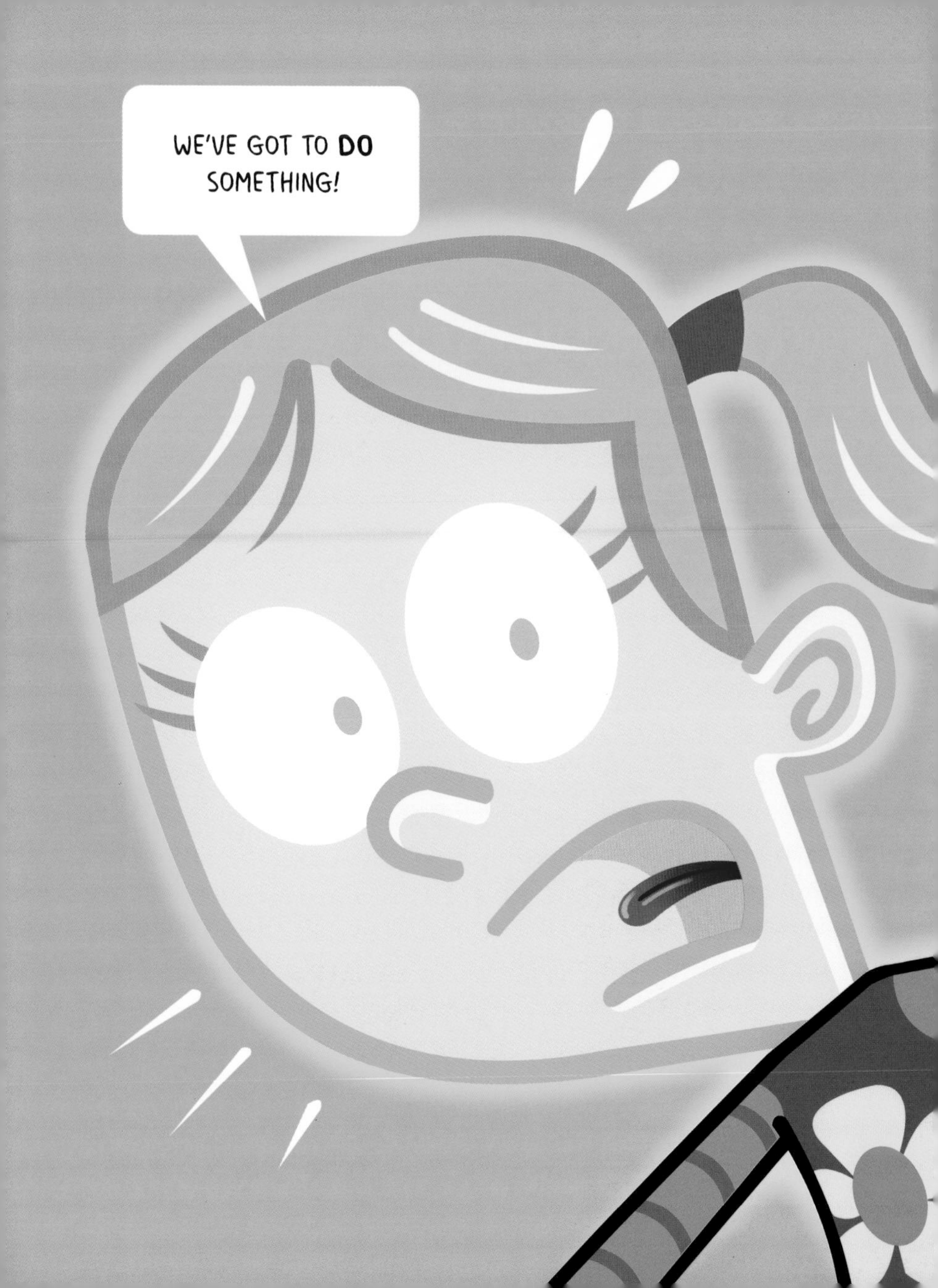
WE'VE GOT TO **DO** SOMETHING!

CHAPTER 3

Even More Stuff

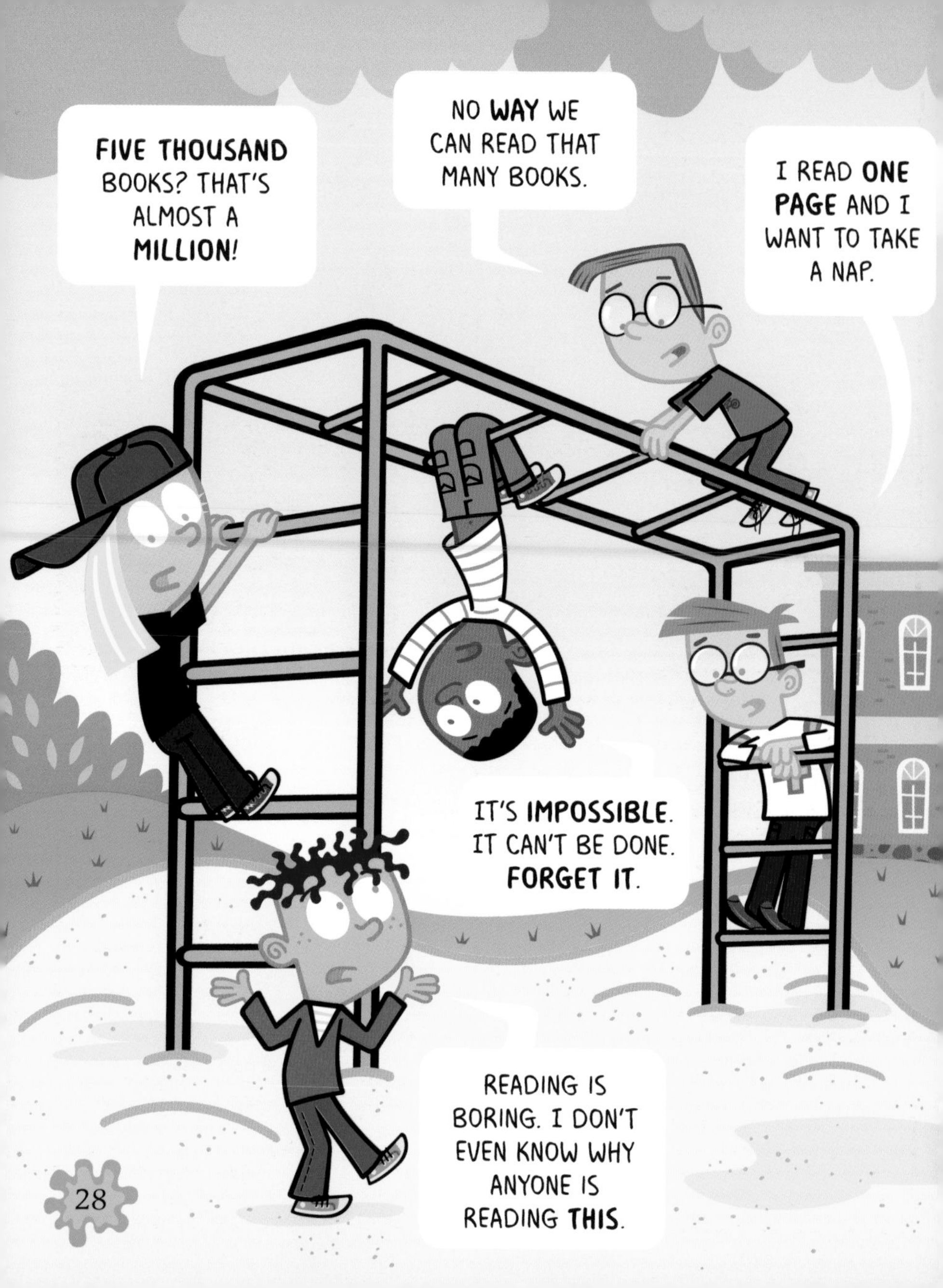
FIVE THOUSAND BOOKS? THAT'S ALMOST A MILLION!
NO WAY WE CAN READ THAT MANY BOOKS.
I READ ONE PAGE AND I WANT TO TAKE A NAP.
IT'S IMPOSSIBLE. IT CAN'T BE DONE. FORGET IT.
READING IS BORING. I DON'T EVEN KNOW WHY ANYONE IS READING THIS.

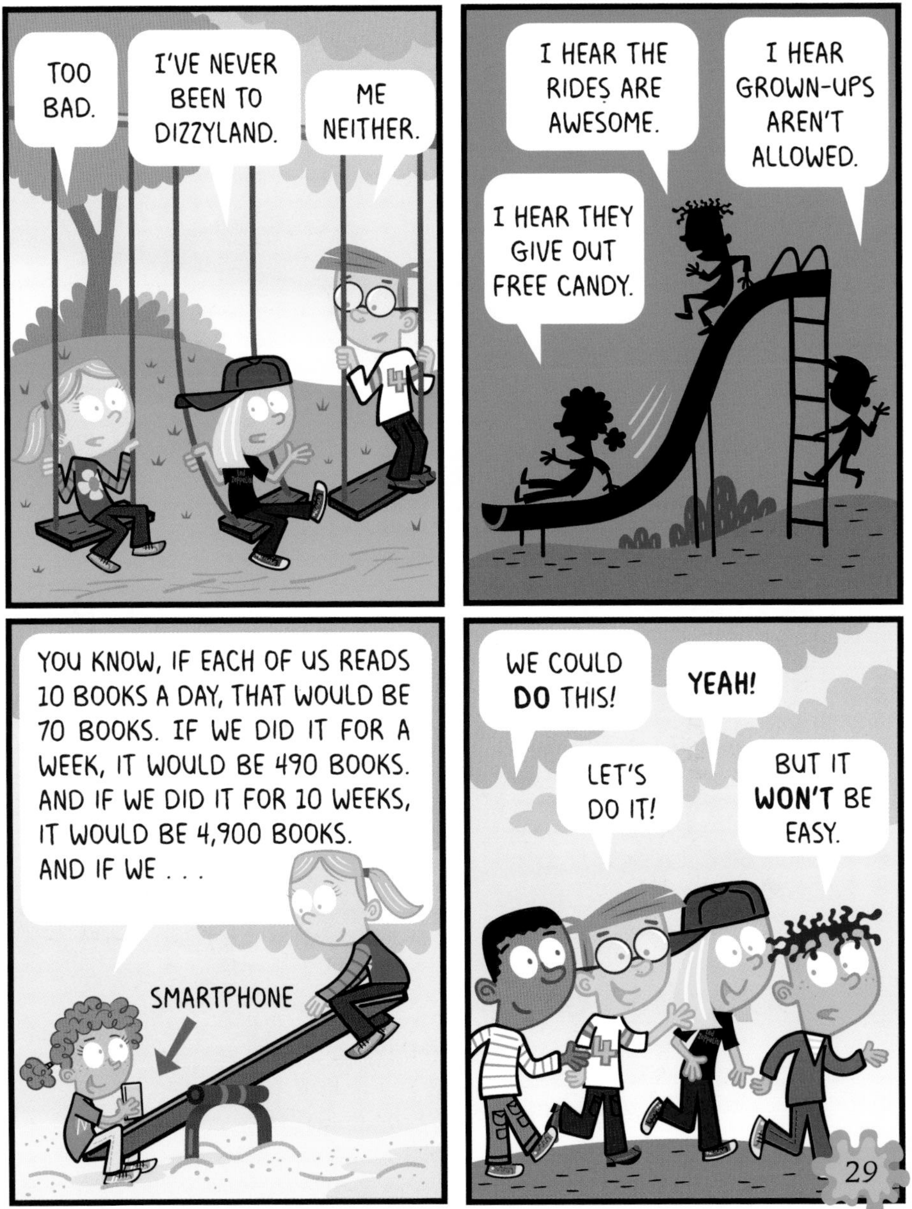
TOO BAD.
I'VE NEVER BEEN TO DIZZYLAND.
ME NEITHER.
I HEAR THE RIDES ARE AWESOME.
I HEAR GROWN-UPS AREN'T ALLOWED.
I HEAR THEY GIVE OUT FREE CANDY.
YOU KNOW, IF EACH OF US READS 10 BOOKS A DAY, THAT WOULD BE 70 BOOKS. IF WE DID IT FOR A WEEK, IT WOULD BE 490 BOOKS. AND IF WE DID IT FOR 10 WEEKS, IT WOULD BE 4,900 BOOKS. AND IF WE . . .
SMARTPHONE
WE COULD **DO** THIS!
YEAH!
LET'S DO IT!
BUT IT **WON'T** BE EASY.

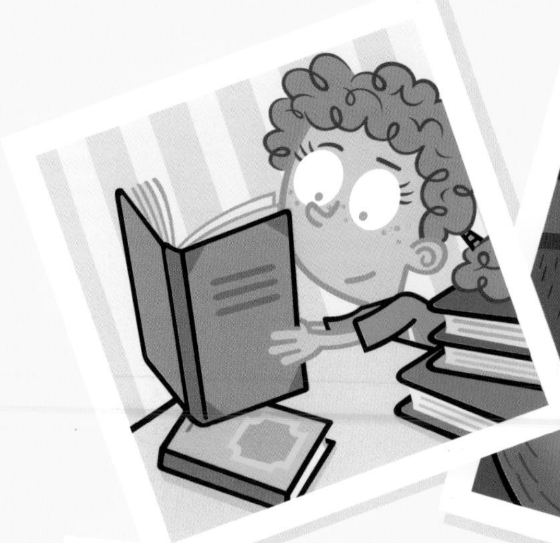
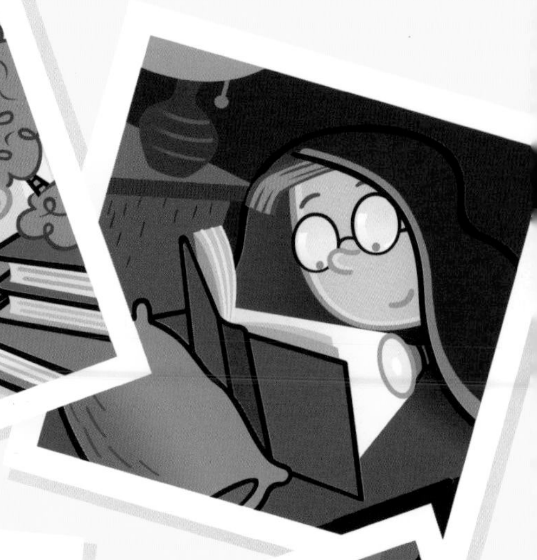
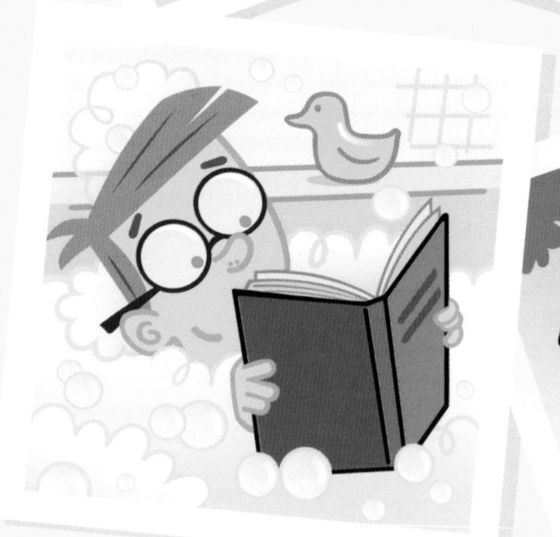
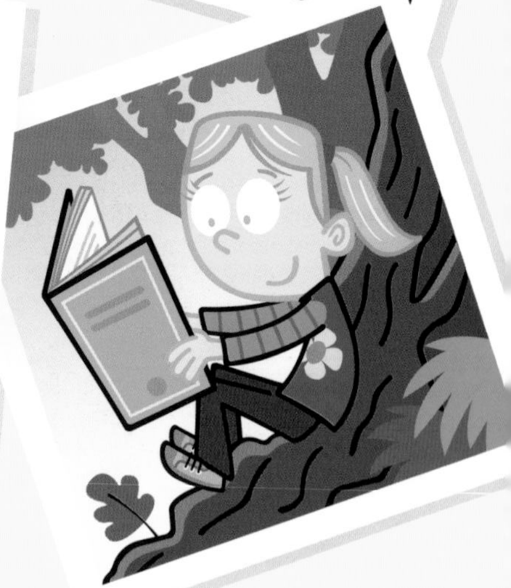

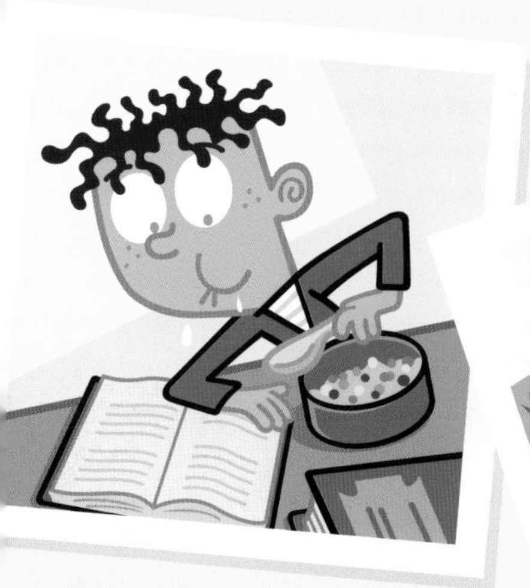

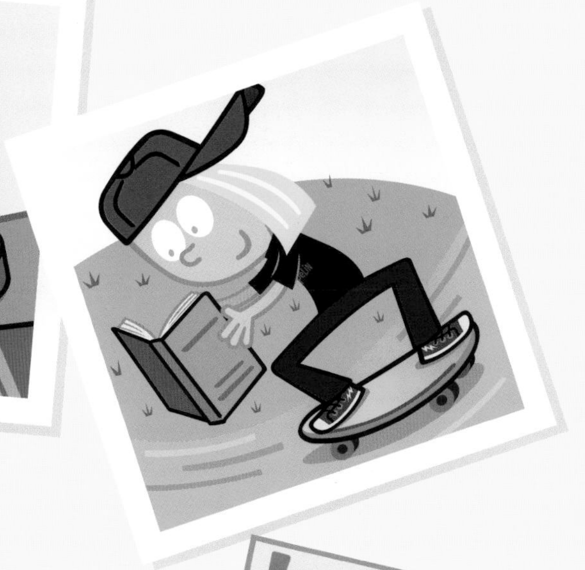

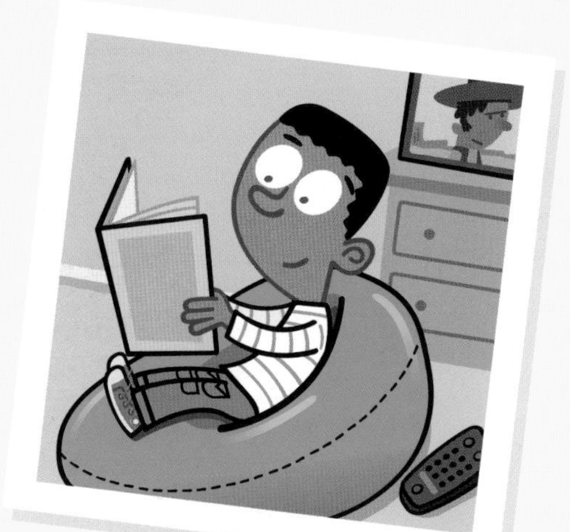

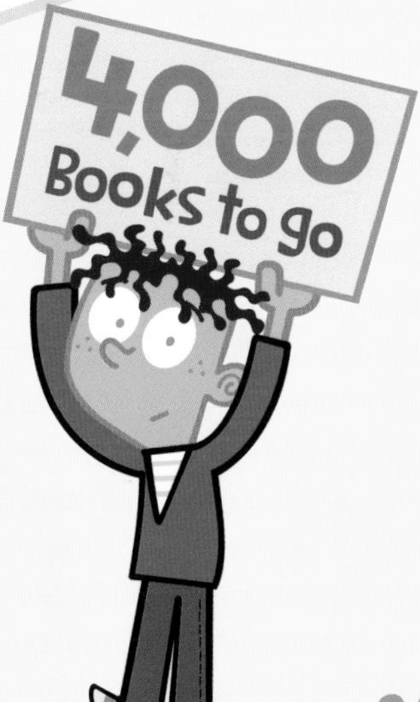
4,000
Books to go

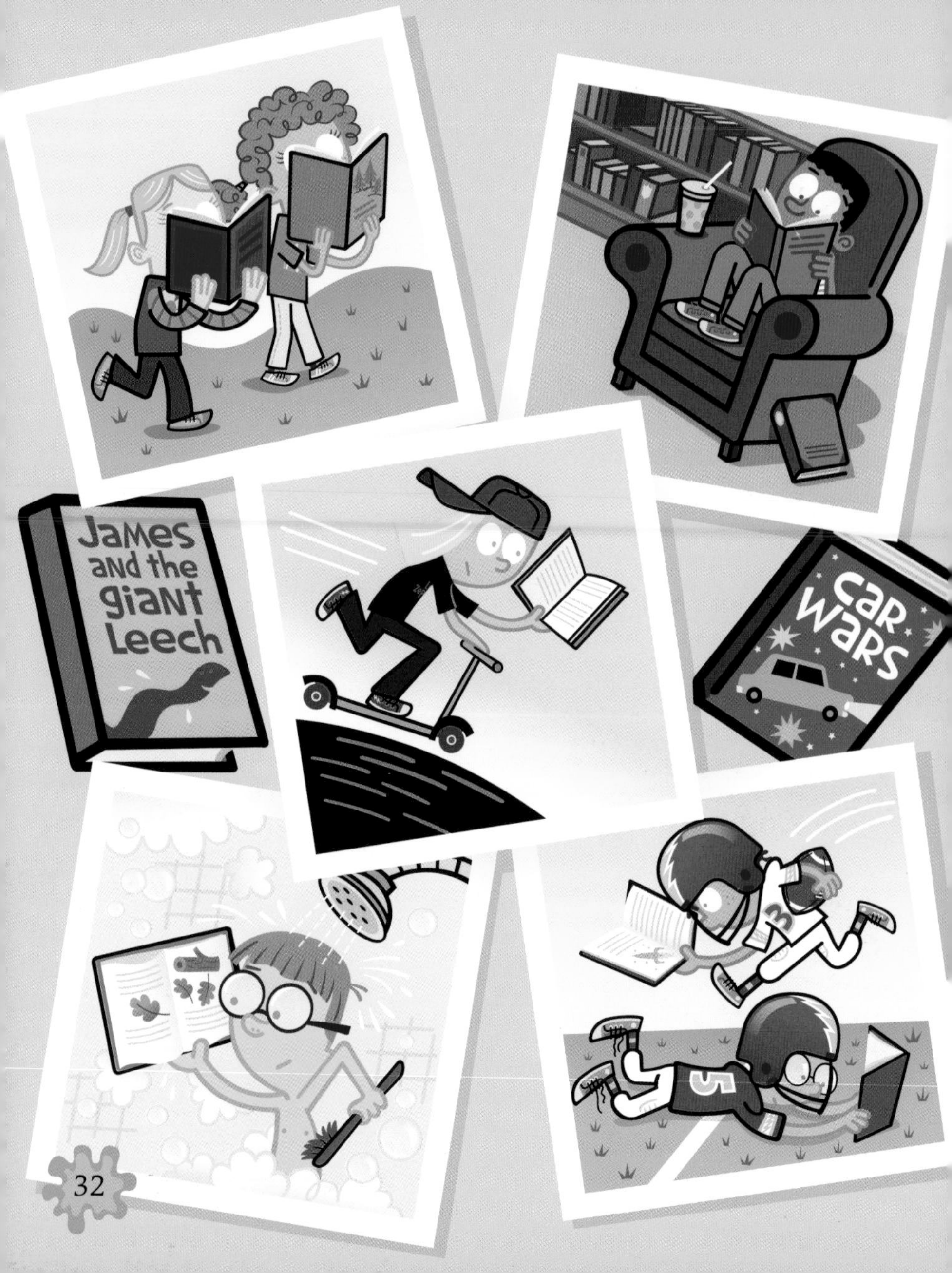
James and the giant Leech
Car Wars

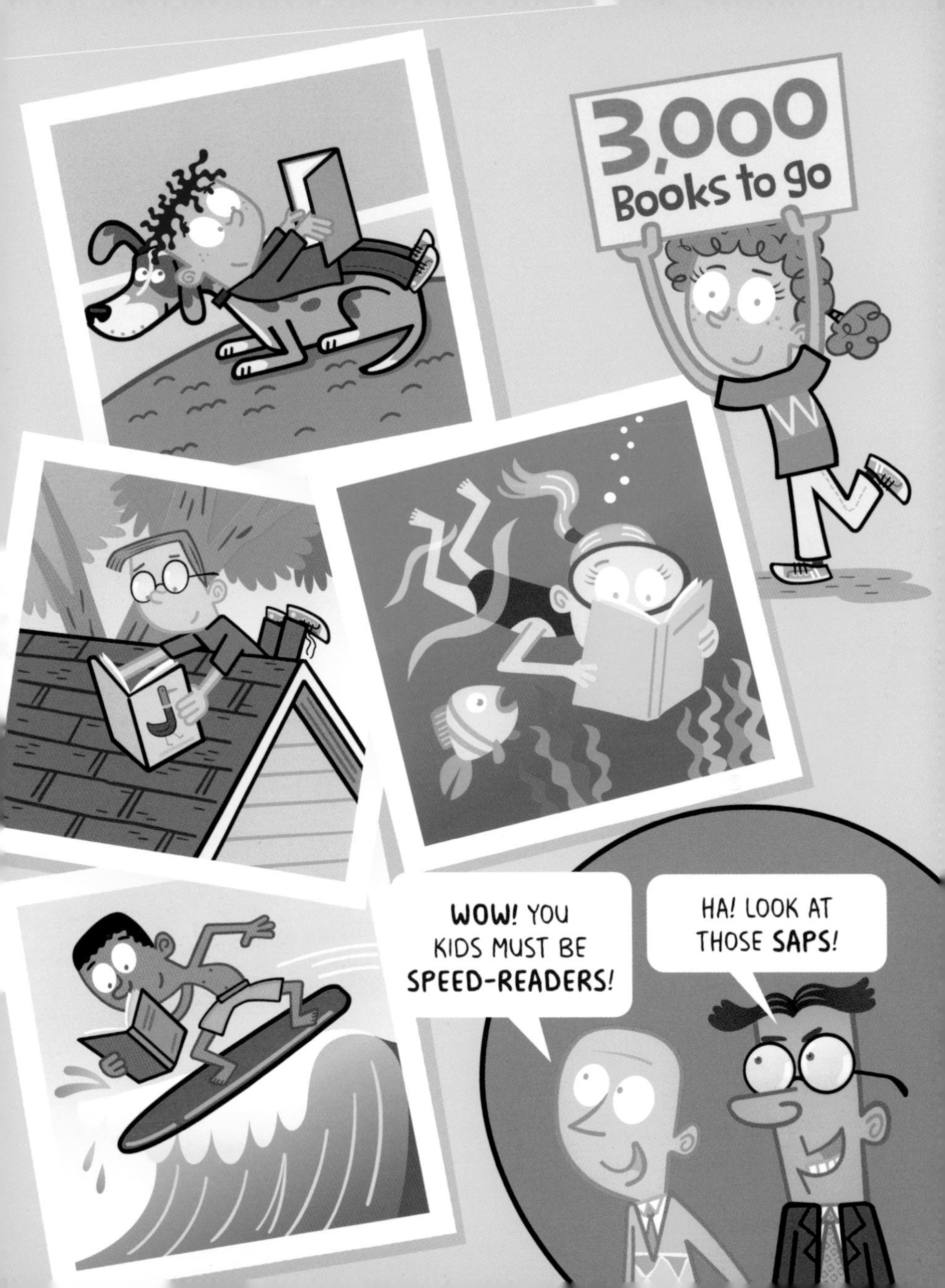
3,000 Books to go
WOW! YOU KIDS MUST BE SPEED-READERS!
HA! LOOK AT THOSE SAPS!

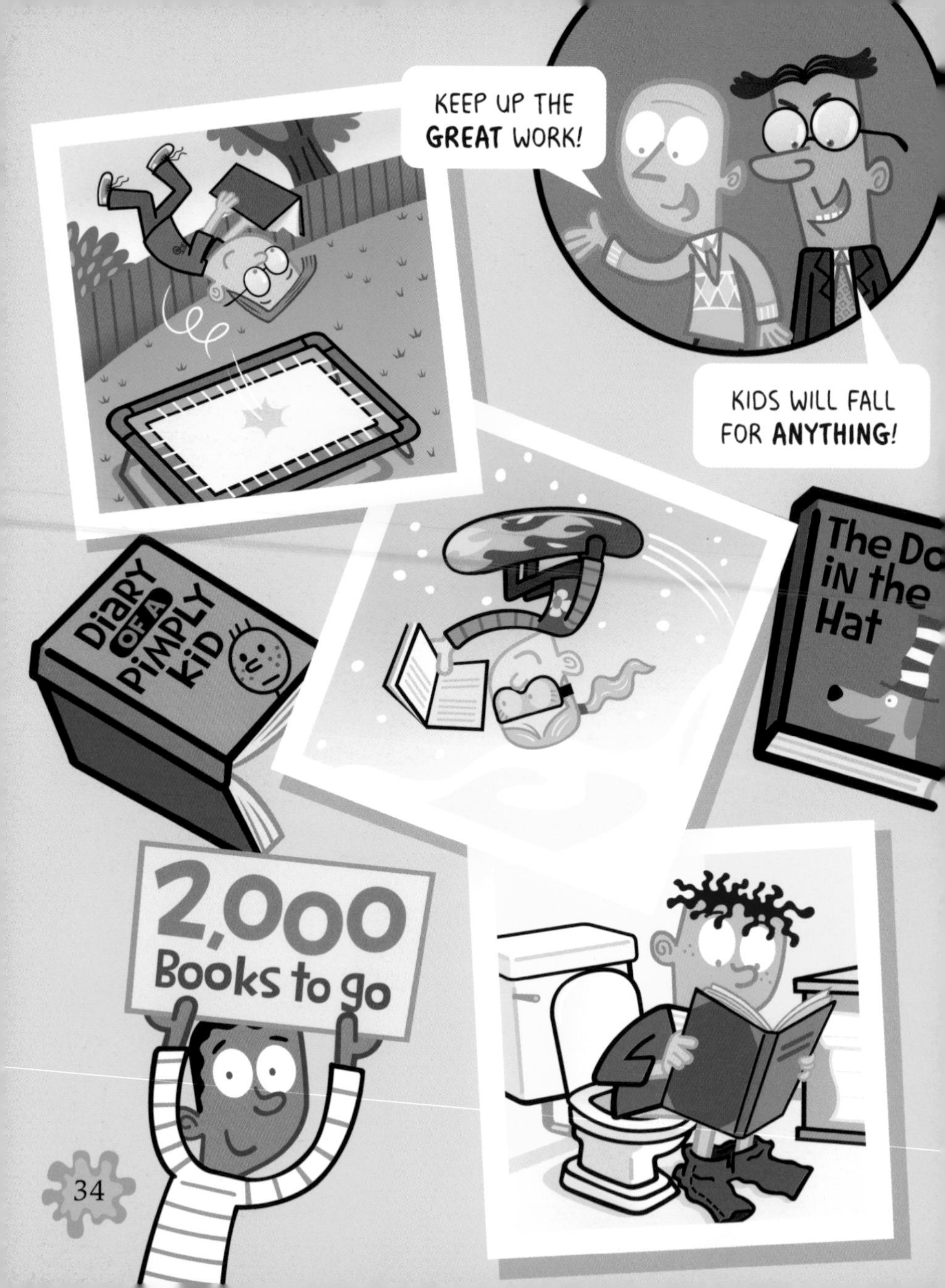
KEEP UP THE GREAT WORK!
KIDS WILL FALL FOR ANYTHING!
DiARY OF A PiMPLY KiD
The Do iN the Hat
2,000 Books to go

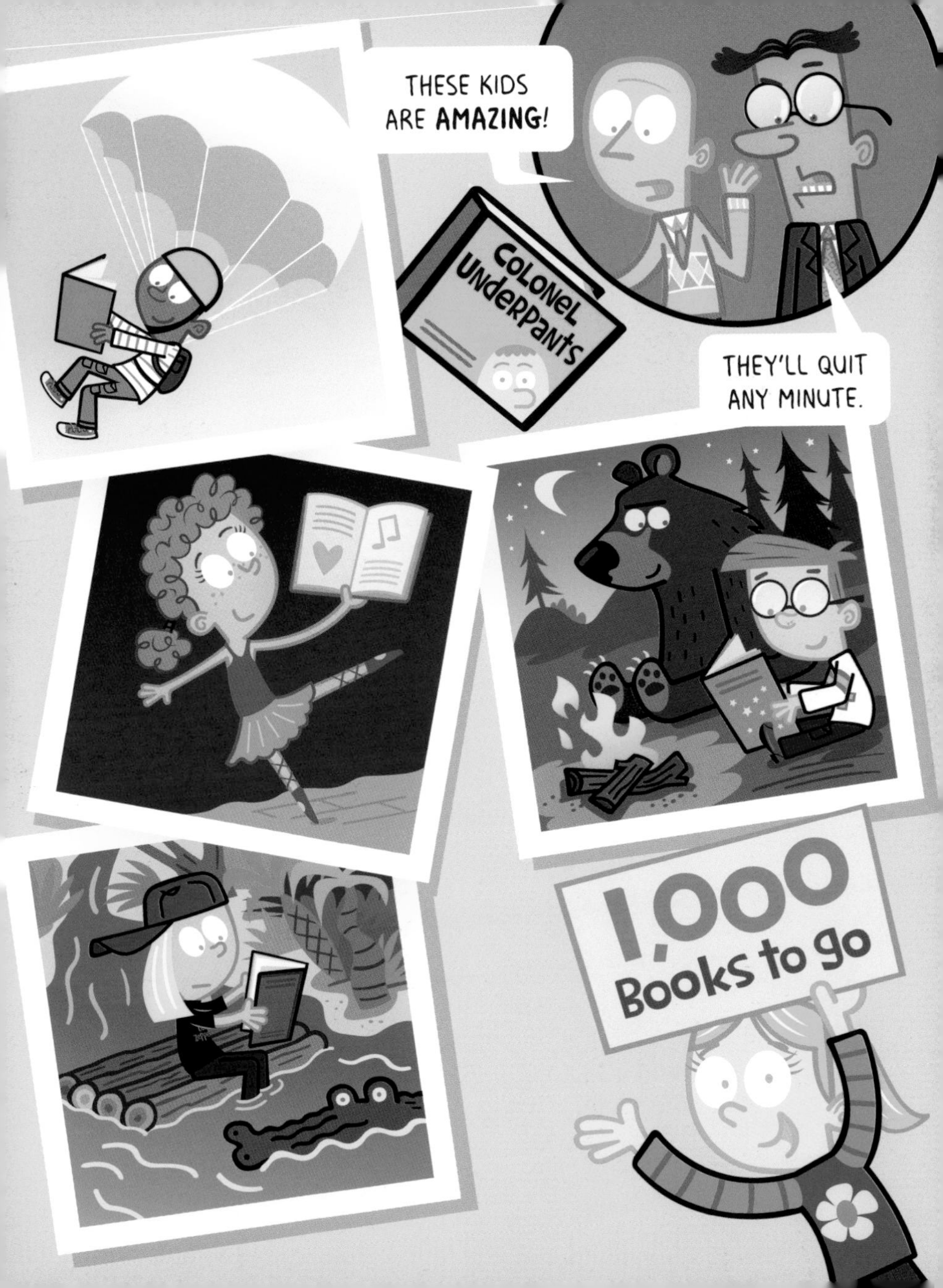
THESE KIDS ARE AMAZING!
COLONEL UNDERPANTS
THEY'LL QUIT ANY MINUTE.
1,000 Books to go

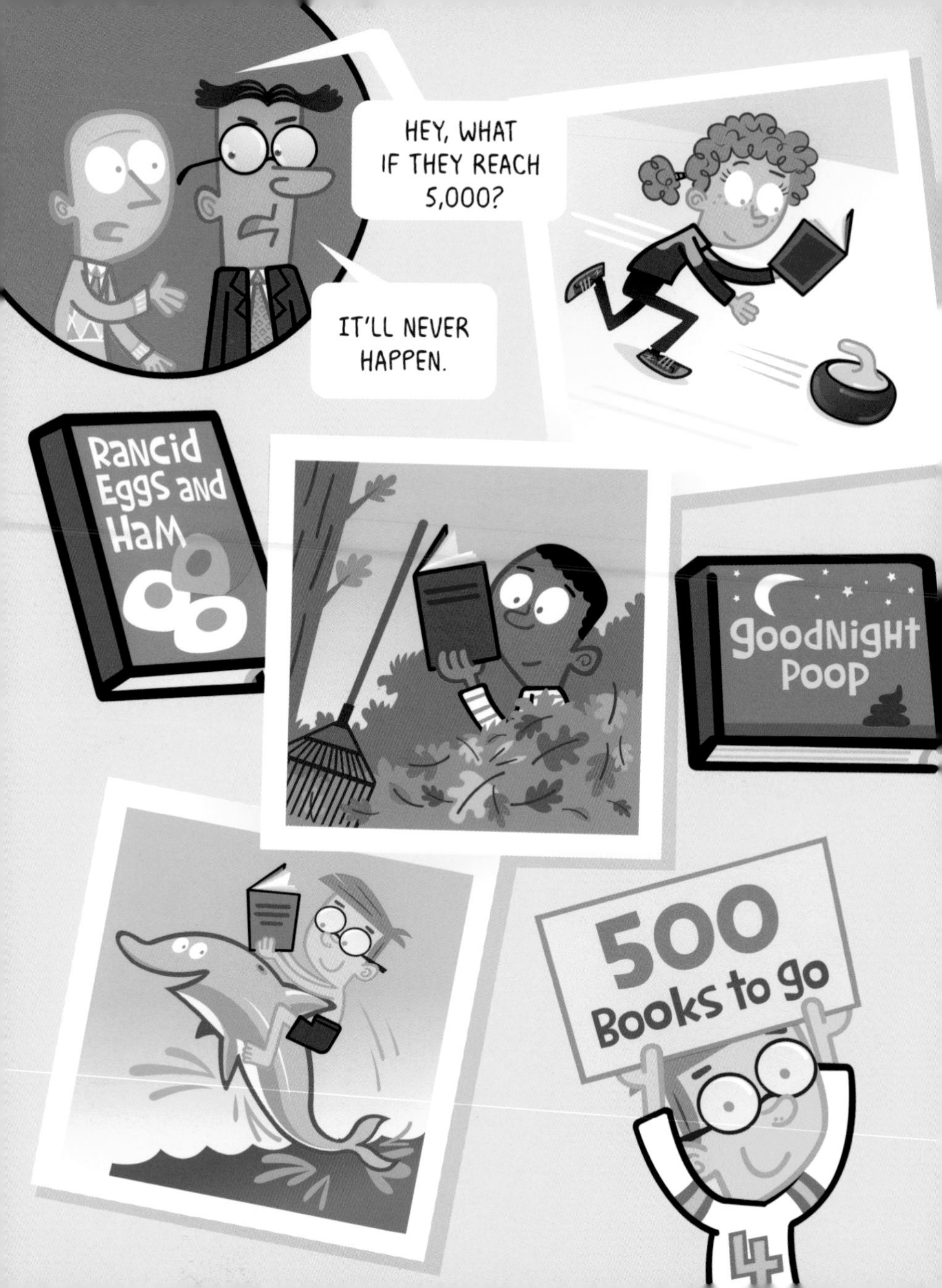
HEY, WHAT IF THEY REACH 5,000?
IT'LL NEVER HAPPEN.
Rancid Eggs and Ham
goodNight Poop
500 Books to go

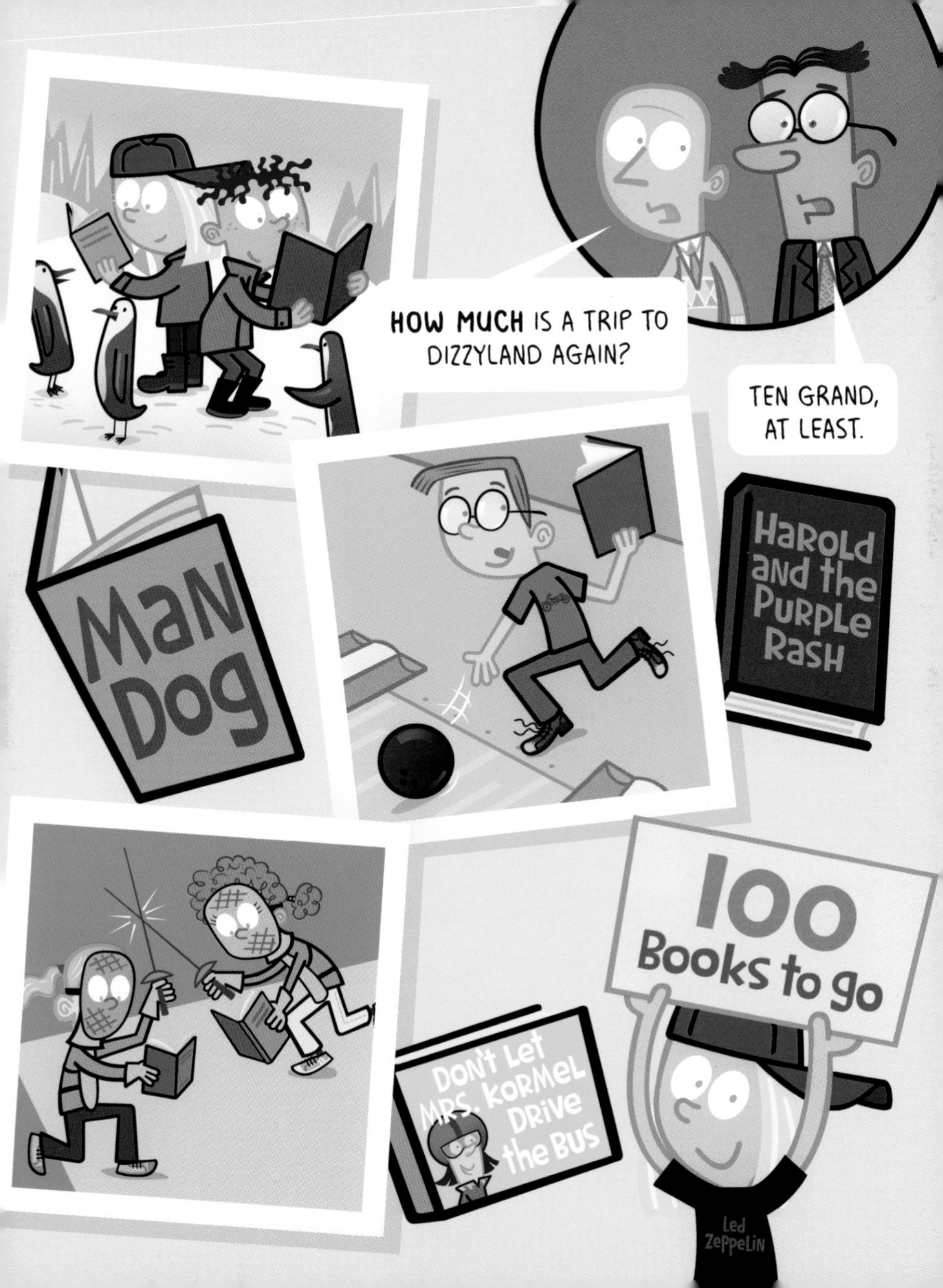
HOW MUCH IS A TRIP TO DIZZYLAND AGAIN?
TEN GRAND, AT LEAST.
Man Dog
Harold and the Purple Rash
100 Books to go
Don't Let Mrs. Kormel Drive the Bus
Led Zeppelin

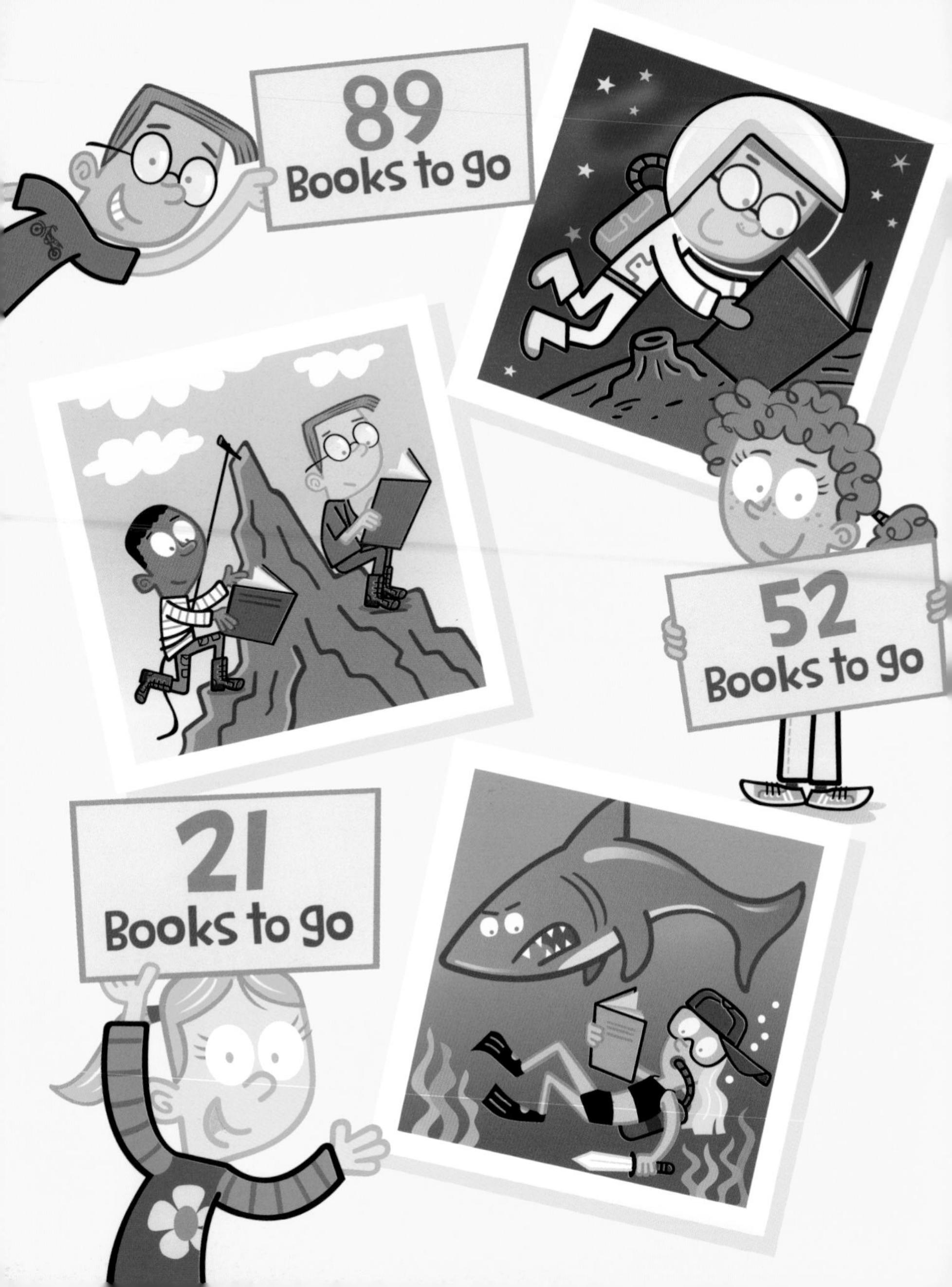
89
Books to go
52
Books to go
21
Books to go

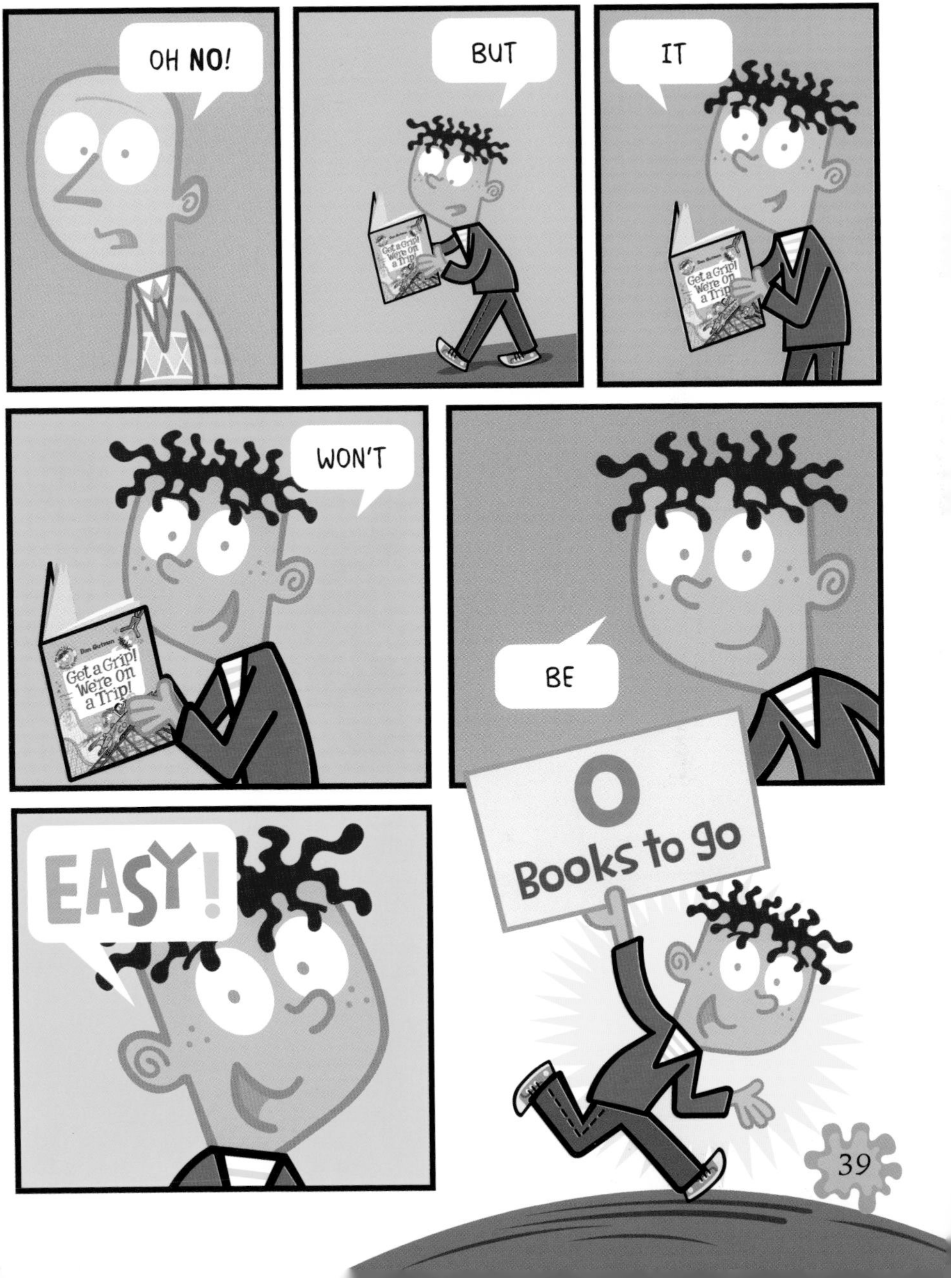
OH NO!
BUT
IT
WON'T
Get a Grip! We're On a Trip!
BE
EASY!
0
Books to go

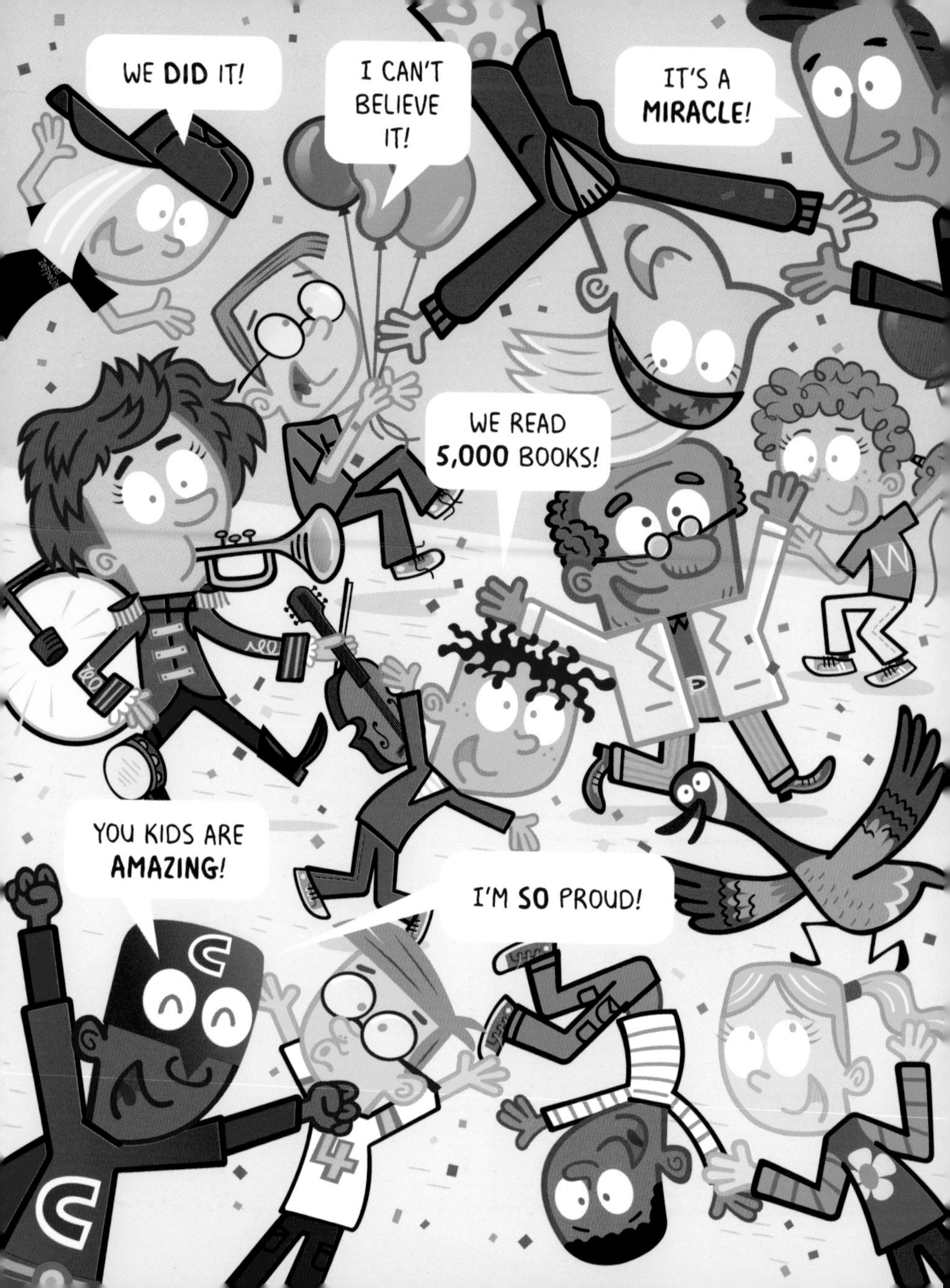
WE DID IT!
I CAN'T BELIEVE IT!
IT'S A MIRACLE!
WE READ 5,000 BOOKS!
YOU KIDS ARE AMAZING!
I'M SO PROUD!

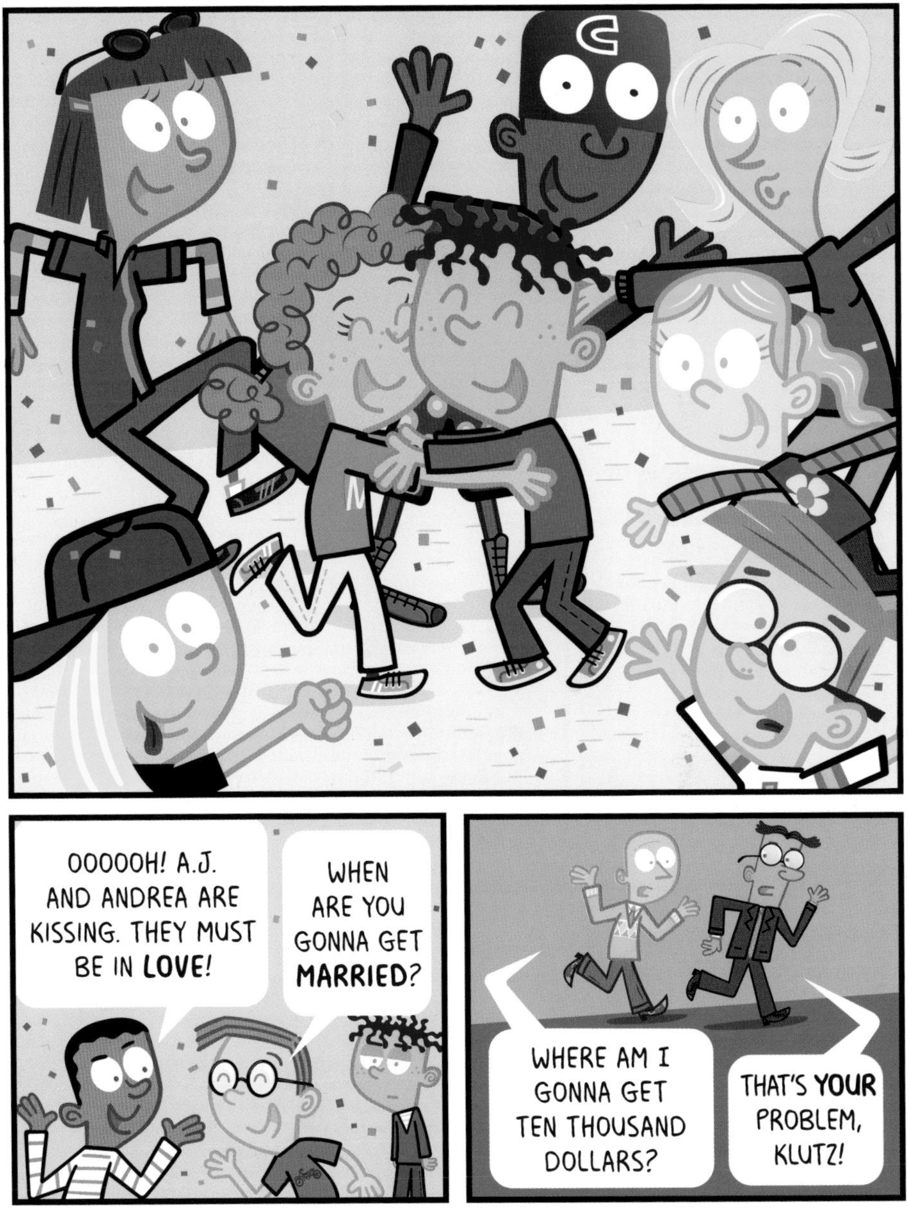
OOOOOH! A.J. AND ANDREA ARE KISSING. THEY MUST BE IN LOVE!
WHEN ARE YOU GONNA GET MARRIED?
WHERE AM I GONNA GET TEN THOUSAND DOLLARS?
THAT'S YOUR PROBLEM, KLUTZ!

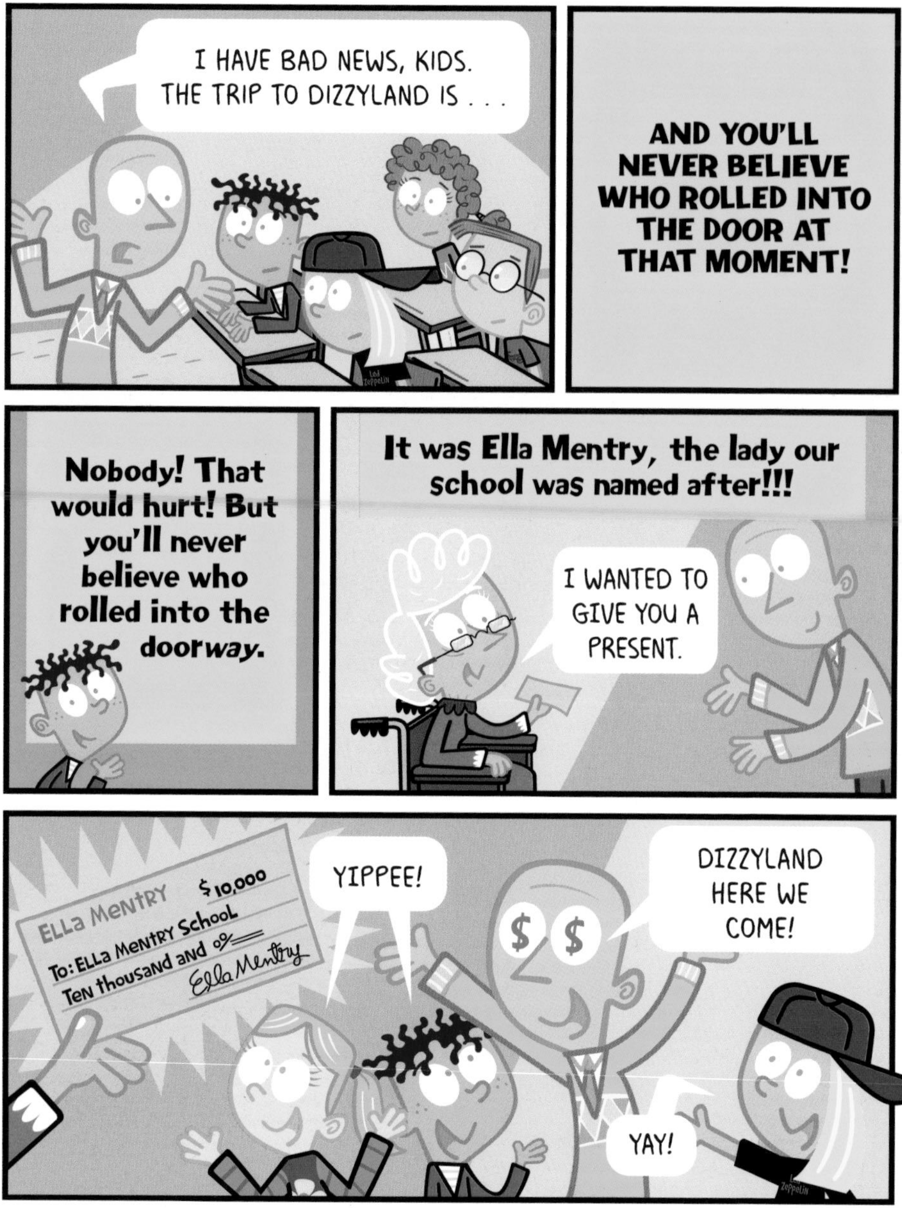
I HAVE BAD NEWS, KIDS. THE TRIP TO DIZZYLAND IS . . .
AND YOU'LL NEVER BELIEVE WHO ROLLED INTO THE DOOR AT THAT MOMENT!
Nobody! That would hurt! But you'll never believe who rolled into the doorway.
It was Ella Mentry, the lady our school was named after!!!
I WANTED TO GIVE YOU A PRESENT.
ELLa MENTRY
$10,000
To: ELLa MENTRY SchooL
Ten thousand and 0%
Ella Mentry
YIPPEE!
DIZZYLAND HERE WE COME!
YAY!

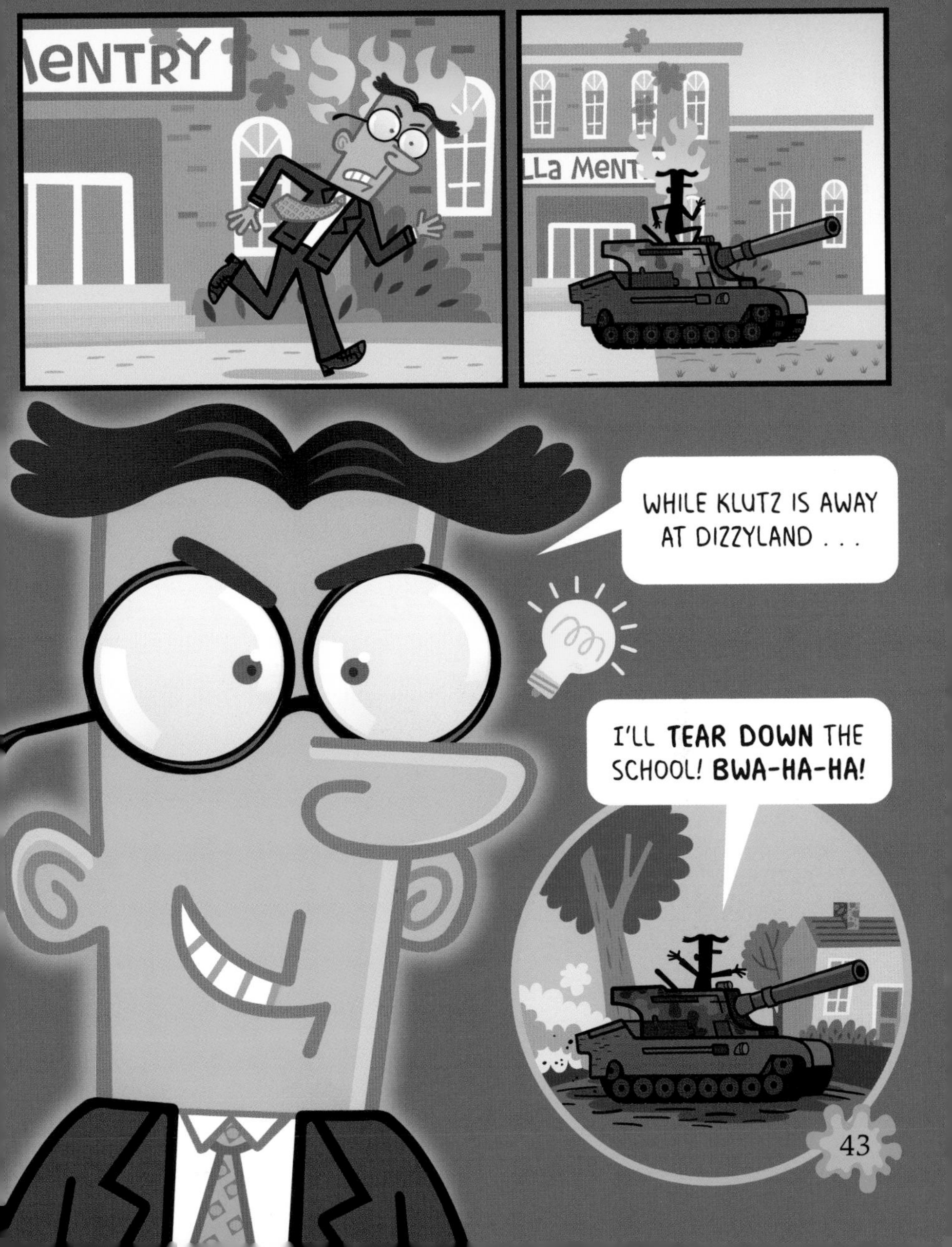

MENTRY
LLA MENT
WHILE KLUTZ IS AWAY AT DIZZYLAND . . .
I'LL **TEAR DOWN** THE SCHOOL! **BWA-HA-HA!**

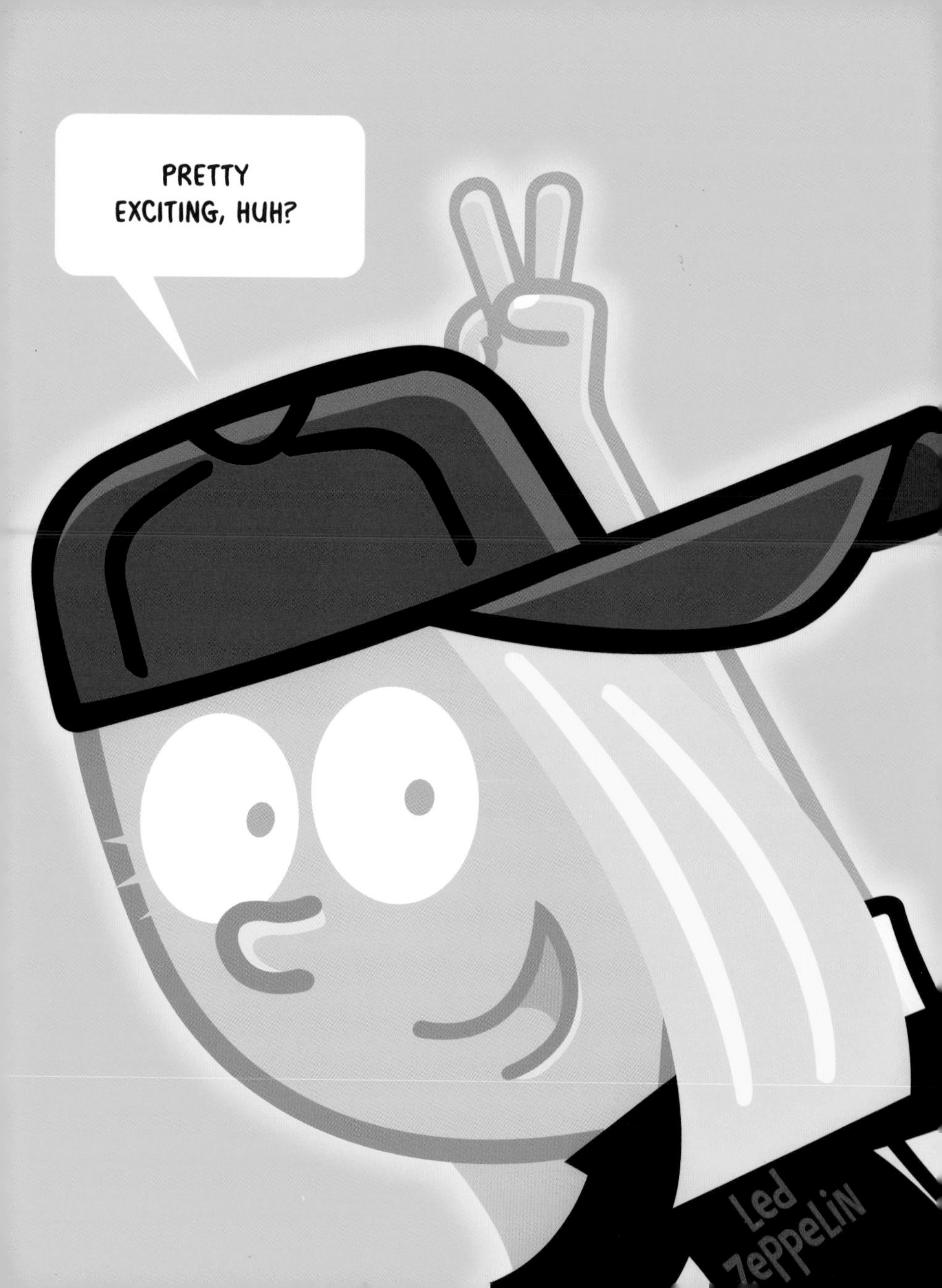
PRETTY EXCITING, HUH?
Led ZEPPELIN

CHAPTER 4
A Ridorkulous Amount of Stuff

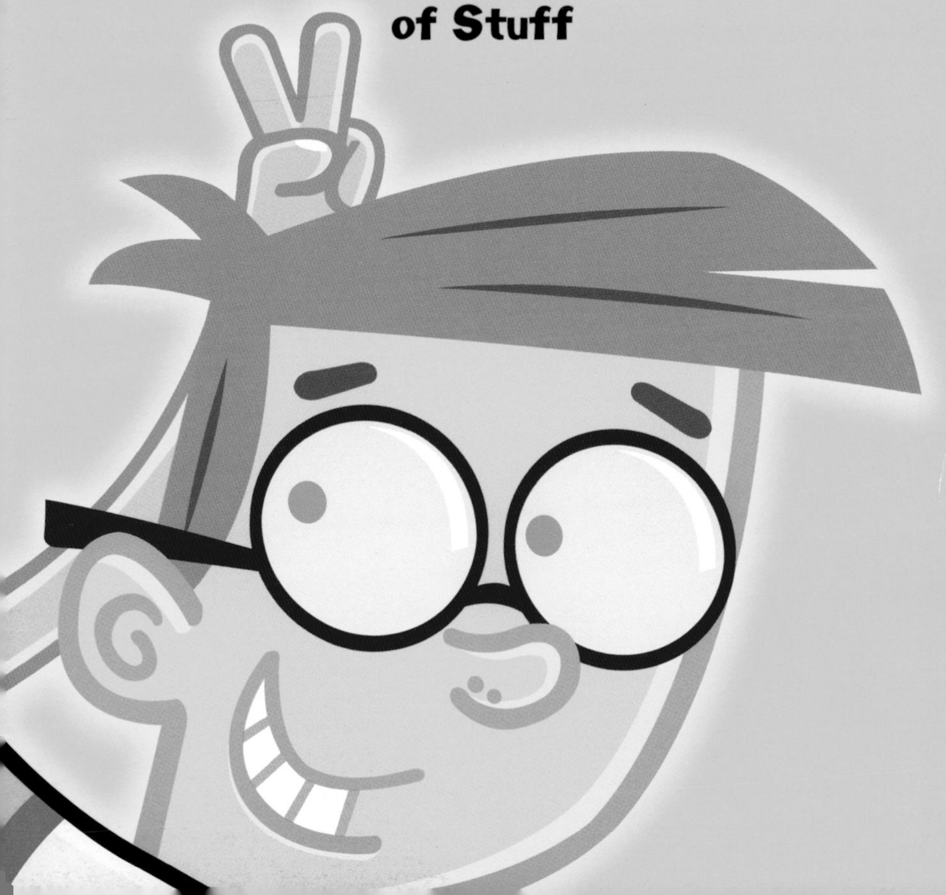

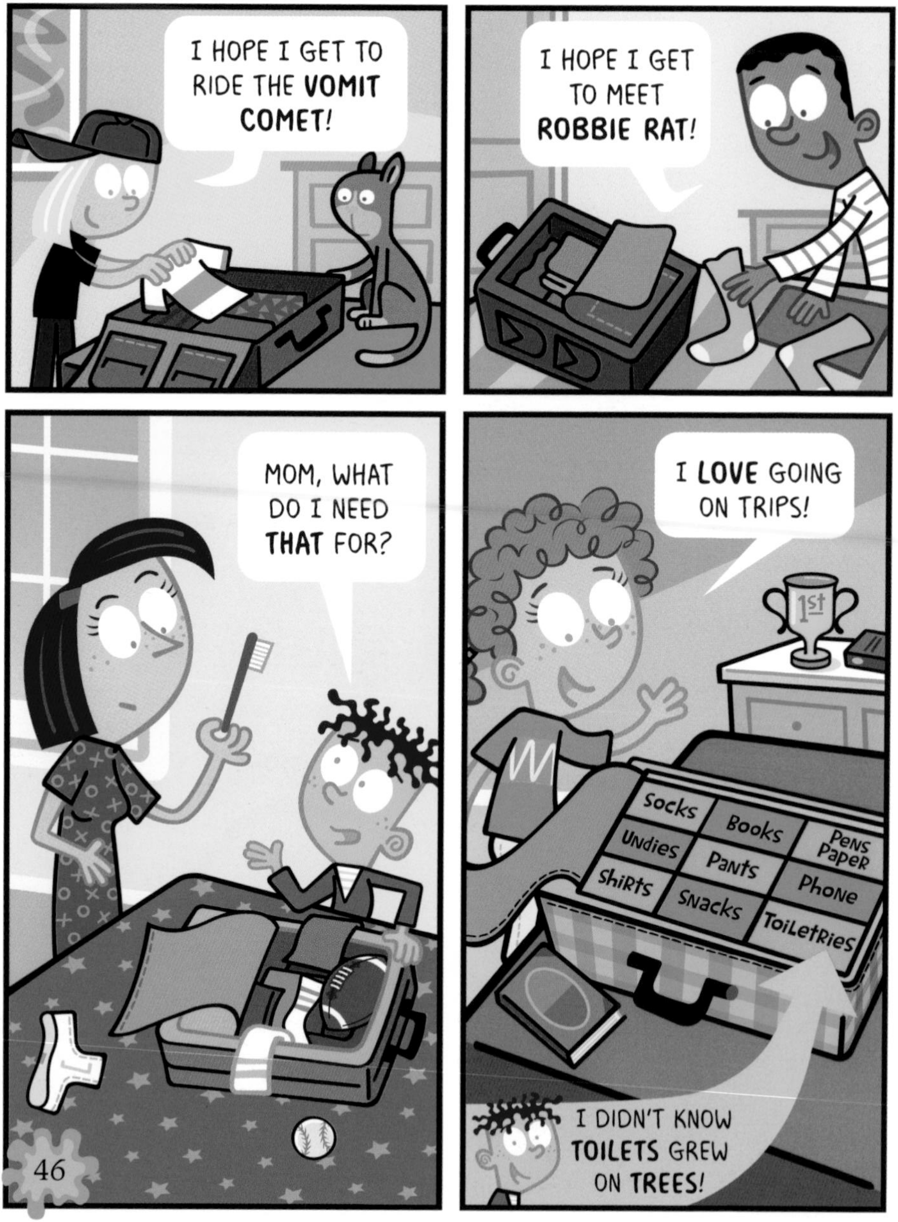
I HOPE I GET TO RIDE THE VOMIT COMET!
I HOPE I GET TO MEET ROBBIE RAT!
MOM, WHAT DO I NEED THAT FOR?
I LOVE GOING ON TRIPS!
1st
Socks
Books
Pens Paper
Undies
Pants
Shirts
Phone
Snacks
Toiletries
I DIDN'T KNOW TOILETS GREW ON TREES!

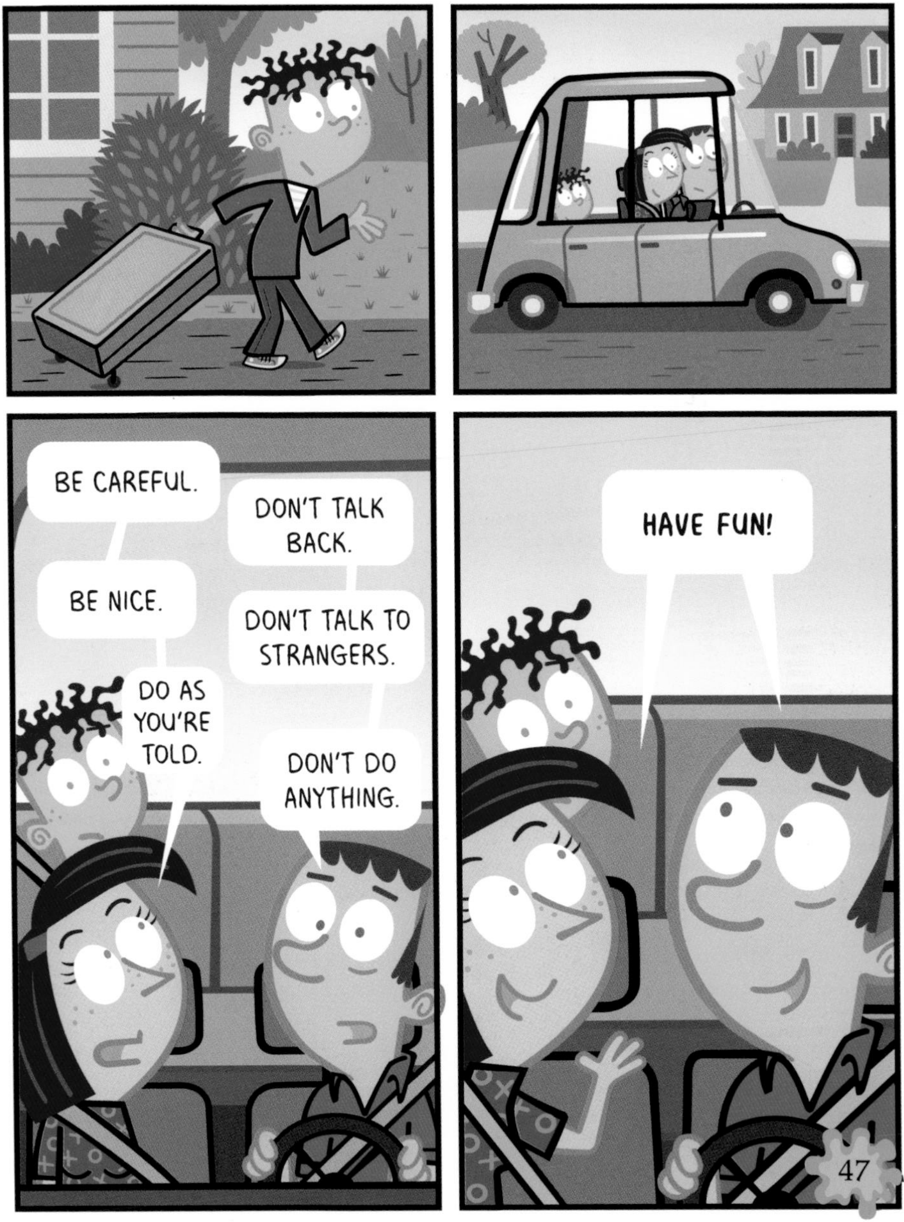
BE CAREFUL.
DON'T TALK BACK.
BE NICE.
DON'T TALK TO STRANGERS.
DO AS YOU'RE TOLD.
DON'T DO ANYTHING.
HAVE FUN!

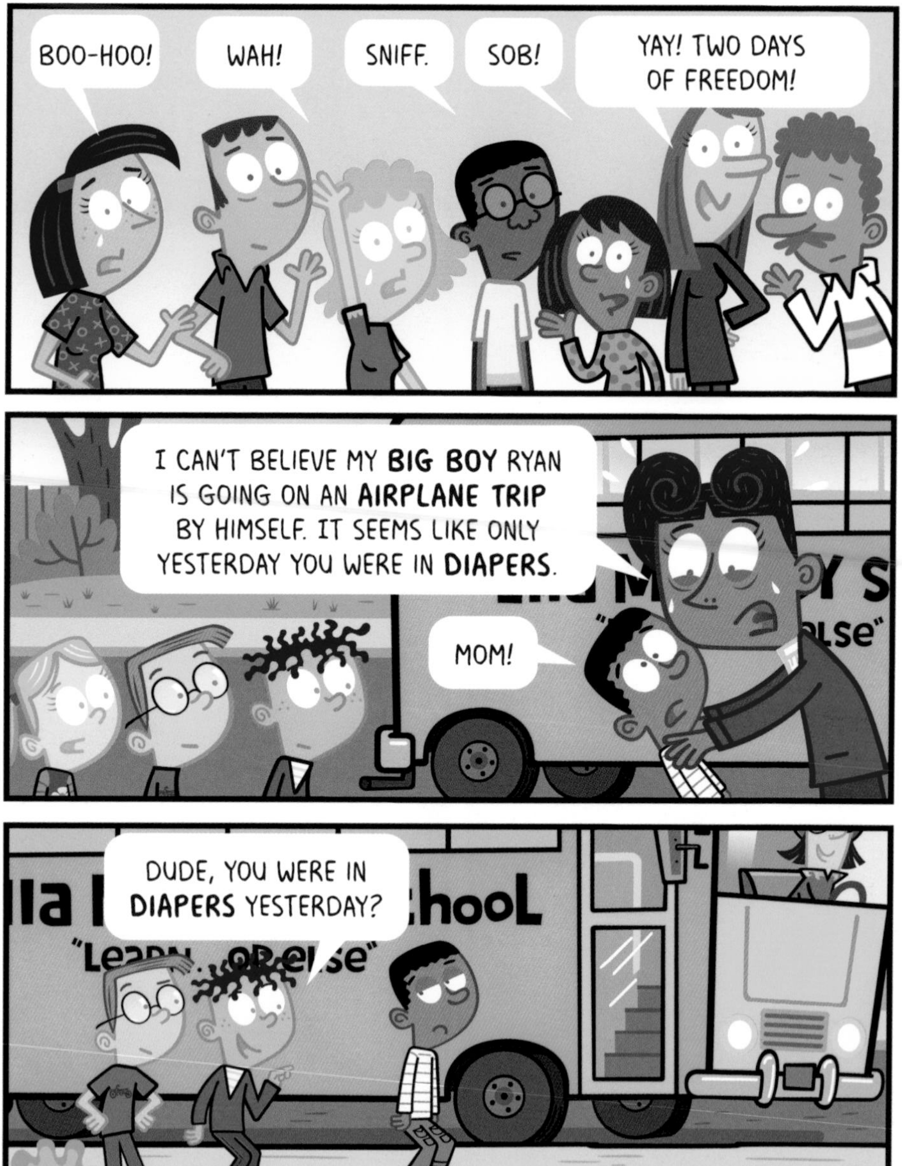
BOO-HOO!
WAH!
SNIFF.
SOB!
YAY! TWO DAYS OF FREEDOM!
I CAN'T BELIEVE MY **BIG BOY** RYAN IS GOING ON AN **AIRPLANE TRIP** BY HIMSELF. IT SEEMS LIKE ONLY YESTERDAY YOU WERE IN **DIAPERS**.
MOM!
DUDE, YOU WERE IN **DIAPERS** YESTERDAY?

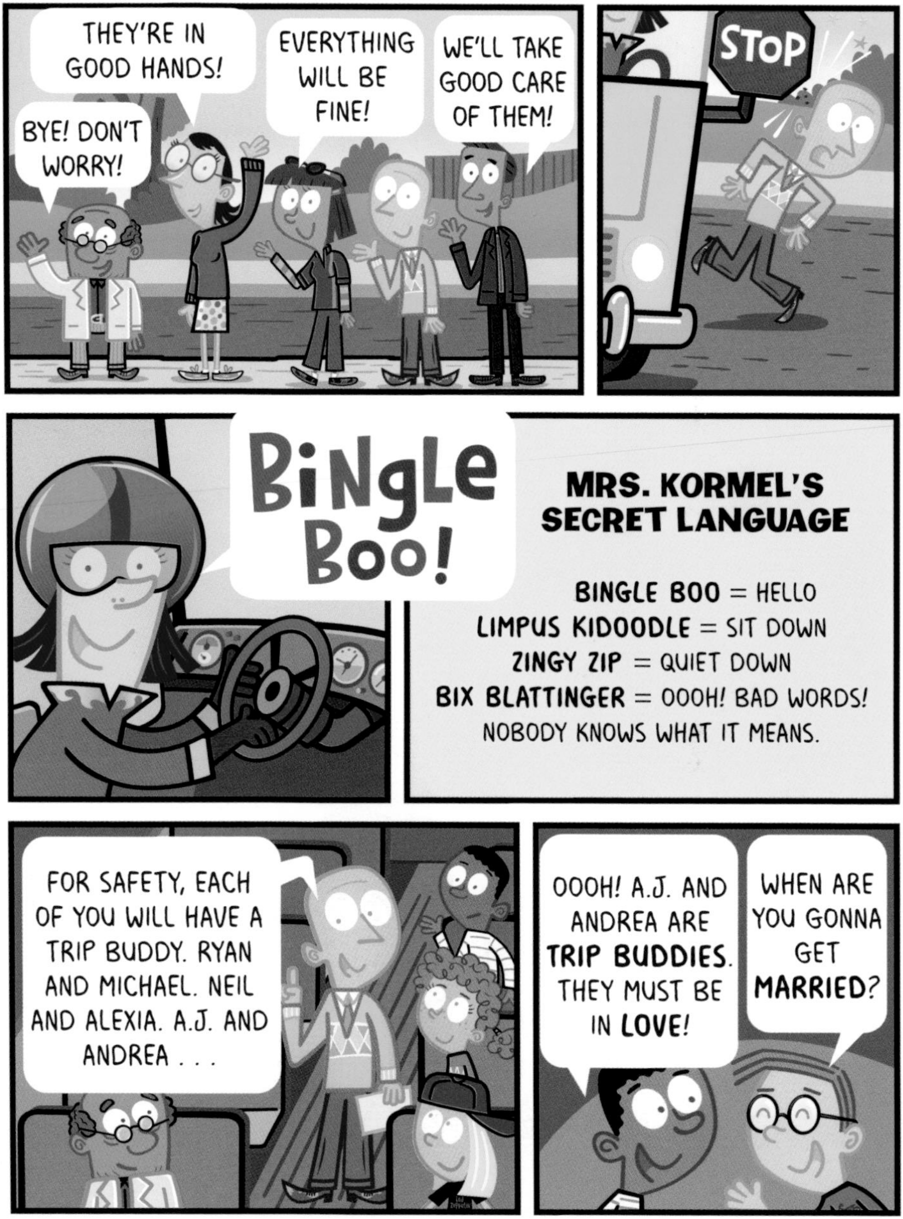
BYE! DON'T WORRY!
THEY'RE IN GOOD HANDS!
EVERYTHING WILL BE FINE!
WE'LL TAKE GOOD CARE OF THEM!
STOP
BiNgLe Boo!
MRS. KORMEL'S SECRET LANGUAGE
BINGLE BOO = HELLO
LIMPUS KIDOODLE = SIT DOWN
ZINGY ZIP = QUIET DOWN
BIX BLATTINGER = OOOH! BAD WORDS! NOBODY KNOWS WHAT IT MEANS.
FOR SAFETY, EACH OF YOU WILL HAVE A TRIP BUDDY. RYAN AND MICHAEL. NEIL AND ALEXIA. A.J. AND ANDREA . . .
OOOH! A.J. AND ANDREA ARE TRIP BUDDIES. THEY MUST BE IN LOVE!
WHEN ARE YOU GONNA GET MARRIED?

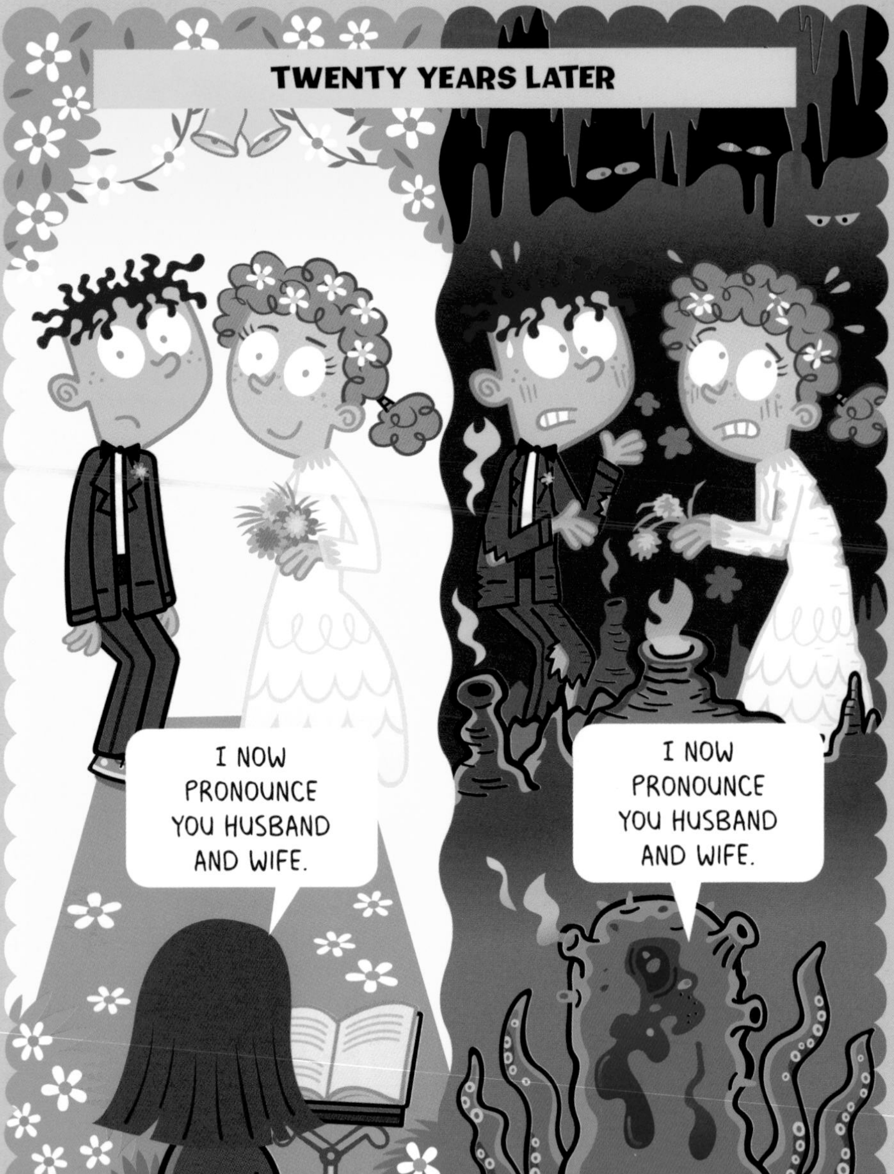
TWENTY YEARS LATER
I NOW PRONOUNCE YOU HUSBAND AND WIFE.
I NOW PRONOUNCE YOU HUSBAND AND WIFE.

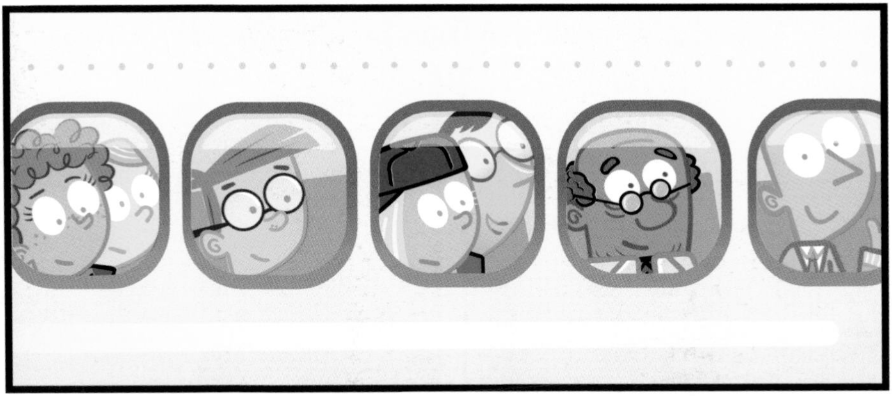

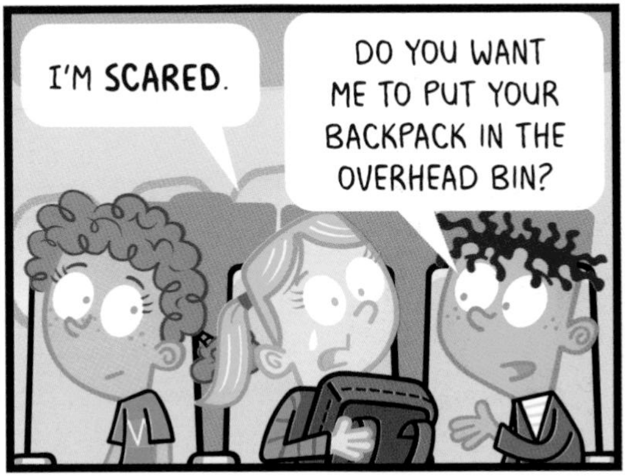
I'M **SCARED**.
DO YOU WANT ME TO PUT YOUR BACKPACK IN THE OVERHEAD BIN?

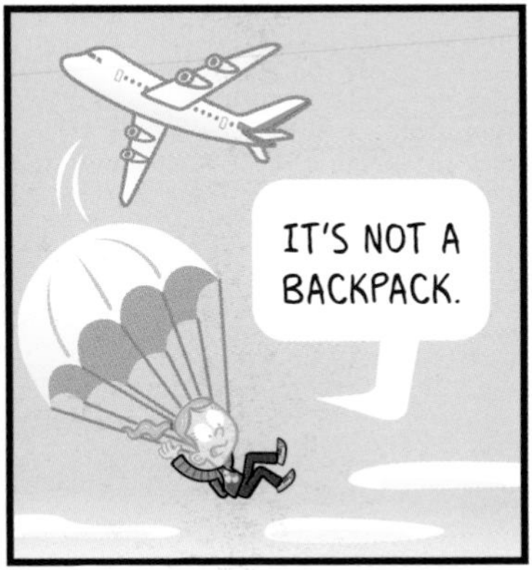
IT'S NOT A BACKPACK.

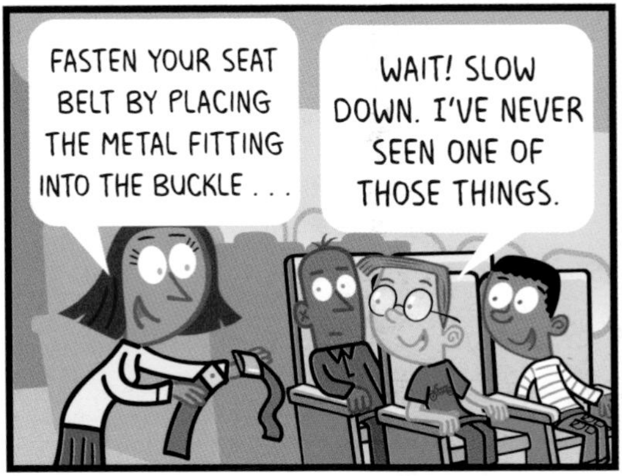
FASTEN YOUR SEAT BELT BY PLACING THE METAL FITTING INTO THE BUCKLE . . .
WAIT! SLOW DOWN. I'VE NEVER SEEN ONE OF THOSE THINGS.

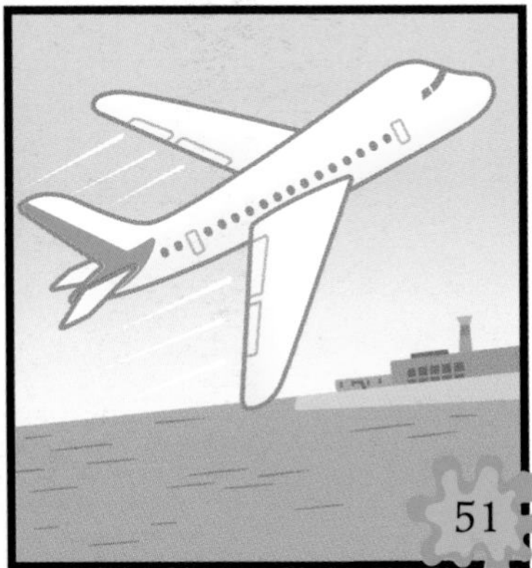

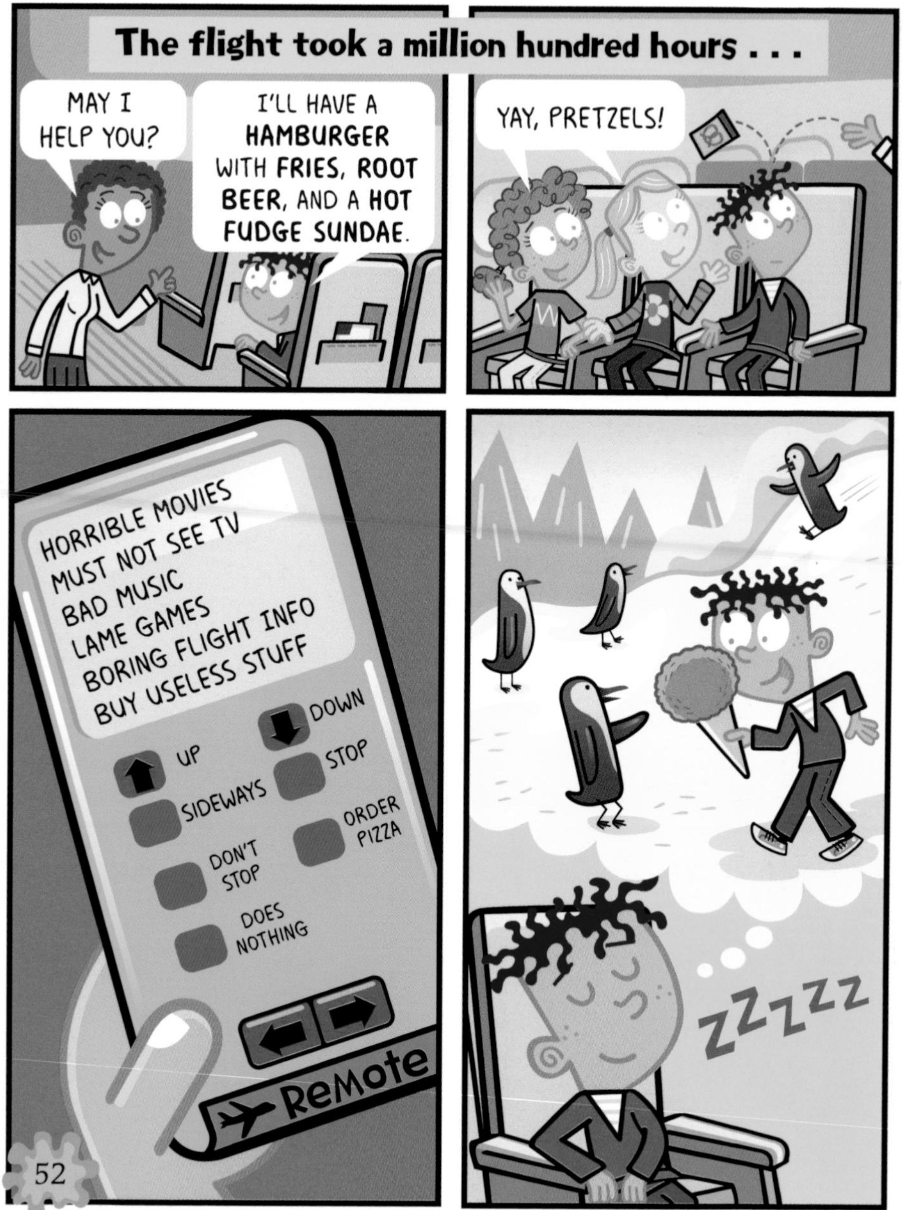
The flight took a million hundred hours . . .
MAY I HELP YOU?
I'LL HAVE A HAMBURGER WITH FRIES, ROOT BEER, AND A HOT FUDGE SUNDAE.
YAY, PRETZELS!
HORRIBLE MOVIES
MUST NOT SEE TV
BAD MUSIC
LAME GAMES
BORING FLIGHT INFO
BUY USELESS STUFF
UP
DOWN
SIDEWAYS
STOP
DON'T STOP
ORDER PIZZA
DOES NOTHING
ReMote
ZZZZZ

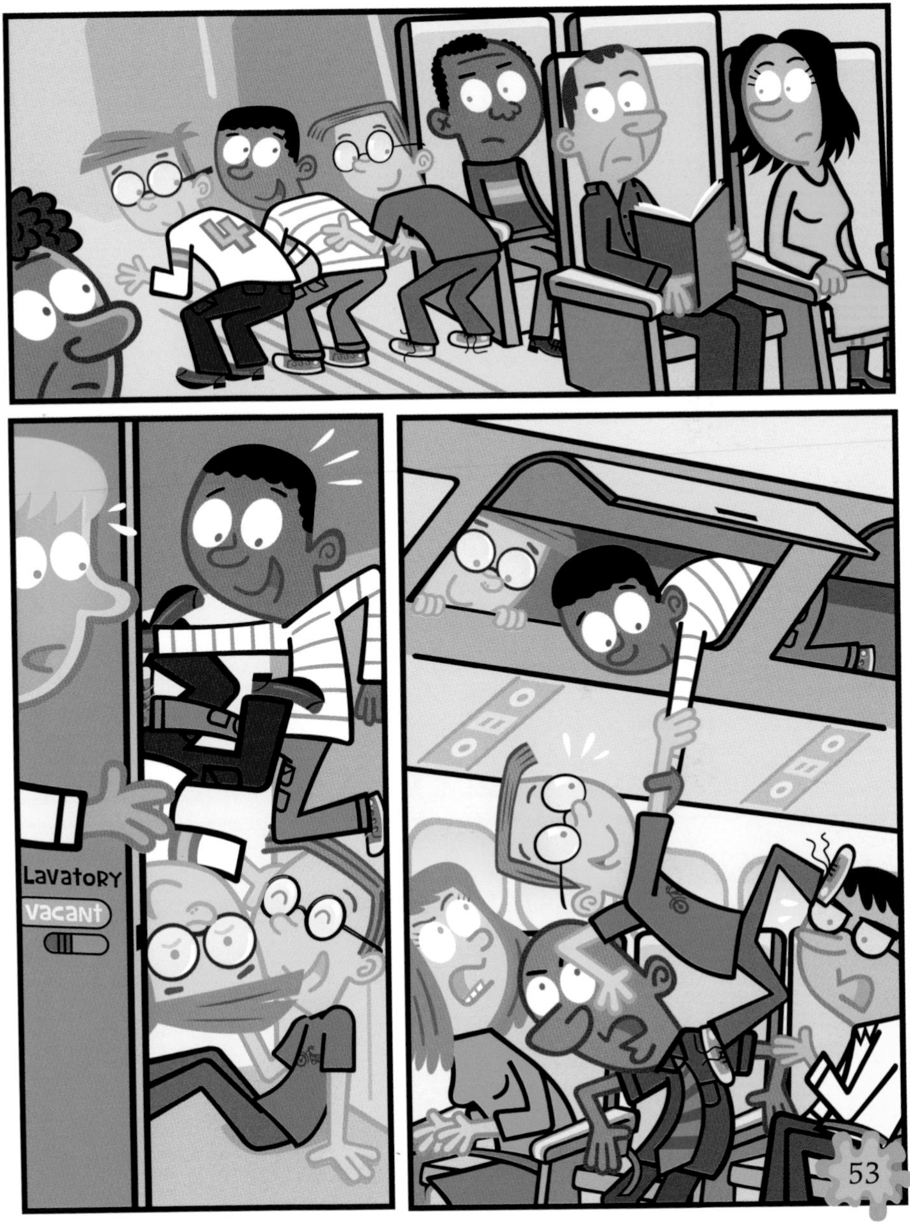
LAVATORY
VACANT

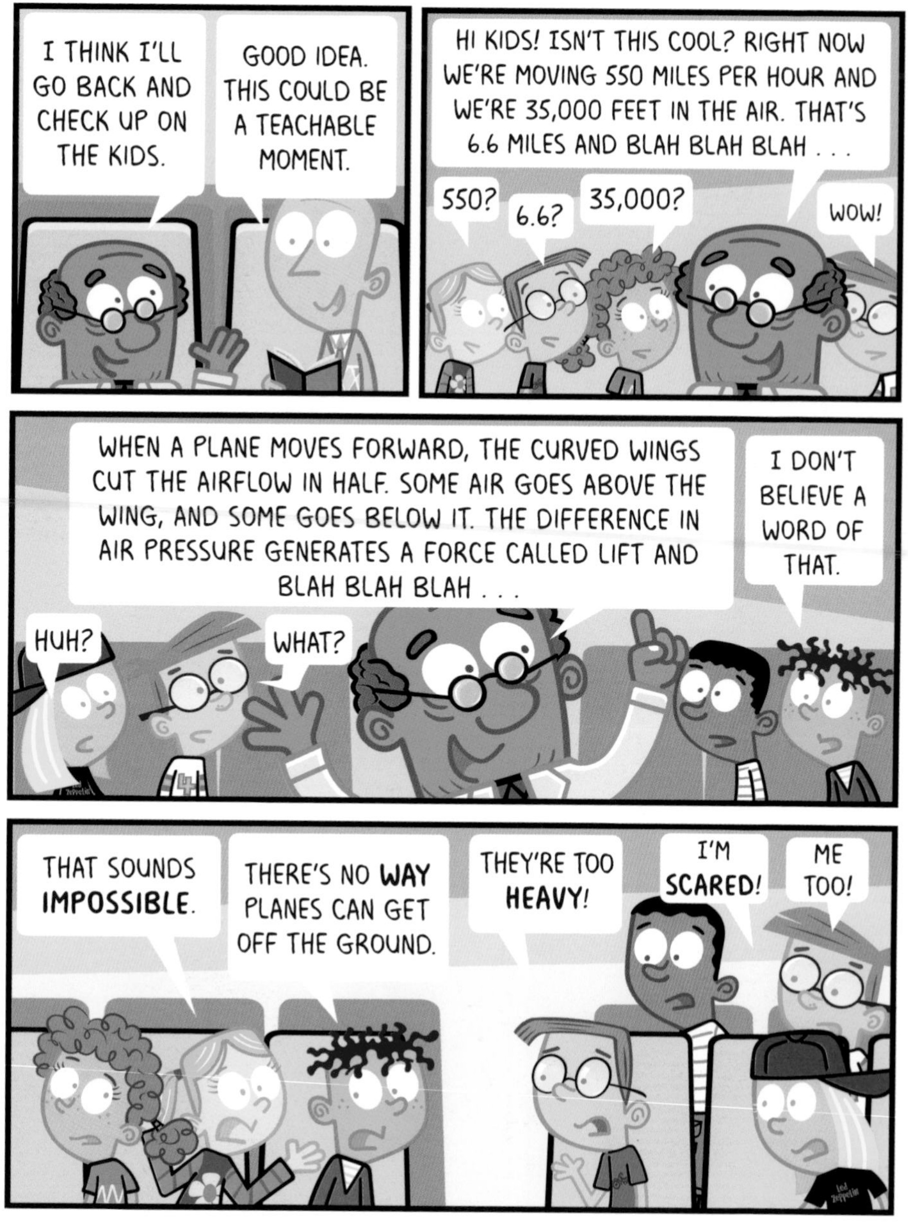
I THINK I'LL GO BACK AND CHECK UP ON THE KIDS.
GOOD IDEA. THIS COULD BE A TEACHABLE MOMENT.
HI KIDS! ISN'T THIS COOL? RIGHT NOW WE'RE MOVING 550 MILES PER HOUR AND WE'RE 35,000 FEET IN THE AIR. THAT'S 6.6 MILES AND BLAH BLAH BLAH . . .
550?
6.6?
35,000?
WOW!
WHEN A PLANE MOVES FORWARD, THE CURVED WINGS CUT THE AIRFLOW IN HALF. SOME AIR GOES ABOVE THE WING, AND SOME GOES BELOW IT. THE DIFFERENCE IN AIR PRESSURE GENERATES A FORCE CALLED LIFT AND BLAH BLAH BLAH . . .
I DON'T BELIEVE A WORD OF THAT.
HUH?
WHAT?
THAT SOUNDS **IMPOSSIBLE**.
THERE'S NO **WAY** PLANES CAN GET OFF THE GROUND.
THEY'RE TOO **HEAVY**!
I'M **SCARED**!
ME TOO!

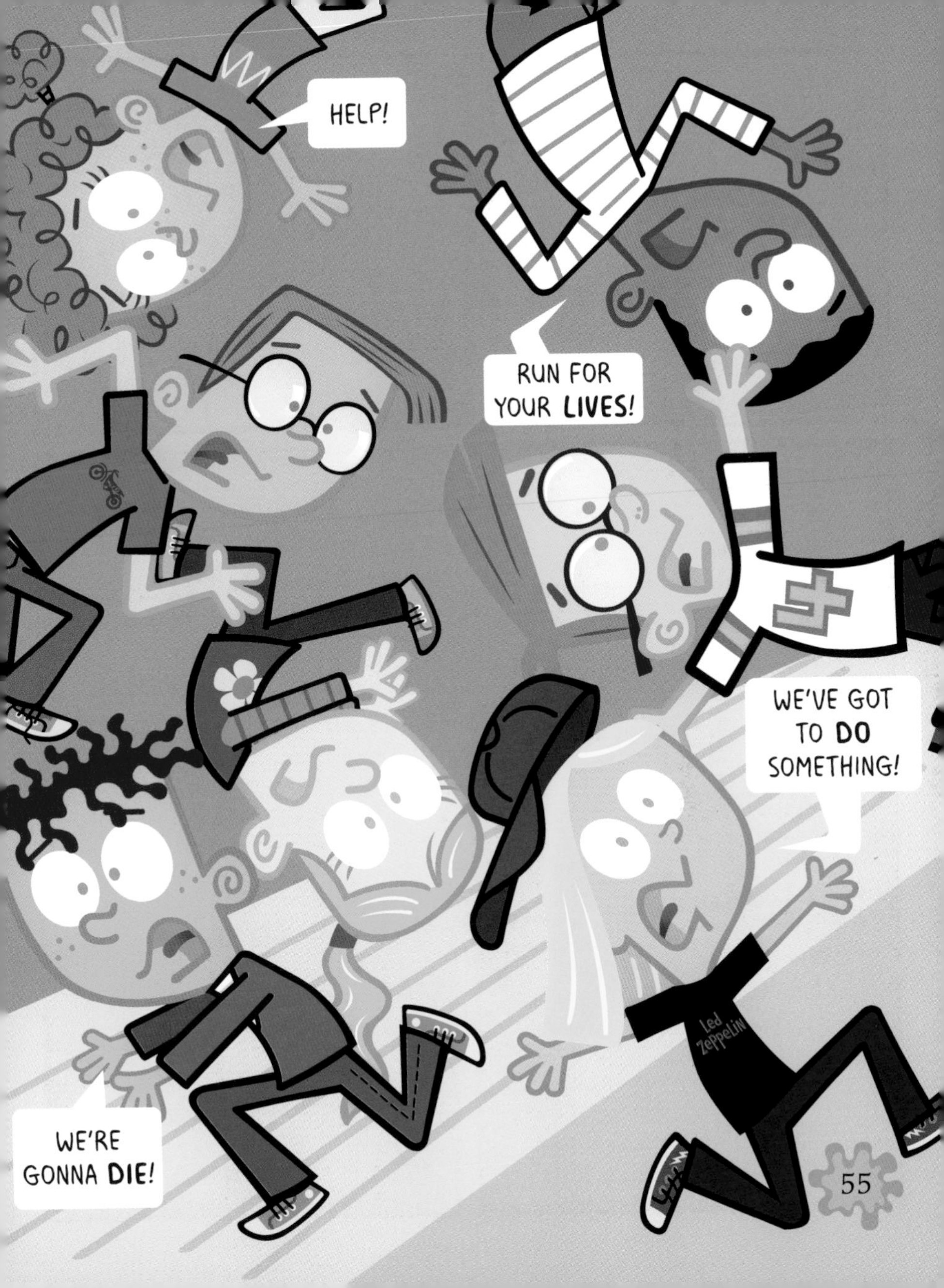
HELP!
RUN FOR YOUR LIVES!
WE'VE GOT TO DO SOMETHING!
WE'RE GONNA DIE!
Led Zeppelin

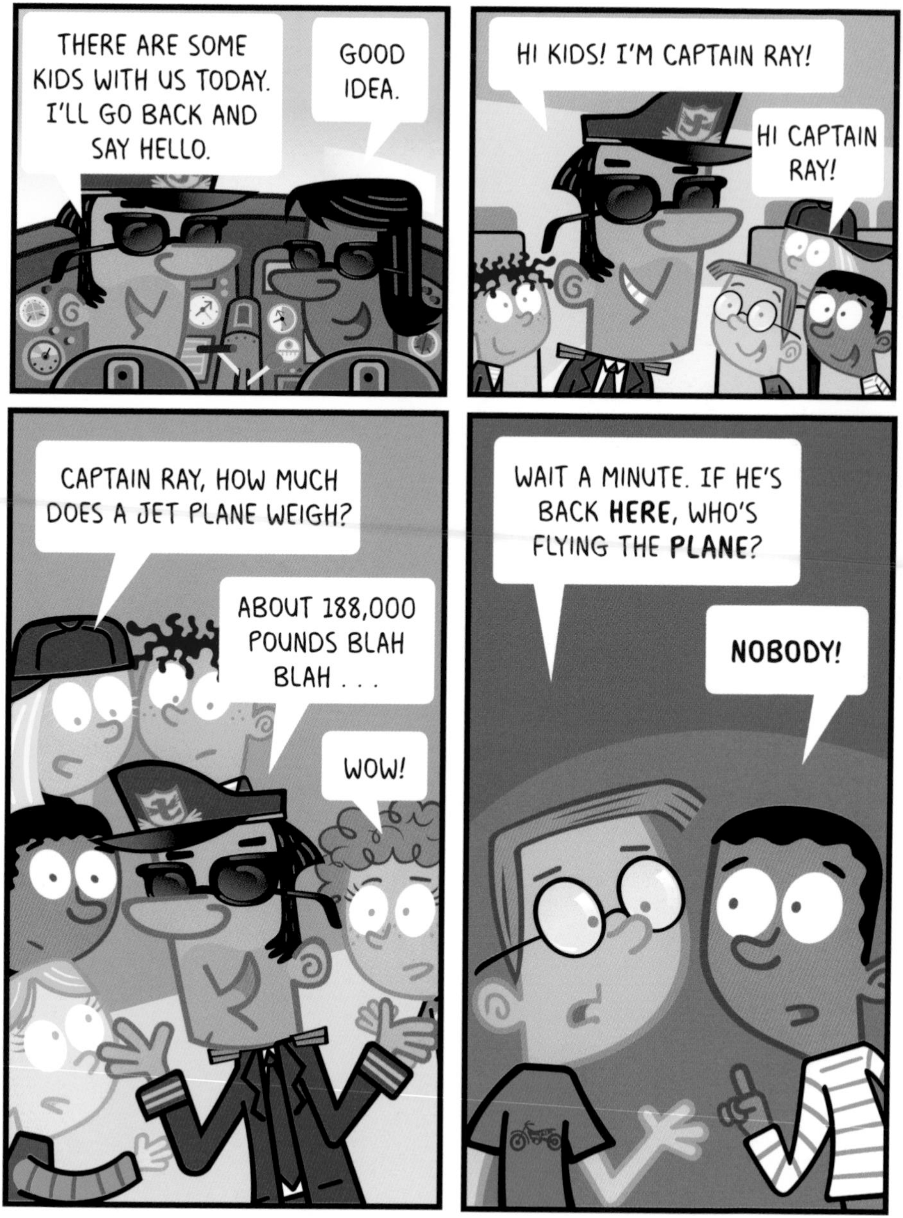
THERE ARE SOME KIDS WITH US TODAY. I'LL GO BACK AND SAY HELLO.
GOOD IDEA.
HI KIDS! I'M CAPTAIN RAY!
HI CAPTAIN RAY!
CAPTAIN RAY, HOW MUCH DOES A JET PLANE WEIGH?
ABOUT 188,000 POUNDS BLAH BLAH . . .
WOW!
WAIT A MINUTE. IF HE'S BACK **HERE**, WHO'S FLYING THE **PLANE**?
NOBODY!

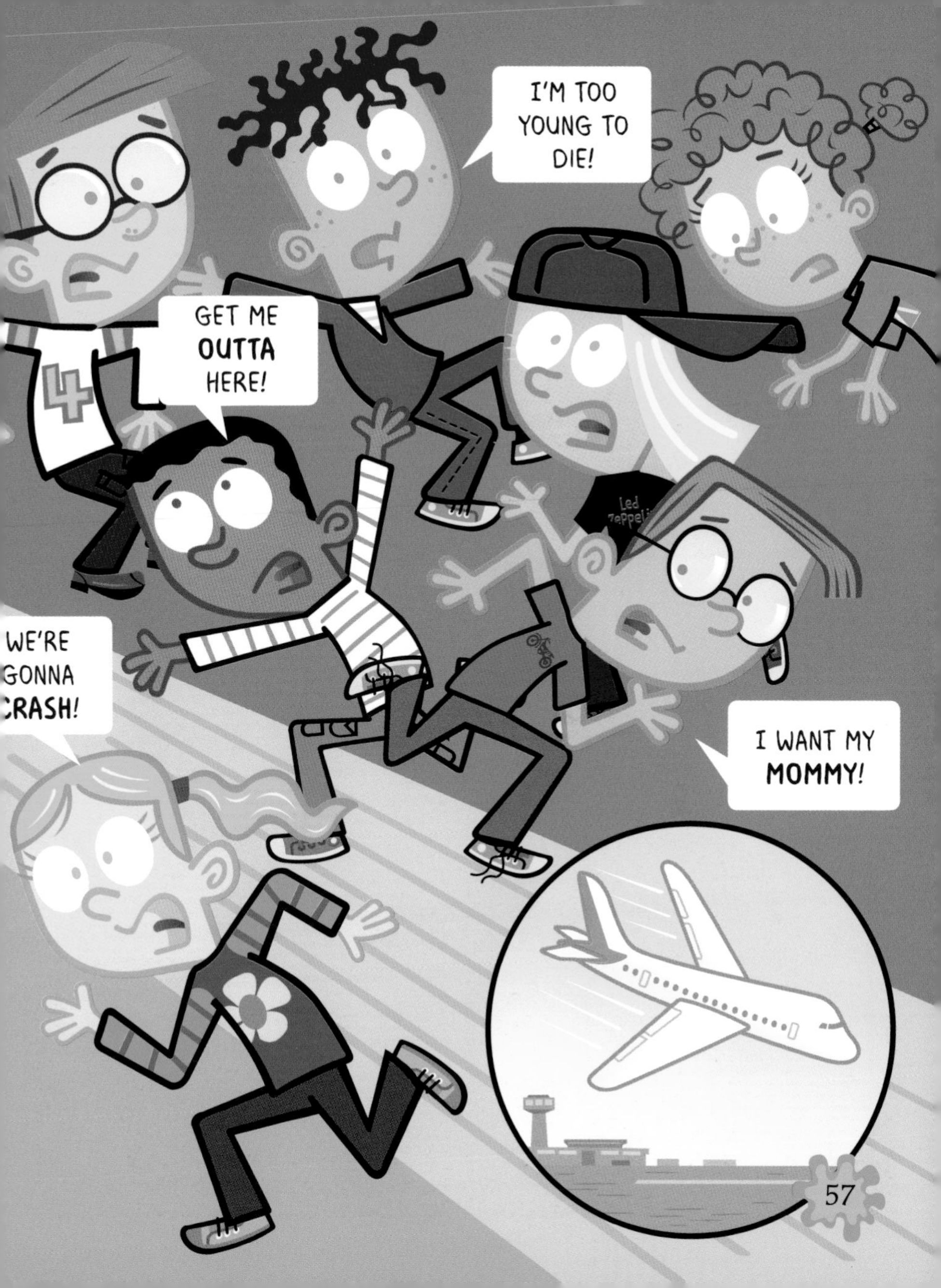
I'M TOO YOUNG TO DIE!
GET ME OUTTA HERE!
WE'RE GONNA CRASH!
I WANT MY MOMMY!
Led Zeppelin

ADVERTISEMENT

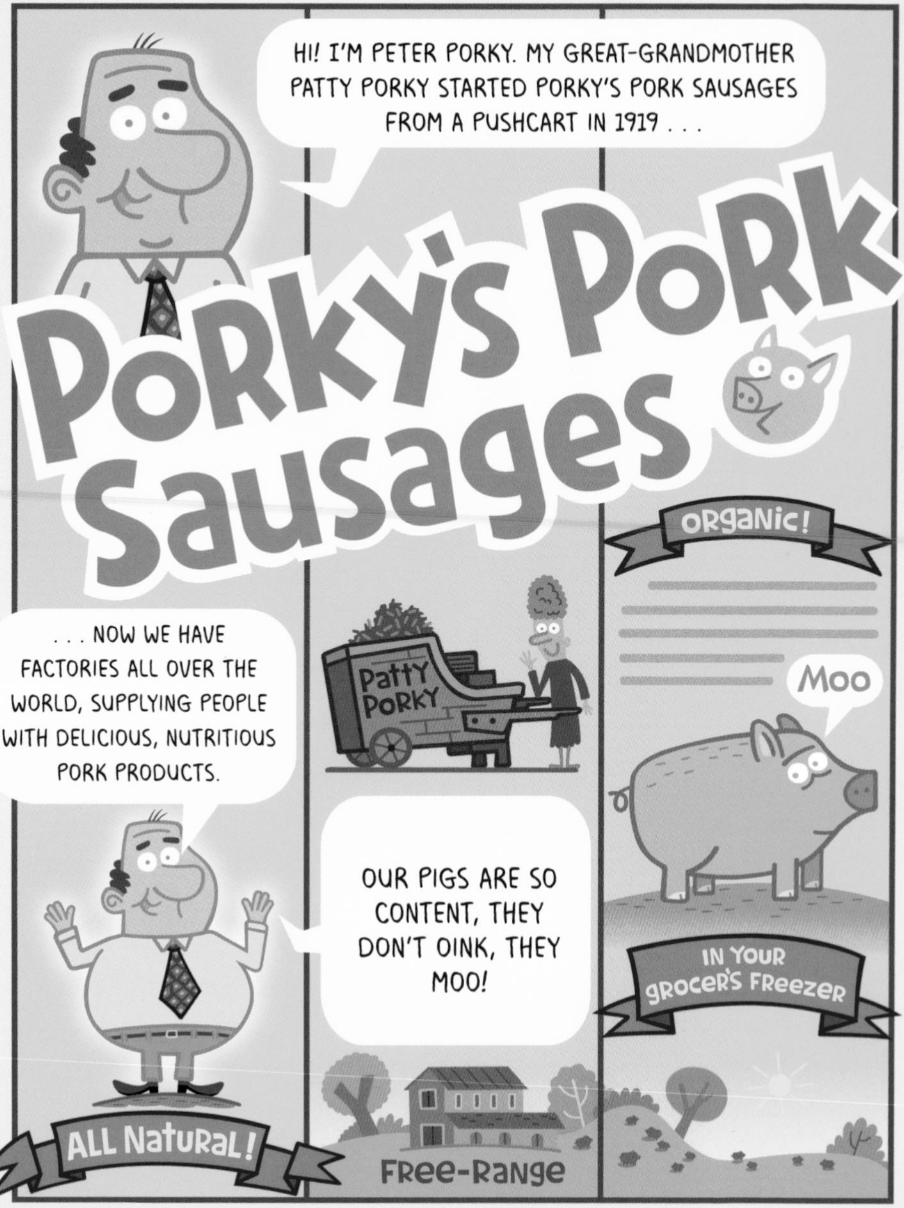

HI! I'M PETER PORKY. MY GREAT-GRANDMOTHER PATTY PORKY STARTED PORKY'S PORK SAUSAGES FROM A PUSHCART IN 1919 . . .
Porky's Pork Sausages
ORGANIC!
Patty Porky
. . . NOW WE HAVE FACTORIES ALL OVER THE WORLD, SUPPLYING PEOPLE WITH DELICIOUS, NUTRITIOUS PORK PRODUCTS.
Moo
OUR PIGS ARE SO CONTENT, THEY DON'T OINK, THEY MOO!
IN YOUR grocer's Freezer
ALL Natural!
Free-Range

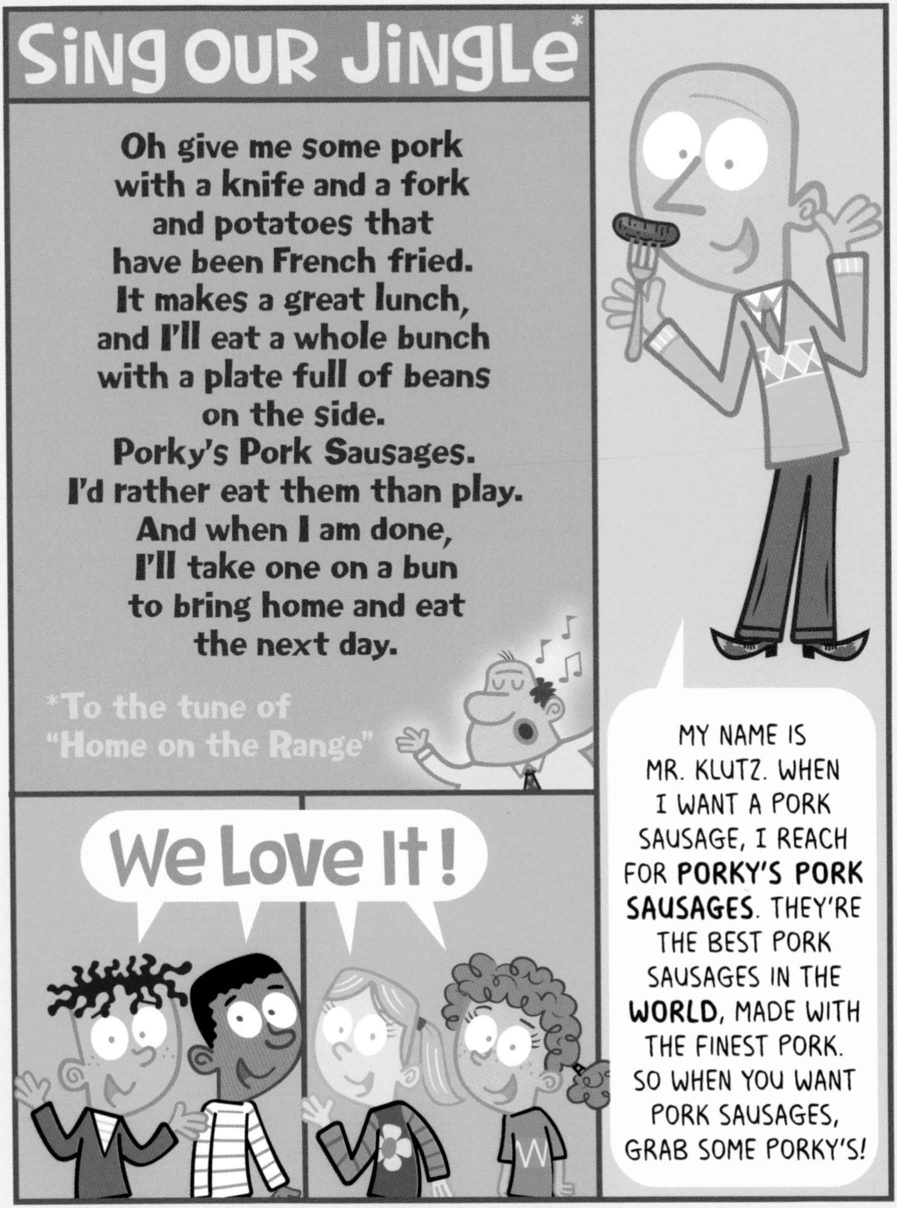
Sing Our Jingle*
Oh give me some pork
with a knife and a fork
and potatoes that
have been French fried.
It makes a great lunch,
and I'll eat a whole bunch
with a plate full of beans
on the side.
Porky's Pork Sausages.
I'd rather eat them than play.
And when I am done,
I'll take one on a bun
to bring home and eat
the next day.
*To the tune of "Home on the Range"
MY NAME IS MR. KLUTZ. WHEN I WANT A PORK SAUSAGE, I REACH FOR PORKY'S PORK SAUSAGES. THEY'RE THE BEST PORK SAUSAGES IN THE WORLD, MADE WITH THE FINEST PORK. SO WHEN YOU WANT PORK SAUSAGES, GRAB SOME PORKY'S!
We Love It!

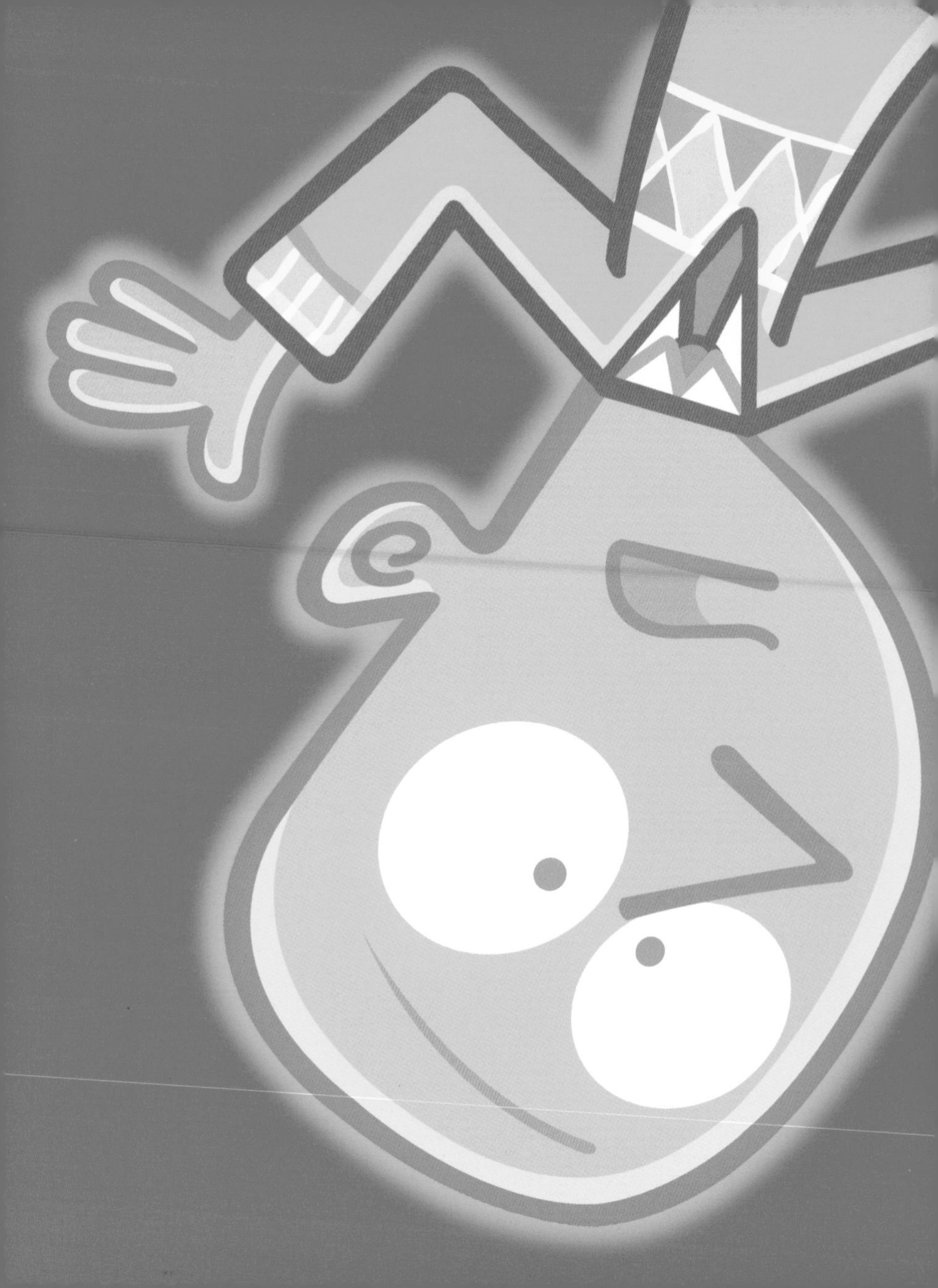

CHAPTER 5

Too Much Stuff

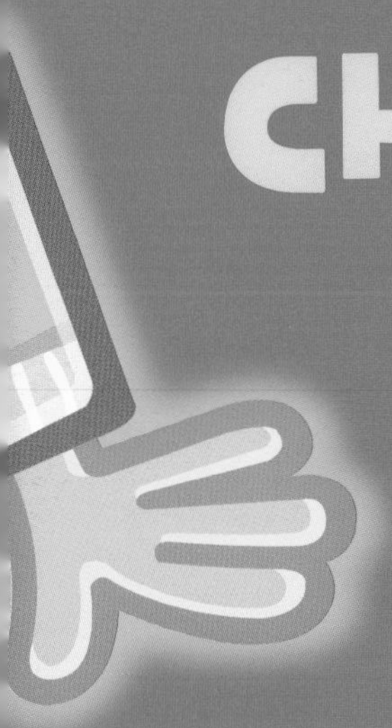

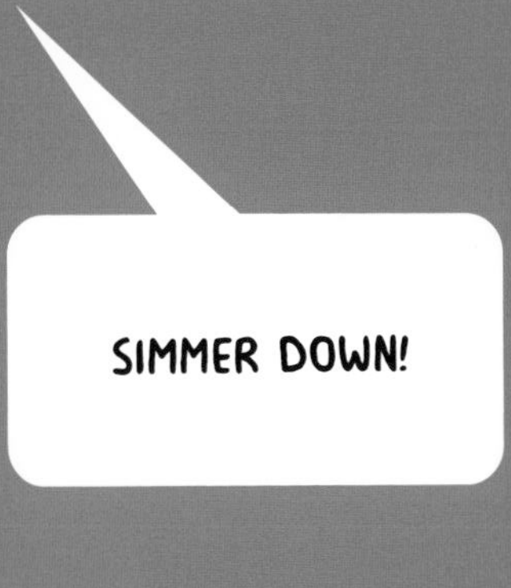
SIMMER DOWN!

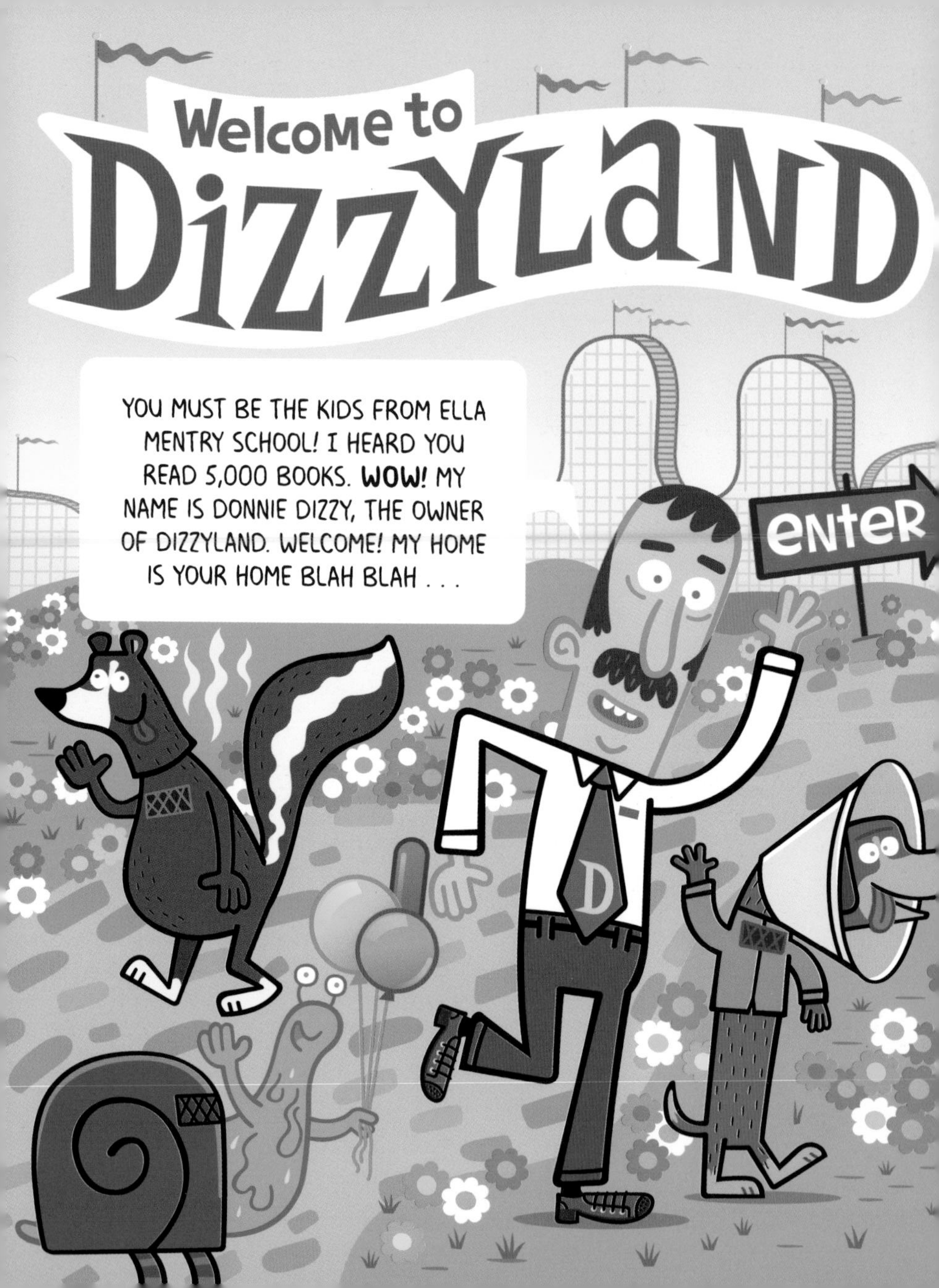
Welcome to
DIZZYLAND
YOU MUST BE THE KIDS FROM ELLA MENTRY SCHOOL! I HEARD YOU READ 5,000 BOOKS. **WOW!** MY NAME IS DONNIE DIZZY, THE OWNER OF DIZZYLAND. WELCOME! MY HOME IS YOUR HOME BLAH BLAH . . .
ENTER

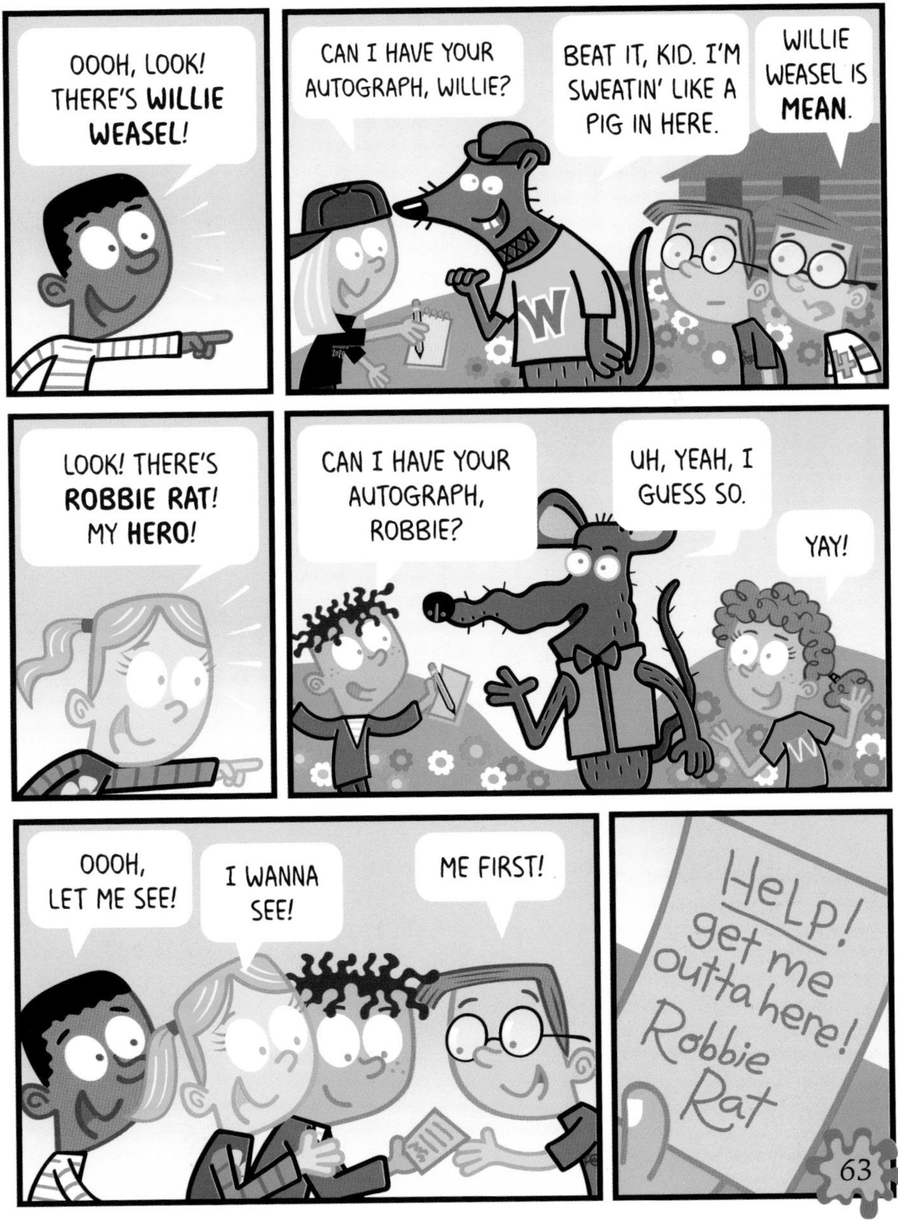

OOOH, LOOK! THERE'S **WILLIE WEASEL**!
CAN I HAVE YOUR AUTOGRAPH, WILLIE?
BEAT IT, KID. I'M SWEATIN' LIKE A PIG IN HERE.
WILLIE WEASEL IS **MEAN**.
LOOK! THERE'S **ROBBIE RAT**! MY **HERO**!
CAN I HAVE YOUR AUTOGRAPH, ROBBIE?
UH, YEAH, I GUESS SO.
YAY!
OOOH, LET ME SEE!
I WANNA SEE!
ME FIRST!
HeLP! get me outta here! Robbie Rat

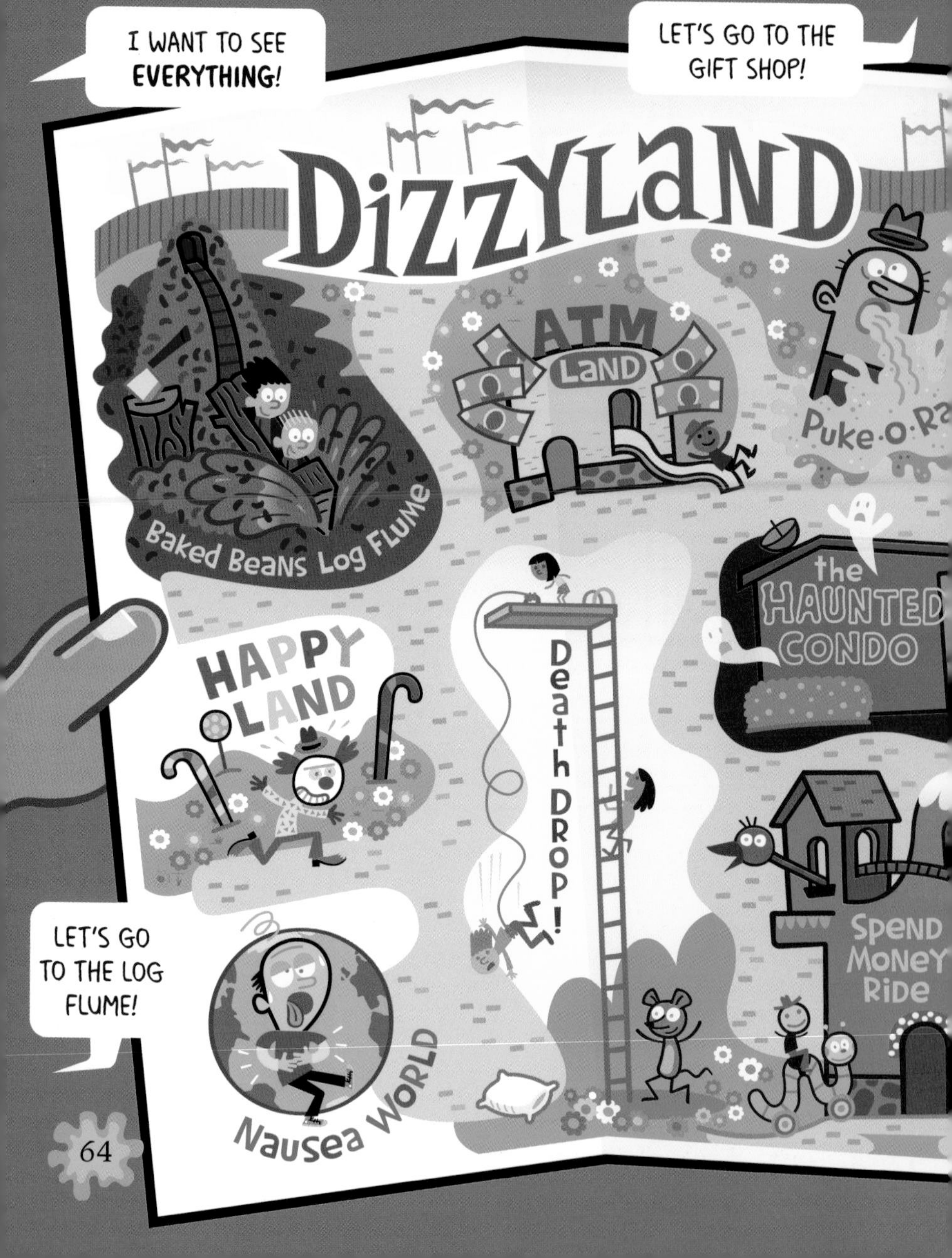
I WANT TO SEE **EVERYTHING**!
LET'S GO TO THE GIFT SHOP!
DIZZYLAND
Baked Beans Log FLUME
ATM LAND
Puke-o-Ra
the HAUNTED CONDO
HAPPY LAND
Death DROP!
Spend Money Ride
LET'S GO TO THE LOG FLUME!
Nausea WORLD

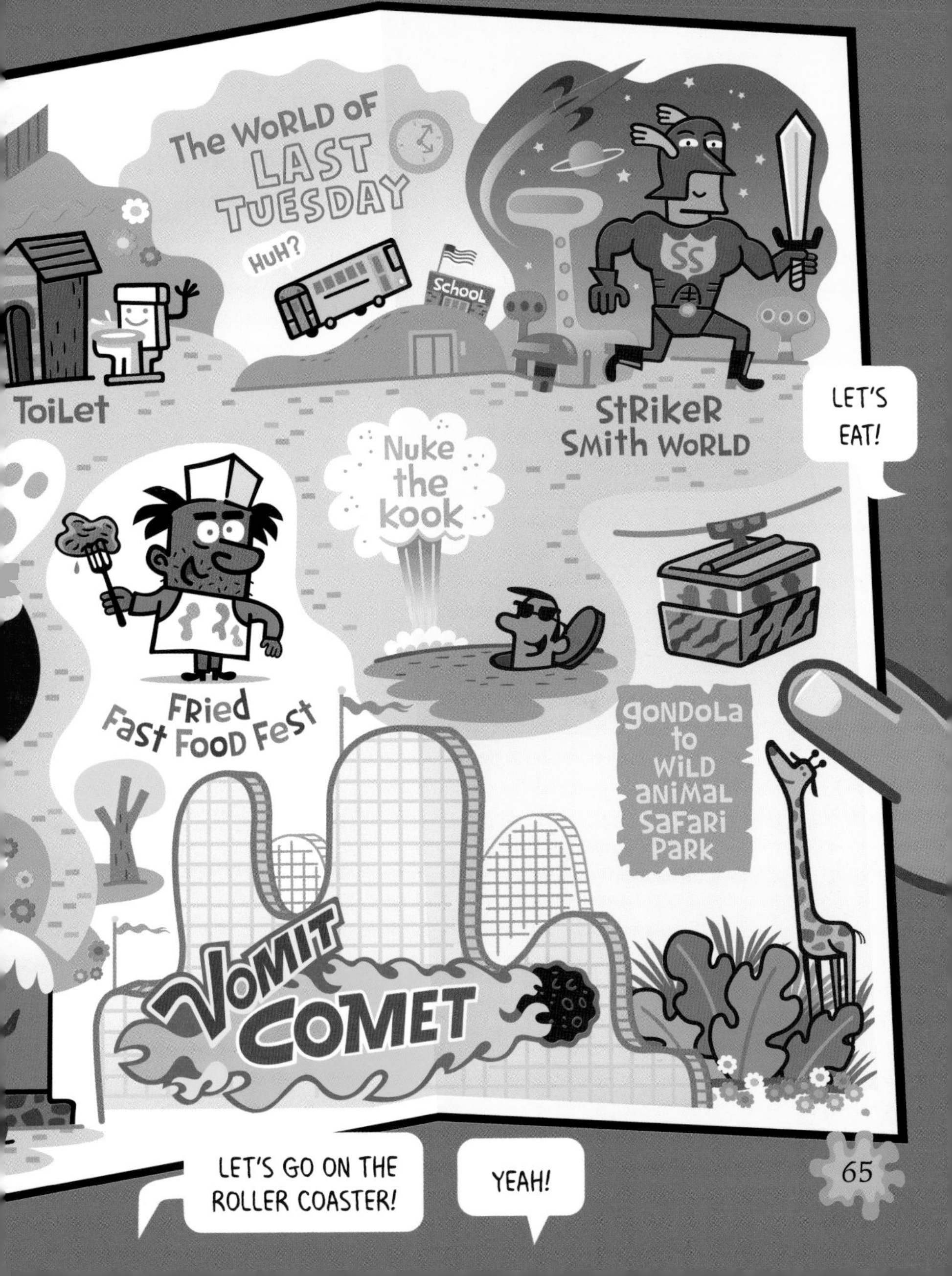
The WORLD OF LAST TUESDAY
HUH?
SCHOOL
TOILET
STRIKER SMITH WORLD
LET'S EAT!
Nuke the kook
FRIED FAST FOOD FEST
GONDOLA to WILD ANIMAL SAFARI PARK
VOMIT COMET
LET'S GO ON THE ROLLER COASTER!
YEAH!

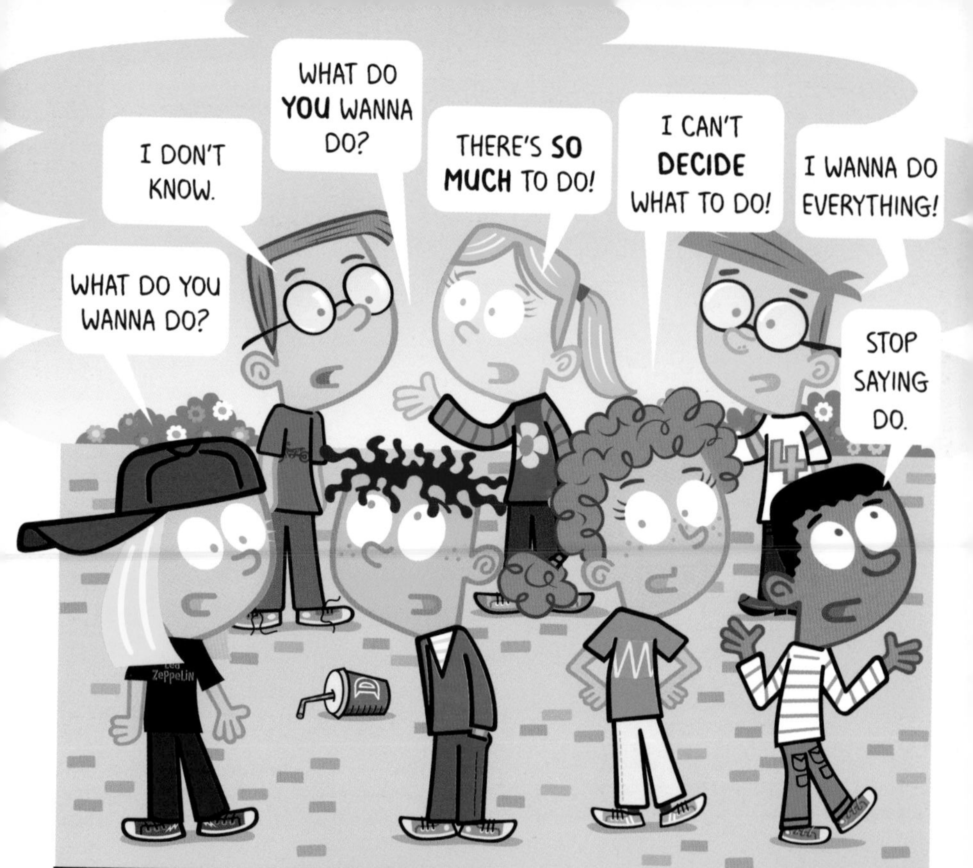
WHAT DO YOU WANNA DO?
I DON'T KNOW.
WHAT DO **YOU** WANNA DO?
THERE'S **SO MUCH** TO DO!
I CAN'T **DECIDE** WHAT TO DO!
I WANNA DO EVERYTHING!
STOP SAYING DO.
Led Zeppelin

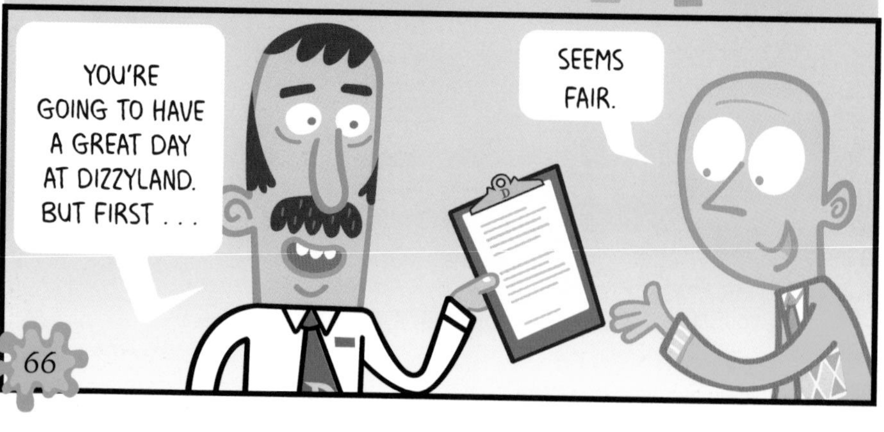
YOU'RE GOING TO HAVE A GREAT DAY AT DIZZYLAND. BUT FIRST . . .
SEEMS FAIR.

YOU CAN'T SUE US IF:

-Your personal items are lost or stolen.

-Your car is not in the parking lot at the end of the day.

-There is an earthquake, tornado, or natural disaster.

-One of the rides malfunctions.

-You get heat stroke while waiting on line.

-One of our toilets overflows while you're sitting on it.

-You don't have a good time.

-You're bored.

-You die.

-One of your parents is a lawyer.

-We put you in one of our promotional videos.

-We decide you're too ugly to appear in our promotional videos.

-You spend all your money on dumb souvenirs.

-One of our employees farts within five feet of you.

-You choke on your own vomit.

-You choke on somebody else's vomit.

-A mime follows you around, imitating you.

-An anvil falls on your head.

-You're hit by a boomerang.

-You slip on a banana peel.

-A banana peel slips on you.

-You don't like reading long lists of stuff.

-You fall into a sinkhole that suddenly opens up for no reason.

-You get hit by a meteorite from outer space.

-Aliens from the future come and steal your car keys.

-You go blind after staring at a solar eclipse.

-One of the members of your party spontaneously combusts.

-You're trampled by a stampeding herd of buffalo.

-An atomic bomb wipes out the park while you're here.

-You get hit by a tranquilizing dart.

-Your intestines explode after you eat at our snack bar.

-Your body is dismembered by hungry wild animals.

-You get a paper cut signing this waiver.

Mr. Klutz

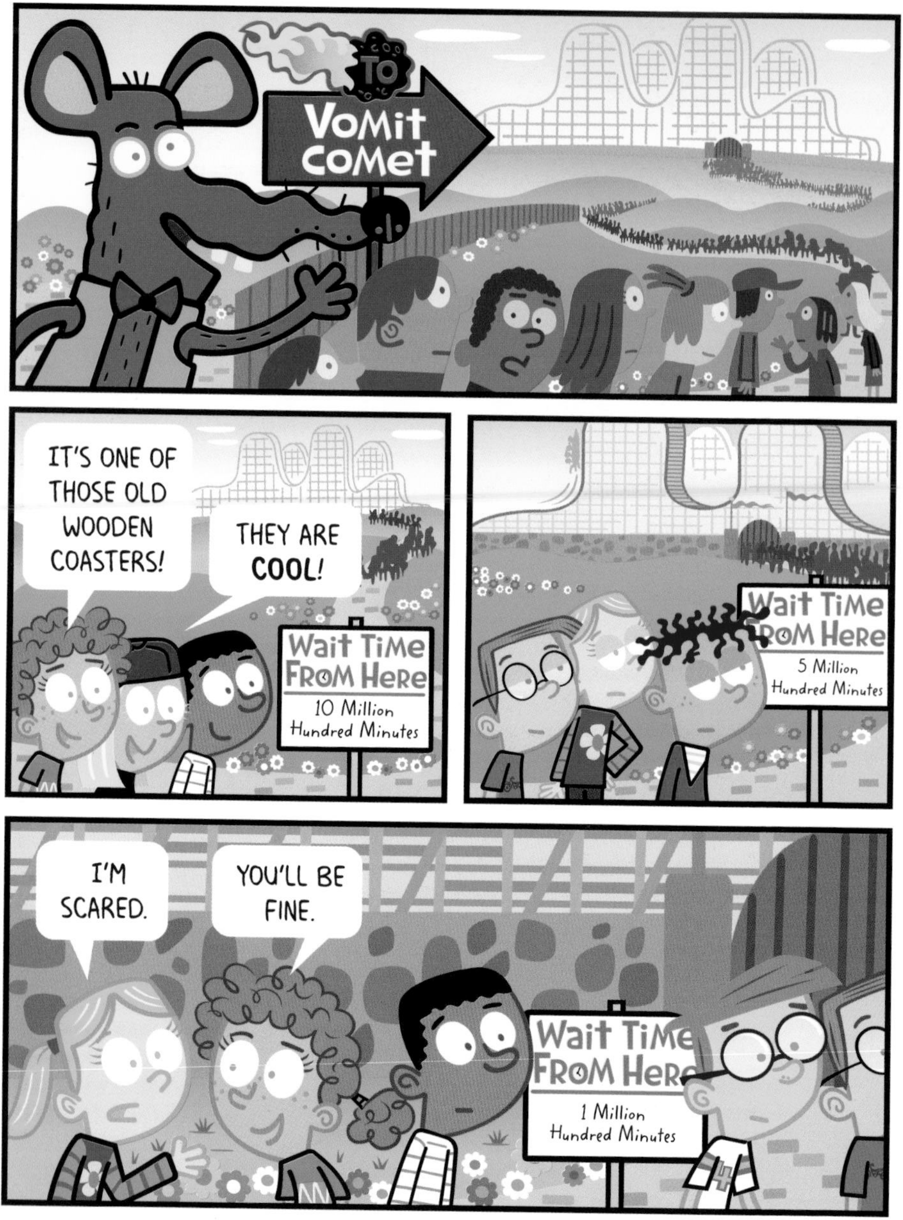
TO
VoMit CoMet
IT'S ONE OF THOSE OLD WOODEN COASTERS!
THEY ARE **COOL!**
Wait TiMe FRoM Here
10 Million Hundred Minutes
Wait TiMe FRoM Here
5 Million Hundred Minutes
I'M SCARED.
YOU'LL BE FINE.
Wait TiMe FRoM Here
1 Million Hundred Minutes

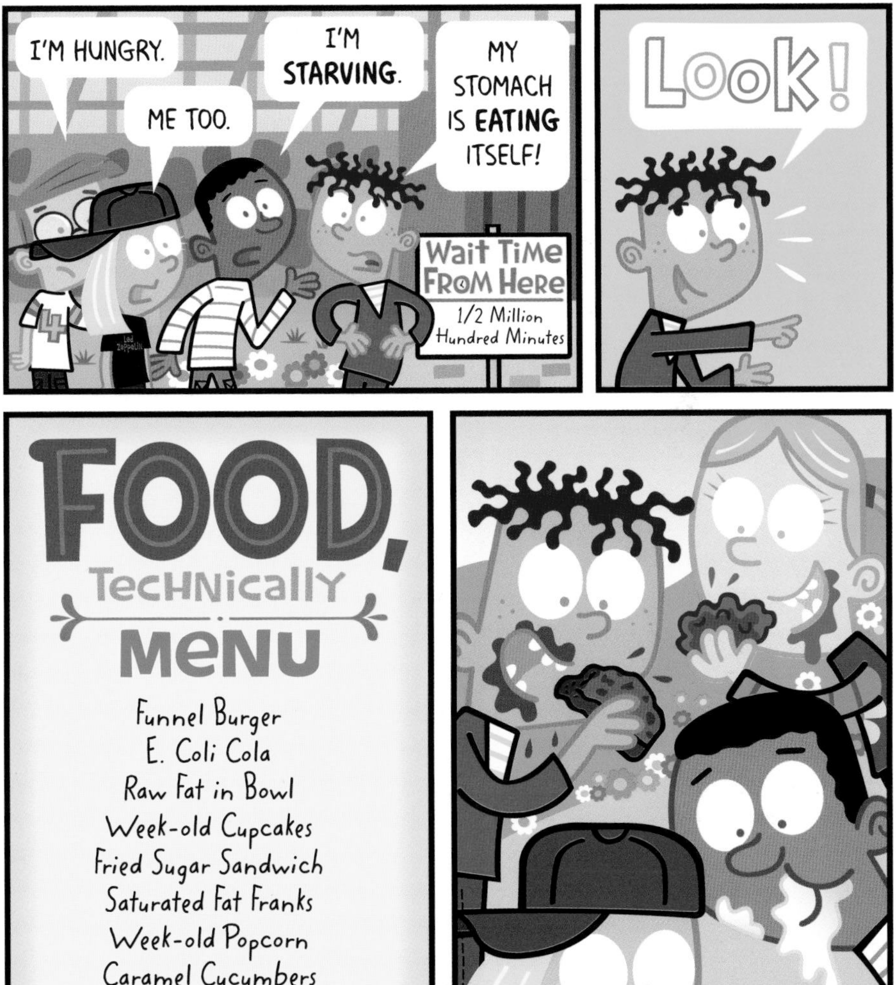
I'M HUNGRY.
ME TOO.
I'M STARVING.
MY STOMACH IS EATING ITSELF!
Wait Time From Here
1/2 Million Hundred Minutes
LOOK!
FOOD, Technically MENU
Funnel Burger
E. Coli Cola
Raw Fat in Bowl
Week-old Cupcakes
Fried Sugar Sandwich
Saturated Fat Franks
Week-old Popcorn
Caramel Cucumbers
Fructose Pops
Extra Gluten
YAY!
YAY!
YAY!
YAY!

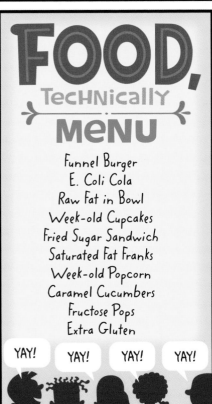

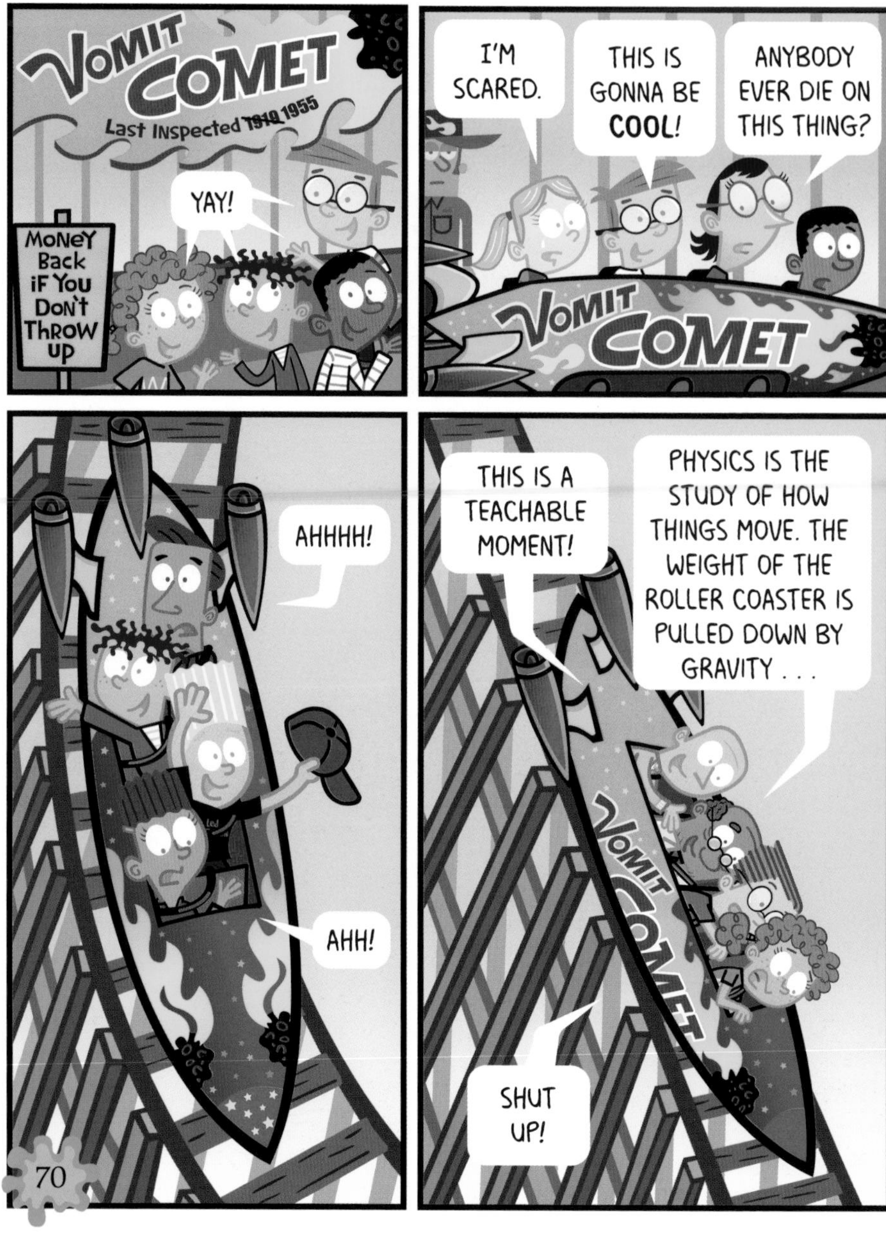
VOMIT COMET
Last Inspected ~~1919~~ 1955
YAY!
MONEY Back iF You DON'T THROW UP
I'M SCARED.
THIS IS GONNA BE **COOL**!
ANYBODY EVER DIE ON THIS THING?
VOMIT COMET
AHHHH!
AHH!
THIS IS A TEACHABLE MOMENT!
PHYSICS IS THE STUDY OF HOW THINGS MOVE. THE WEIGHT OF THE ROLLER COASTER IS PULLED DOWN BY GRAVITY . . .
VOMIT COMET
SHUT UP!

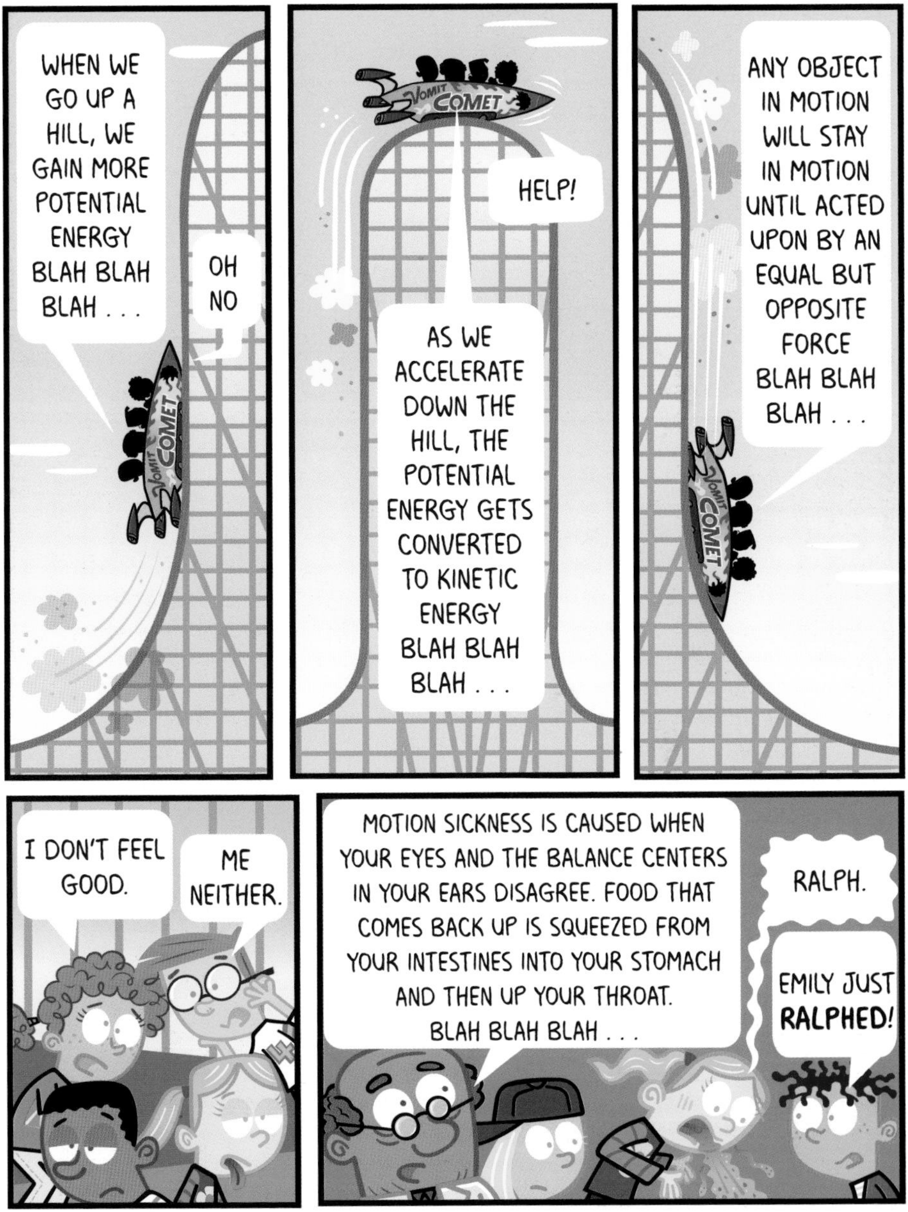
WHEN WE GO UP A HILL, WE GAIN MORE POTENTIAL ENERGY BLAH BLAH BLAH . . .
OH NO
VOMIT COMET
HELP!
AS WE ACCELERATE DOWN THE HILL, THE POTENTIAL ENERGY GETS CONVERTED TO KINETIC ENERGY BLAH BLAH BLAH . . .
ANY OBJECT IN MOTION WILL STAY IN MOTION UNTIL ACTED UPON BY AN EQUAL BUT OPPOSITE FORCE BLAH BLAH BLAH . . .
I DON'T FEEL GOOD.
ME NEITHER.
MOTION SICKNESS IS CAUSED WHEN YOUR EYES AND THE BALANCE CENTERS IN YOUR EARS DISAGREE. FOOD THAT COMES BACK UP IS SQUEEZED FROM YOUR INTESTINES INTO YOUR STOMACH AND THEN UP YOUR THROAT. BLAH BLAH BLAH . . .
RALPH.
EMILY JUST **RALPHED!**

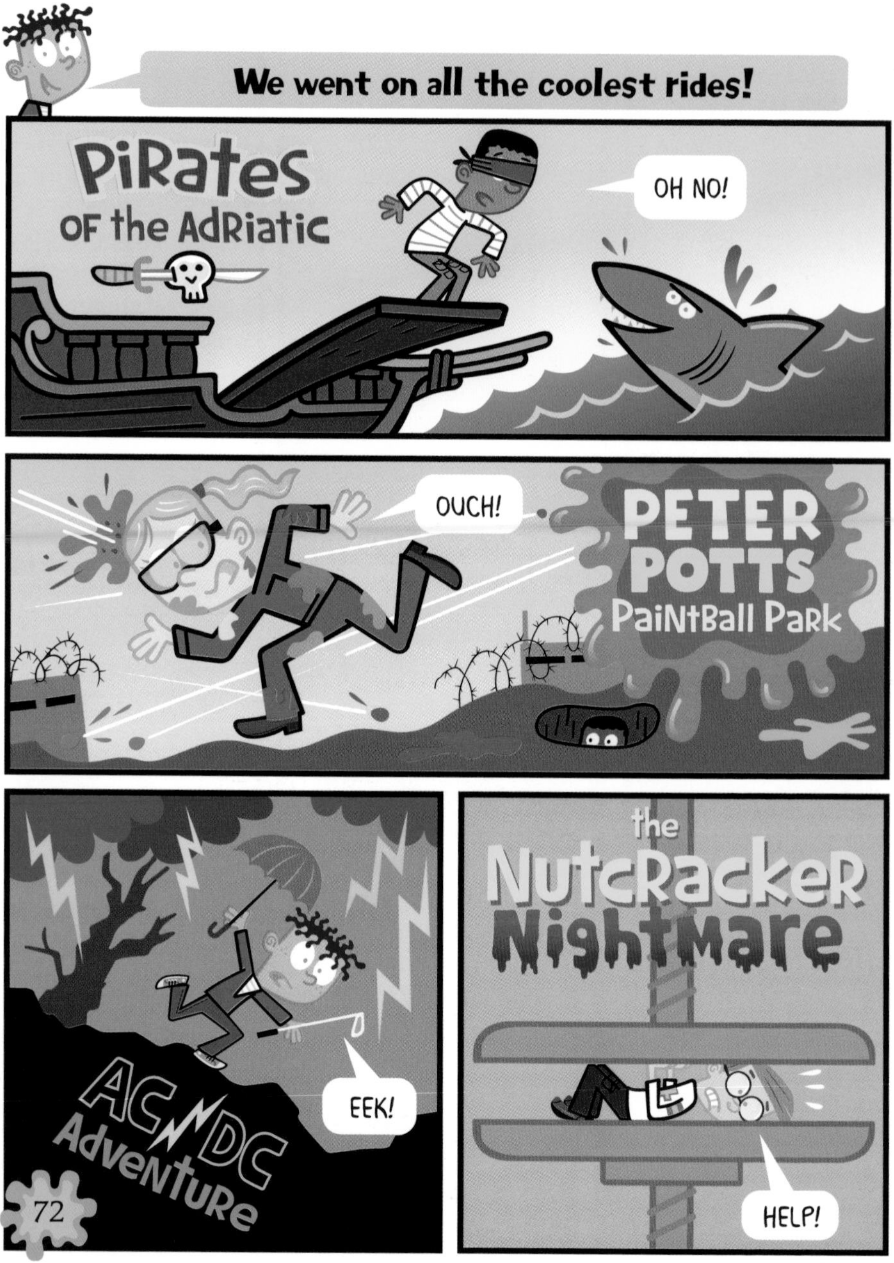
We went on all the coolest rides!
PiRates OF the AdRiatic
OH NO!
OUCH!
PETER POTTS PaiNtBall Park
AC/DC Adventure
EEK!
the NutcRacker Nightmare
HELP!

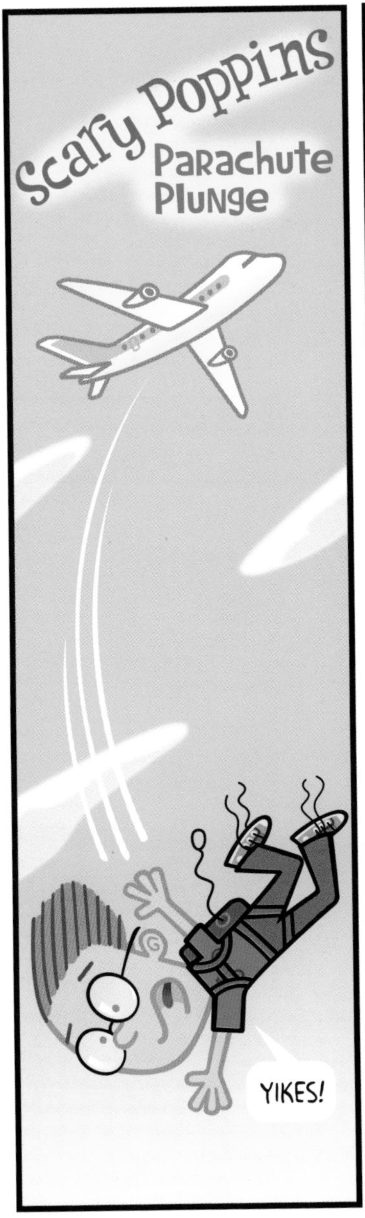
Scary Poppins
Parachute Plunge
YIKES!

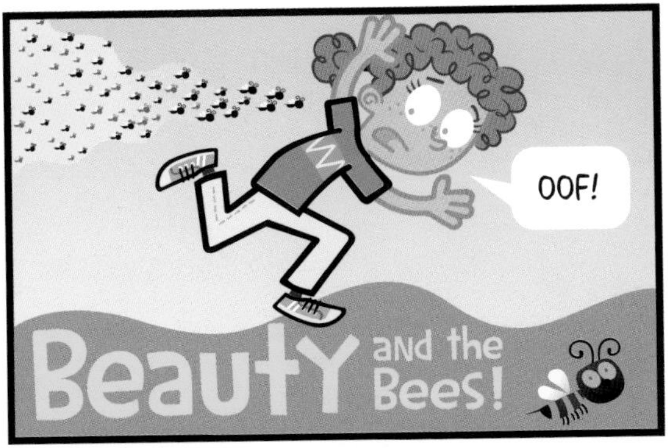
OOF!
Beauty and the Bees!

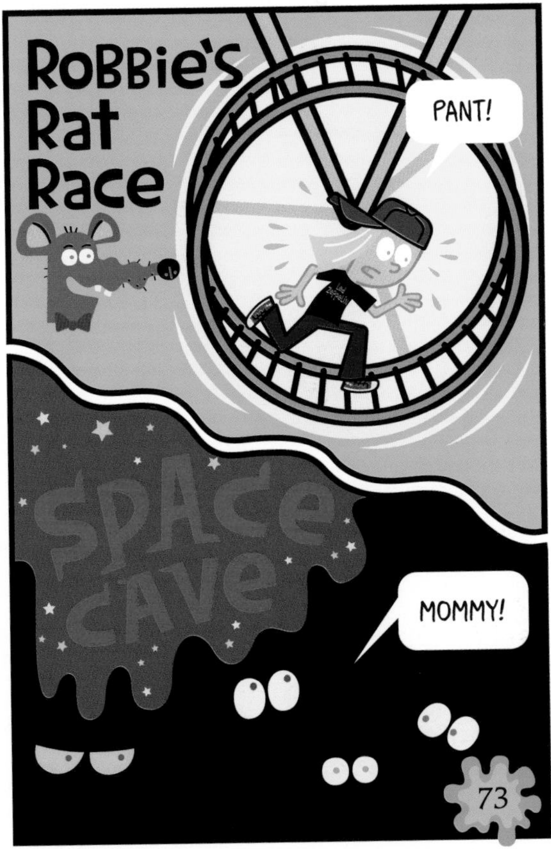
RoBBie's Rat Race
PANT!
SPACE CAVE
MOMMY!

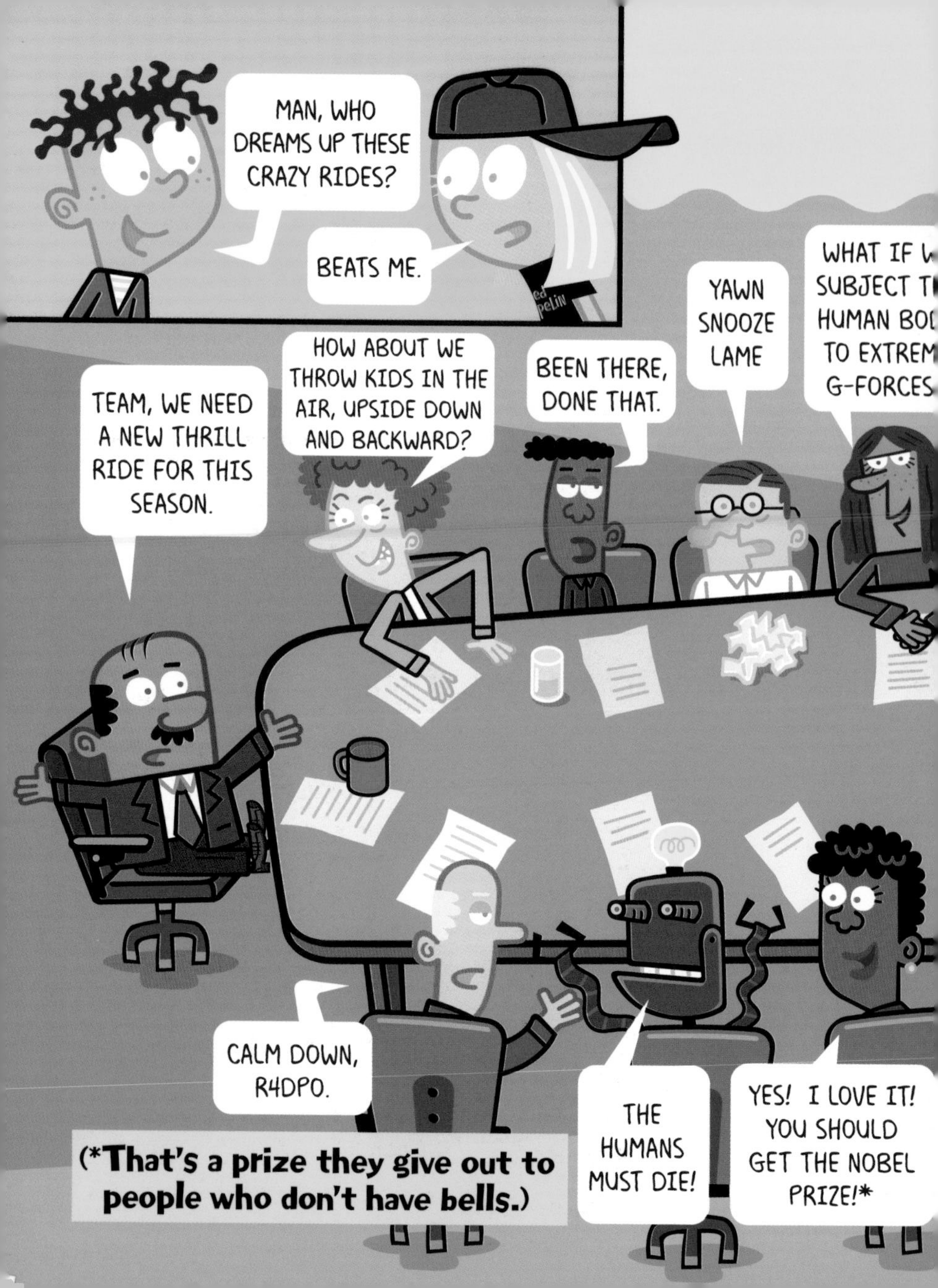
MAN, WHO DREAMS UP THESE CRAZY RIDES?
BEATS ME.
TEAM, WE NEED A NEW THRILL RIDE FOR THIS SEASON.
HOW ABOUT WE THROW KIDS IN THE AIR, UPSIDE DOWN AND BACKWARD?
BEEN THERE, DONE THAT.
YAWN SNOOZE LAME
WHAT IF W SUBJECT T HUMAN BOD TO EXTREM G-FORCES
CALM DOWN, R4DPO.
THE HUMANS MUST DIE!
YES! I LOVE IT! YOU SHOULD GET THE NOBEL PRIZE!*
(*That's a prize they give out to people who don't have bells.)

Deep within the bowels* of Dizzyland is a top secret office where skilled theme park ride designers work on their latest creations . . .

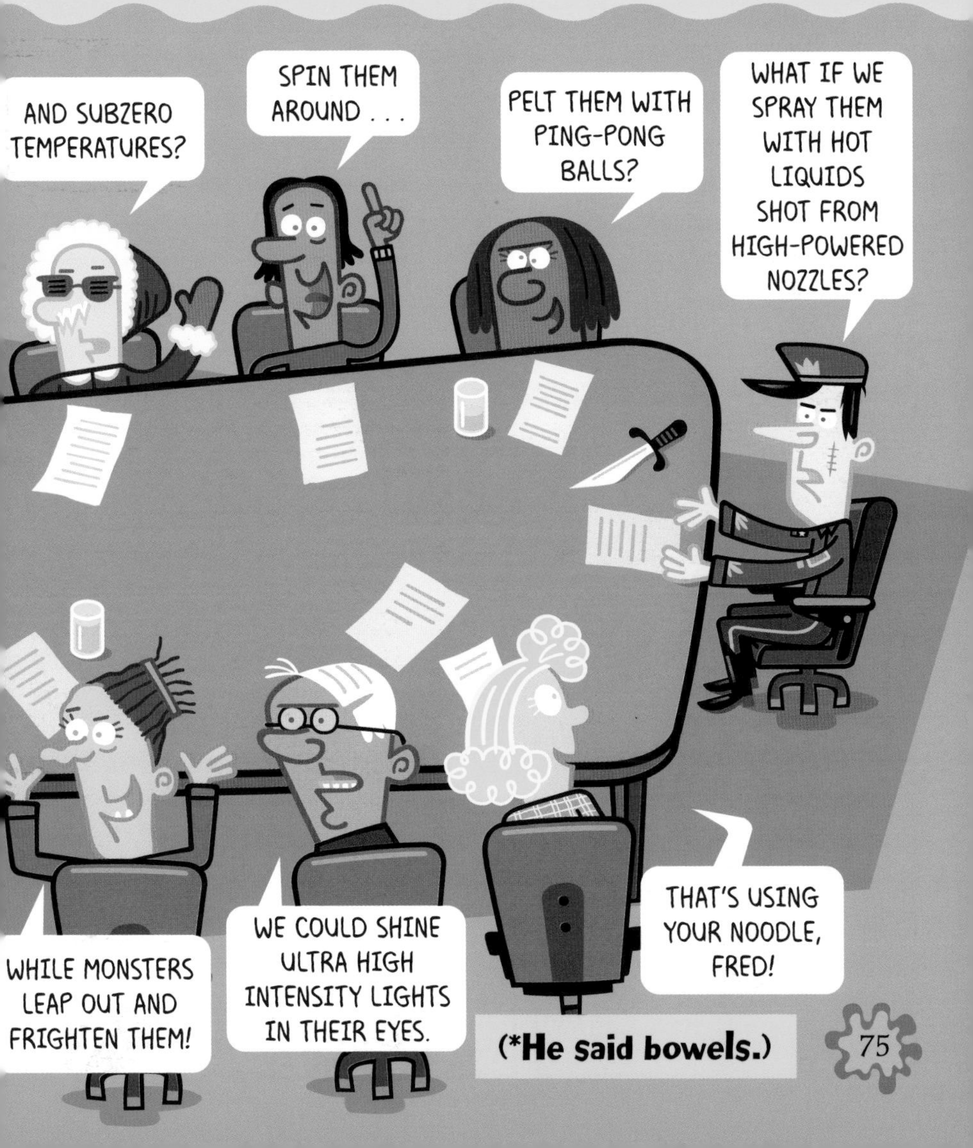

AND SUBZERO TEMPERATURES?
SPIN THEM AROUND . . .
PELT THEM WITH PING-PONG BALLS?
WHAT IF WE SPRAY THEM WITH HOT LIQUIDS SHOT FROM HIGH-POWERED NOZZLES?
WHILE MONSTERS LEAP OUT AND FRIGHTEN THEM!
WE COULD SHINE ULTRA HIGH INTENSITY LIGHTS IN THEIR EYES.
THAT'S USING YOUR NOODLE, FRED!

(*He said bowels.)

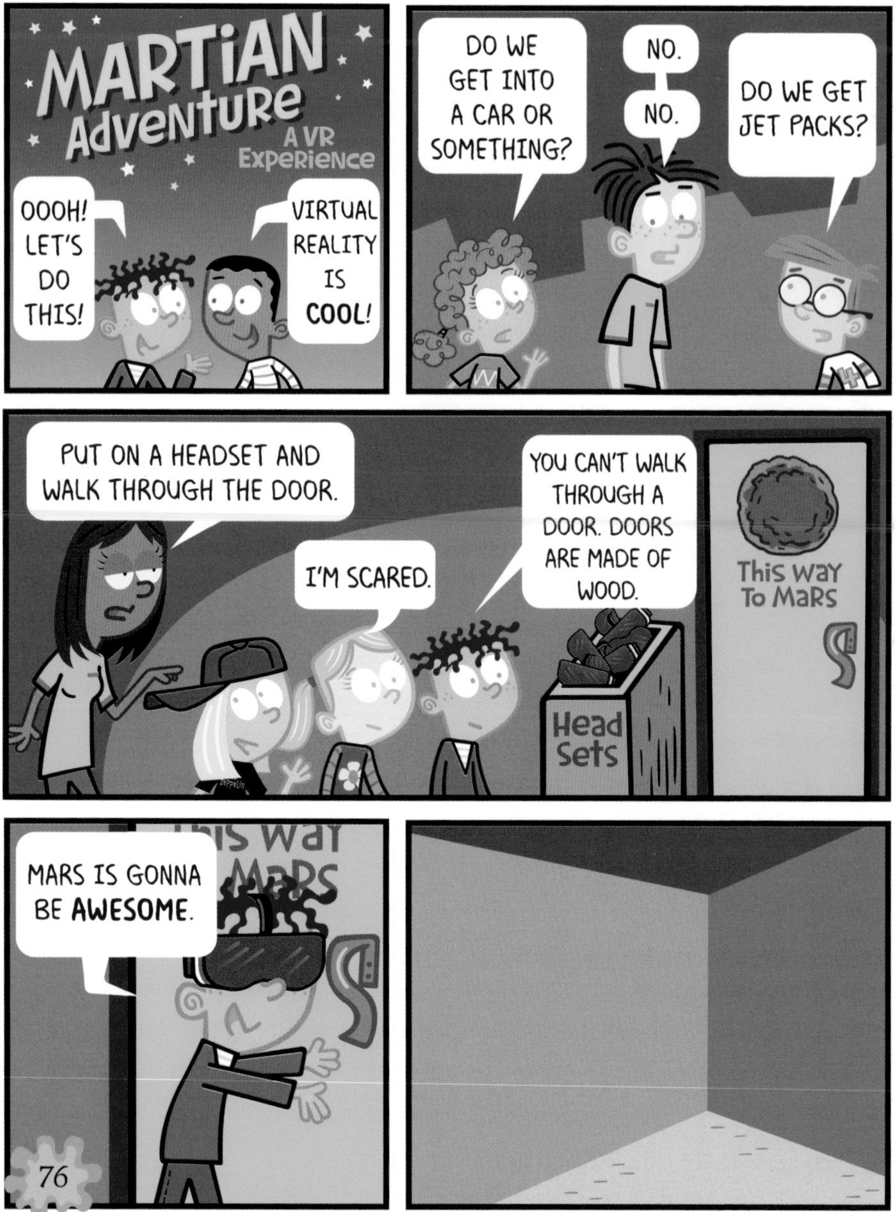
MARTiAN Adventure
A VR Experience
OOOH! LET'S DO THIS!
VIRTUAL REALITY IS **COOL**!
DO WE GET INTO A CAR OR SOMETHING?
NO.
NO.
DO WE GET JET PACKS?
PUT ON A HEADSET AND WALK THROUGH THE DOOR.
I'M SCARED.
YOU CAN'T WALK THROUGH A DOOR. DOORS ARE MADE OF WOOD.
This way To MaRs
Head Sets
MARS IS GONNA BE **AWESOME**.

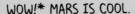

WOW!* MARS IS COOL.

STEP INSIDE THE FUTURE.

(*MOM upside down.)

IT IS THE YEAR 3022. HUMANS WILL LIVE ON MARS.

IN THE FUTURE, HUMANS SUSPEND THEIR DISBELIEF.

WON'T WE BE GROWN-UPS IN THE FUTURE?

IF THIS IS THE FUTURE, WON'T WE MISS OUR FLIGHT HOME?

DOESN'T THIS MEAN WE'RE 1008 YEARS OLD?

Explore Your New Planet

DO WE HAVE TO SAVE MARS?

DO WE GET TO SHOOT LASERS?

OUCH! MY HEAD!

MARS IS CROWDED.

NO

NO

THERE ARE A LOT OF WALLS ON MARS.

THEY'RE NOT WALLS. THEY'RE FORCE FIELDS.

FEELS LIKE A WALL TO ME.

MARS IS BORING. LET'S GET OUTTA HERE.

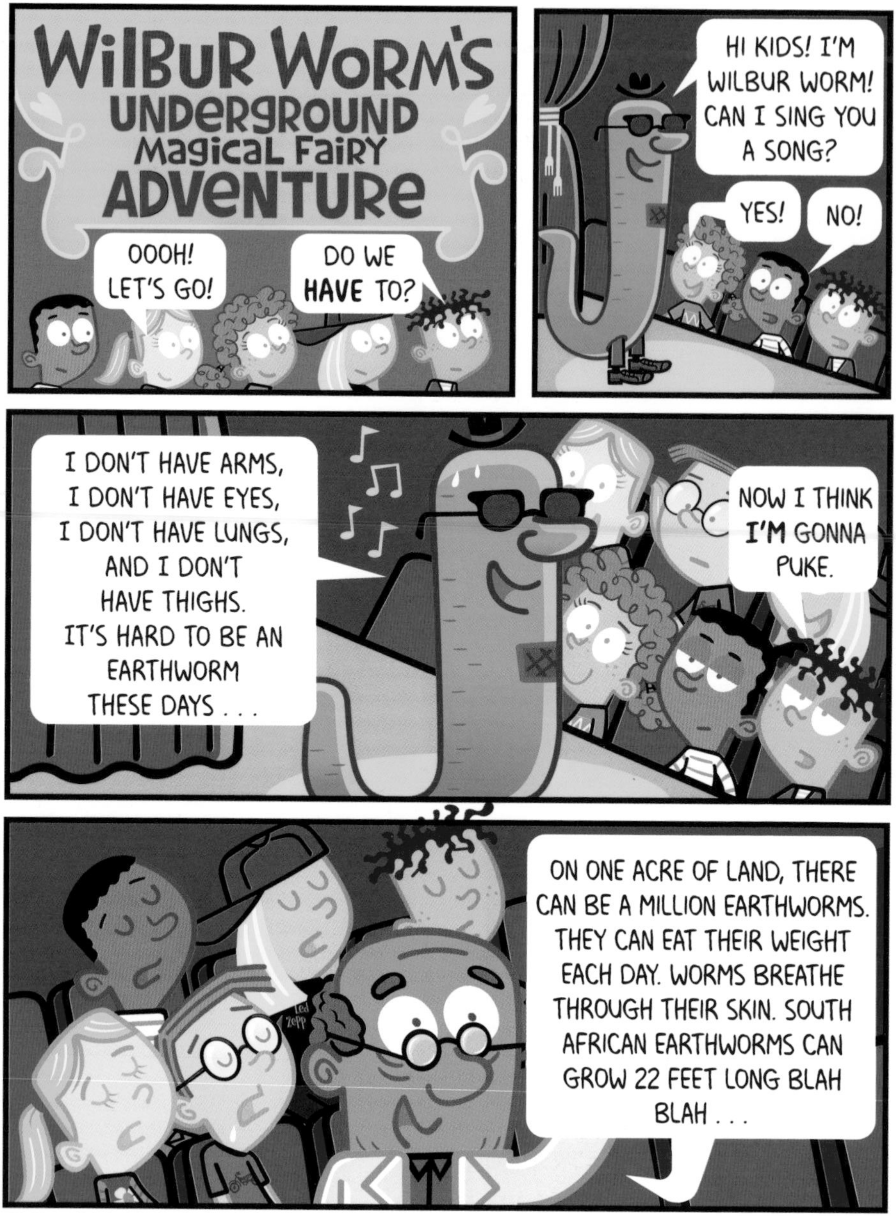
WILBUR WORM'S UNDERGROUND MAGICAL FAIRY ADVENTURE
OOOH! LET'S GO!
DO WE **HAVE** TO?
HI KIDS! I'M WILBUR WORM! CAN I SING YOU A SONG?
YES!
NO!
I DON'T HAVE ARMS, I DON'T HAVE EYES, I DON'T HAVE LUNGS, AND I DON'T HAVE THIGHS. IT'S HARD TO BE AN EARTHWORM THESE DAYS . . .
NOW I THINK **I'M** GONNA PUKE.
ON ONE ACRE OF LAND, THERE CAN BE A MILLION EARTHWORMS. THEY CAN EAT THEIR WEIGHT EACH DAY. WORMS BREATHE THROUGH THEIR SKIN. SOUTH AFRICAN EARTHWORMS CAN GROW 22 FEET LONG BLAH BLAH . . .

Ye Olde Souvenir Shoppe

OOOH! LET'S GO!

MY MOM GAVE ME MONEY.

BUY StuFF

BUY MoRE StuFF

SNOW globes

COFFEE Mugs

Fridge Magnets

COMET COMET COMET COMET COMET

Plastic JUNK

You Need this Like You Need a hole in Your head →

USELESS BOWLS

SAVE TIME! THROW IT AWAY NOW!

MiNi Toilet BOWLS

RoBBie Rat TaiLS

ON SALE

LOOK! THEY HAVE ROBBIE RAT TAILS!

THEY'RE COOL!

I WANT ONE.

ME TOO!

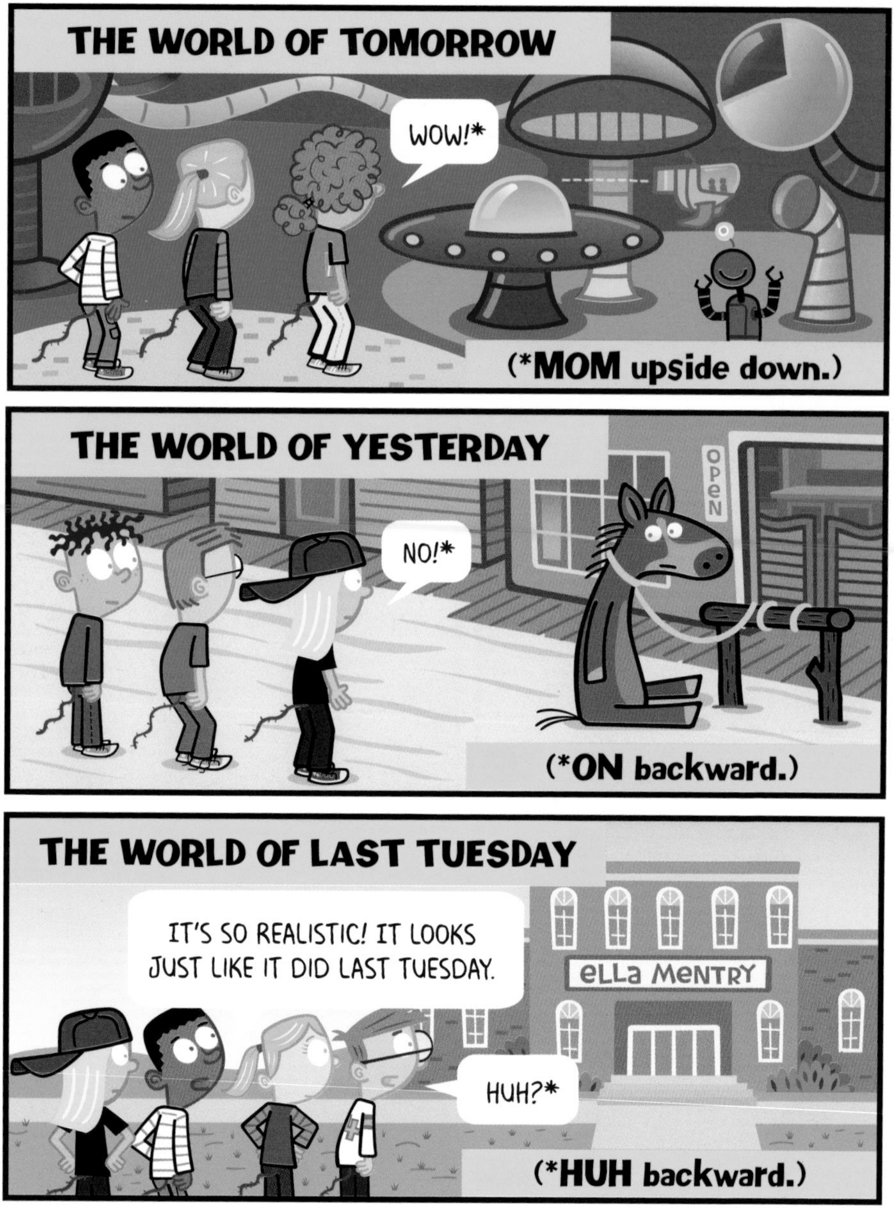
THE WORLD OF TOMORROW
WOW!*
(*MOM upside down.)
THE WORLD OF YESTERDAY
OPeN
NO!*
(*ON backward.)
THE WORLD OF LAST TUESDAY
IT'S SO REALISTIC! IT LOOKS JUST LIKE IT DID LAST TUESDAY.
eLLa MeNTRY
HUH?*
(*HUH backward.)

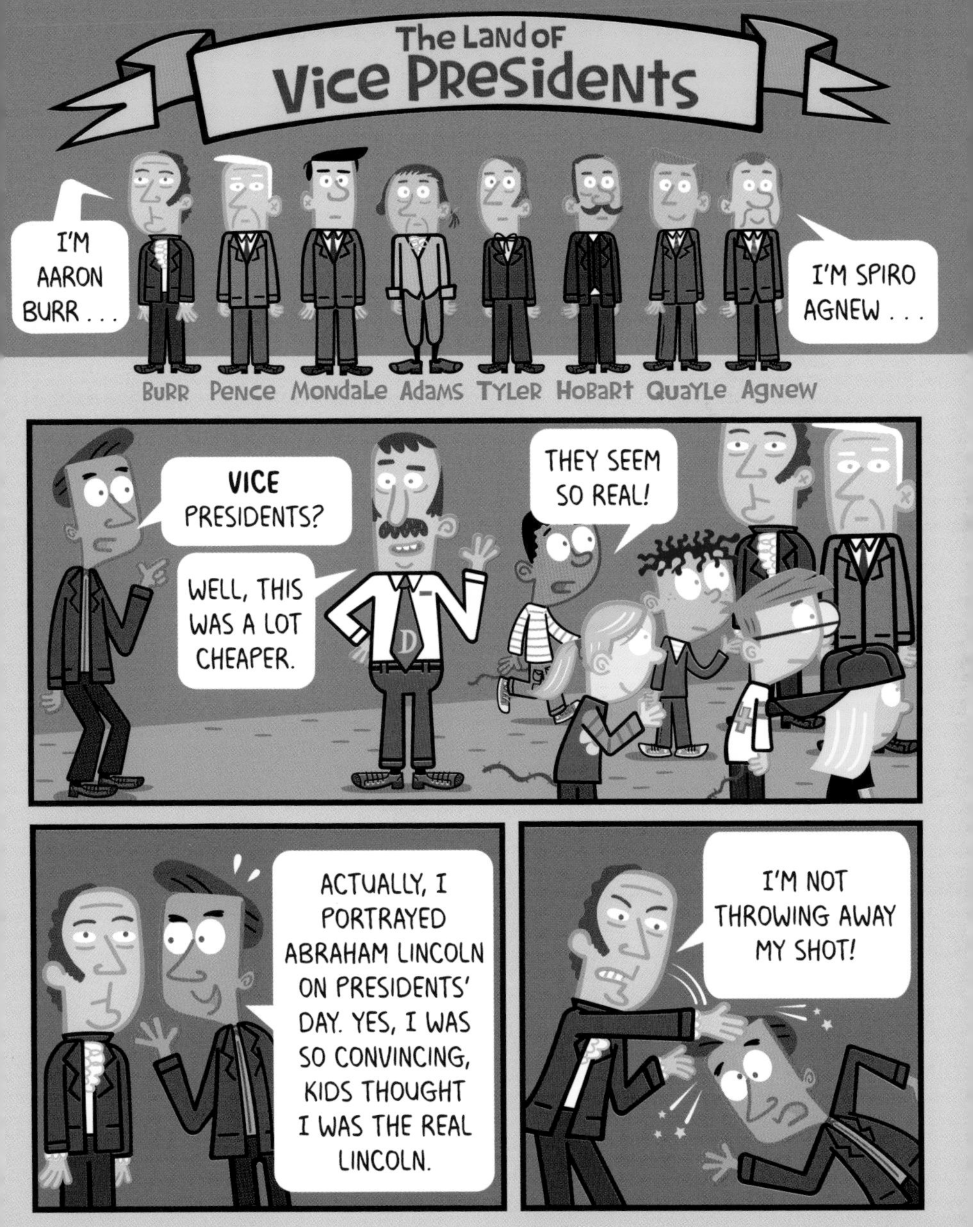
The Land of
Vice Presidents
I'M AARON BURR . . .
I'M SPIRO AGNEW . . .
BURR
PENCE
MONDALE
ADAMS
TYLER
HOBART
QUAYLE
AGNEW
VICE PRESIDENTS?
WELL, THIS WAS A LOT CHEAPER.
THEY SEEM SO REAL!
ACTUALLY, I PORTRAYED ABRAHAM LINCOLN ON PRESIDENTS' DAY. YES, I WAS SO CONVINCING, KIDS THOUGHT I WAS THE REAL LINCOLN.
I'M NOT THROWING AWAY MY SHOT!

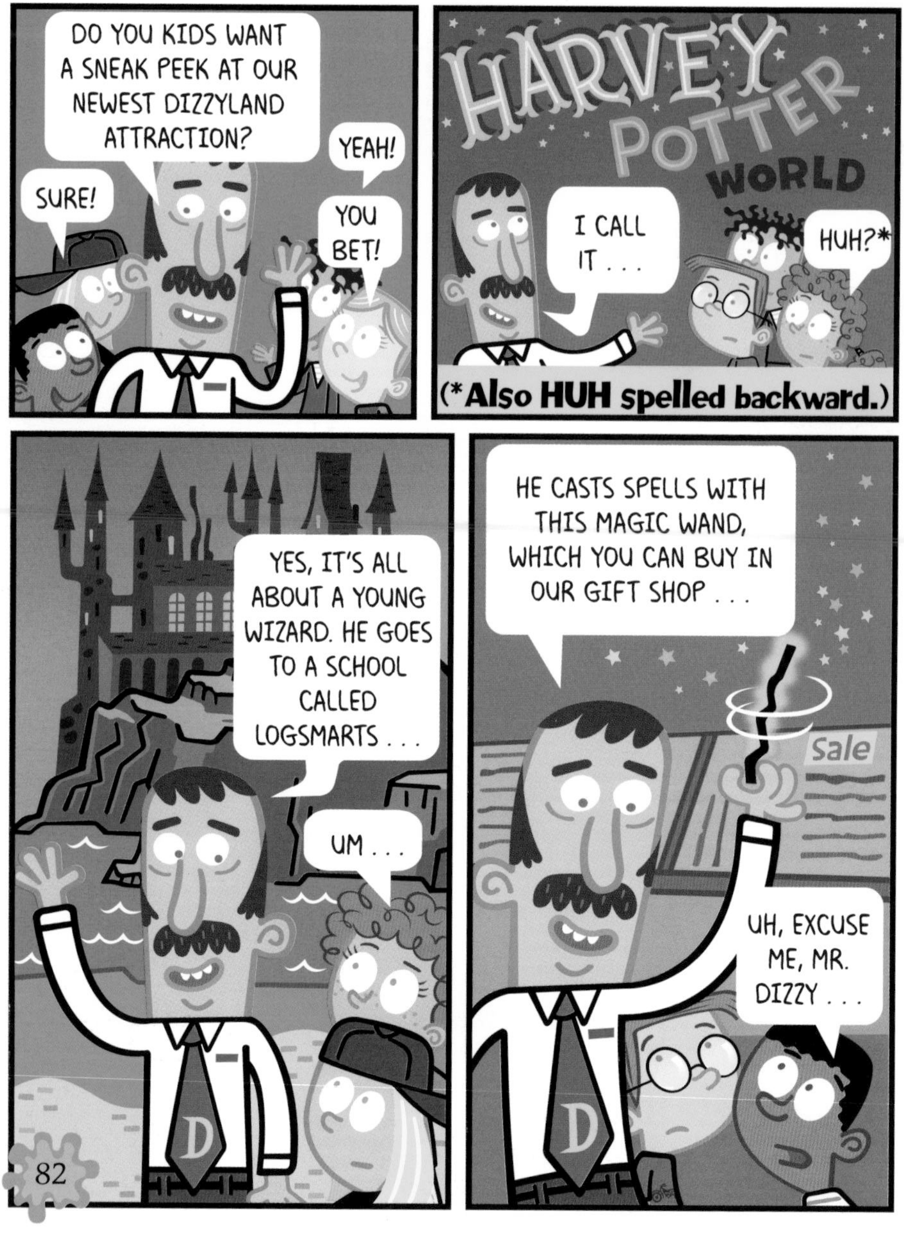
DO YOU KIDS WANT A SNEAK PEEK AT OUR NEWEST DIZZYLAND ATTRACTION?
SURE!
YEAH!
YOU BET!
HARVEY POTTER WORLD
I CALL IT . . .
HUH?*
(*Also HUH spelled backward.)
YES, IT'S ALL ABOUT A YOUNG WIZARD. HE GOES TO A SCHOOL CALLED LOGSMARTS . . .
UM . . .
HE CASTS SPELLS WITH THIS MAGIC WAND, WHICH YOU CAN BUY IN OUR GIFT SHOP . . .
Sale
UH, EXCUSE ME, MR. DIZZY . . .

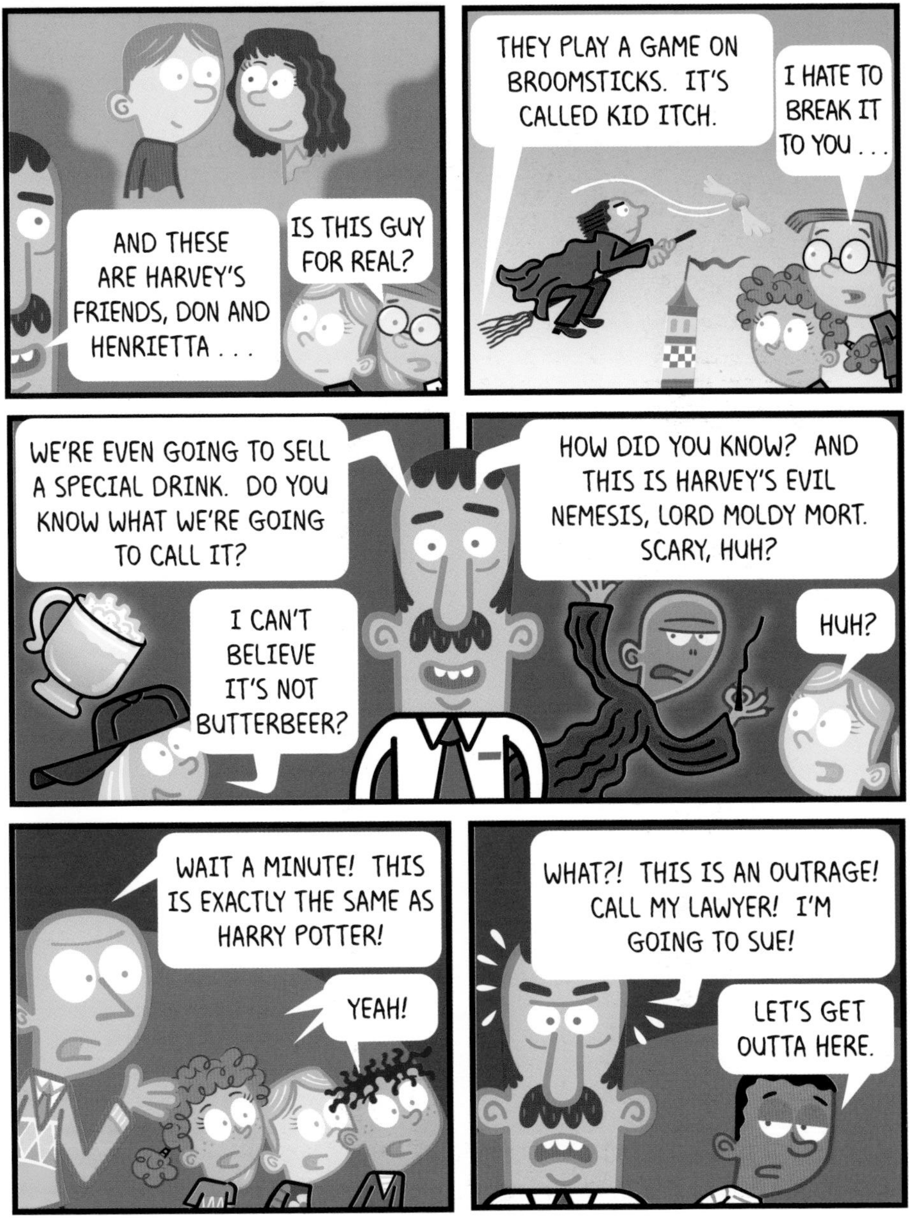
AND THESE ARE HARVEY'S FRIENDS, DON AND HENRIETTA . . .
IS THIS GUY FOR REAL?
THEY PLAY A GAME ON BROOMSTICKS. IT'S CALLED KID ITCH.
I HATE TO BREAK IT TO YOU . . .
WE'RE EVEN GOING TO SELL A SPECIAL DRINK. DO YOU KNOW WHAT WE'RE GOING TO CALL IT?
I CAN'T BELIEVE IT'S NOT BUTTERBEER?
HOW DID YOU KNOW? AND THIS IS HARVEY'S EVIL NEMESIS, LORD MOLDY MORT. SCARY, HUH?
HUH?
WAIT A MINUTE! THIS IS EXACTLY THE SAME AS HARRY POTTER!
YEAH!
WHAT?! THIS IS AN OUTRAGE! CALL MY LAWYER! I'M GOING TO SUE!
LET'S GET OUTTA HERE.

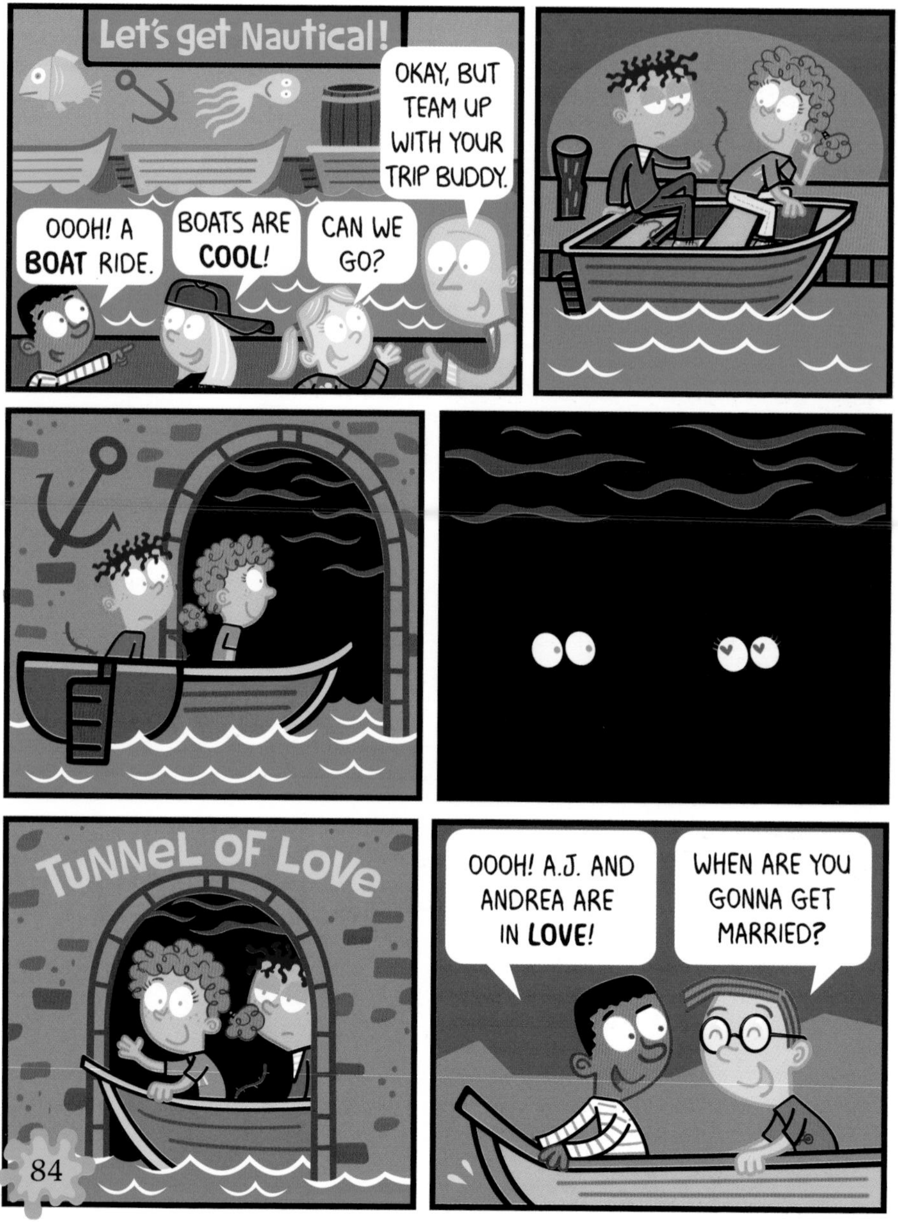
Let's get Nautical!
OKAY, BUT TEAM UP WITH YOUR TRIP BUDDY.
OOOH! A BOAT RIDE.
BOATS ARE COOL!
CAN WE GO?
TUNNEL OF LOVE
OOOH! A.J. AND ANDREA ARE IN LOVE!
WHEN ARE YOU GONNA GET MARRIED?

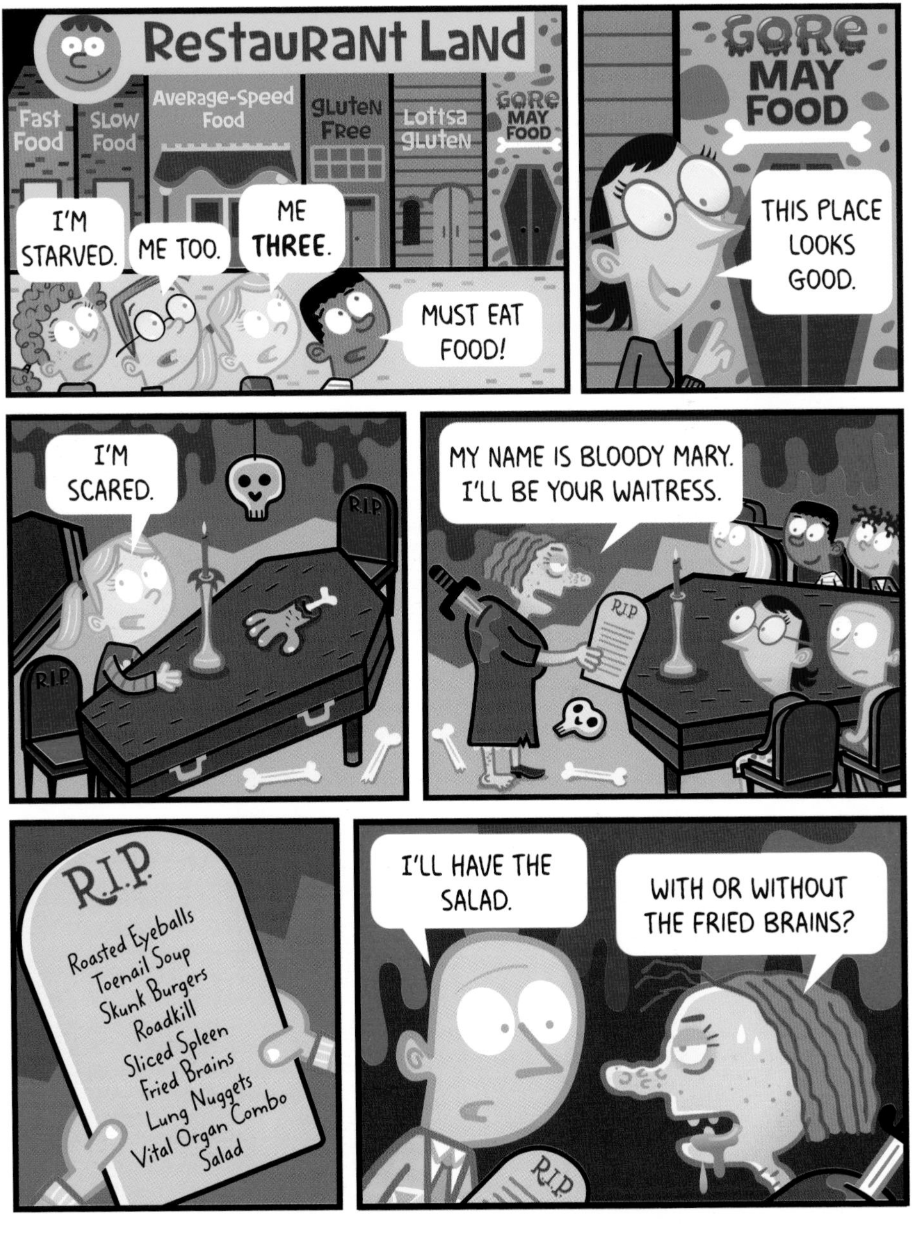
RESTAURANT LAND
Fast Food
SLOW Food
Average-Speed Food
gLUTEN FREE
Lottsa gLUTEN
GORE MAY FOOD
I'M STARVED.
ME TOO.
ME THREE.
MUST EAT FOOD!
GORE MAY FOOD
THIS PLACE LOOKS GOOD.
I'M SCARED.
R.I.P.
R.I.P.
MY NAME IS BLOODY MARY. I'LL BE YOUR WAITRESS.
R.I.P.
R.I.P.
Roasted Eyeballs
Toenail Soup
Skunk Burgers
Roadkill
Sliced Spleen
Fried Brains
Lung Nuggets
Vital Organ Combo
Salad
I'LL HAVE THE SALAD.
WITH OR WITHOUT THE FRIED BRAINS?
R.I.P.

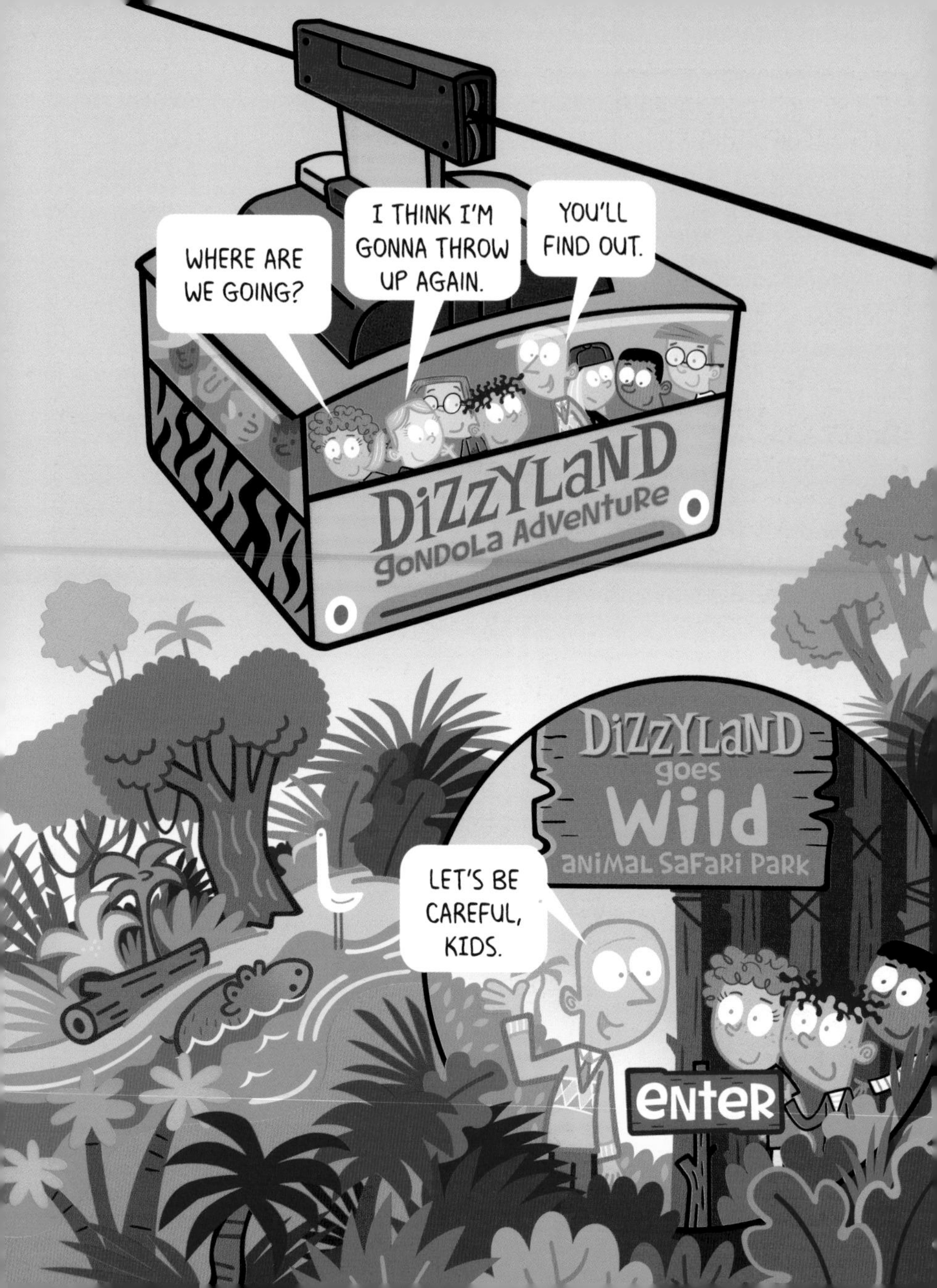
WHERE ARE WE GOING?
I THINK I'M GONNA THROW UP AGAIN.
YOU'LL FIND OUT.
DiZZYLaND
goNDoLa AdveNtuRe
DiZZYLaND goes Wild
aNiMaL SaFaRi PaRk
LET'S BE CAREFUL, KIDS.
eNteR

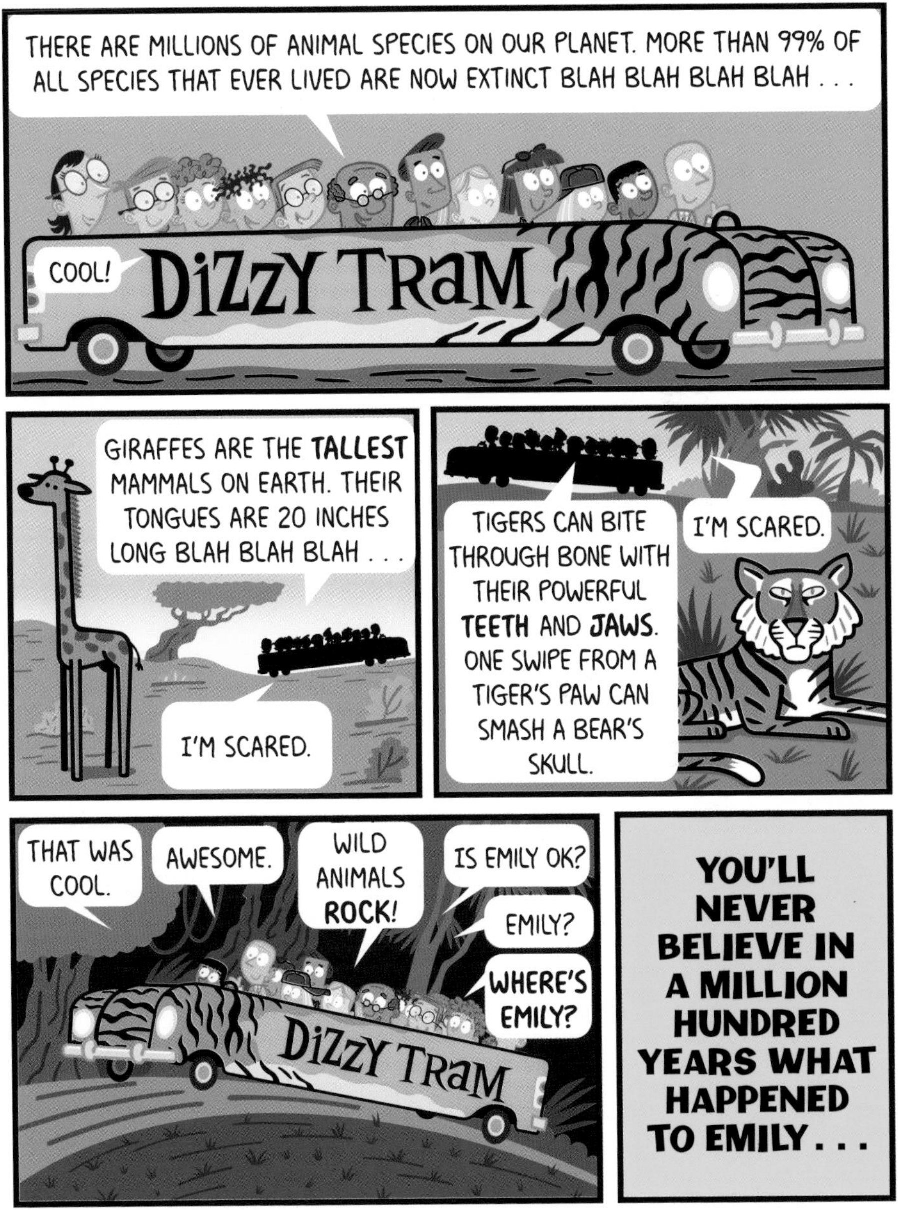
THERE ARE MILLIONS OF ANIMAL SPECIES ON OUR PLANET. MORE THAN 99% OF ALL SPECIES THAT EVER LIVED ARE NOW EXTINCT BLAH BLAH BLAH BLAH . . .
COOL!
DIZZY TRAM
GIRAFFES ARE THE **TALLEST** MAMMALS ON EARTH. THEIR TONGUES ARE 20 INCHES LONG BLAH BLAH BLAH . . .
I'M SCARED.
TIGERS CAN BITE THROUGH BONE WITH THEIR POWERFUL **TEETH** AND **JAWS**. ONE SWIPE FROM A TIGER'S PAW CAN SMASH A BEAR'S SKULL.
I'M SCARED.
THAT WAS COOL.
AWESOME.
WILD ANIMALS **ROCK!**
IS EMILY OK?
EMILY?
WHERE'S EMILY?
DIZZY TRAM
YOU'LL NEVER BELIEVE IN A MILLION HUNDRED YEARS WHAT HAPPENED TO EMILY . . .

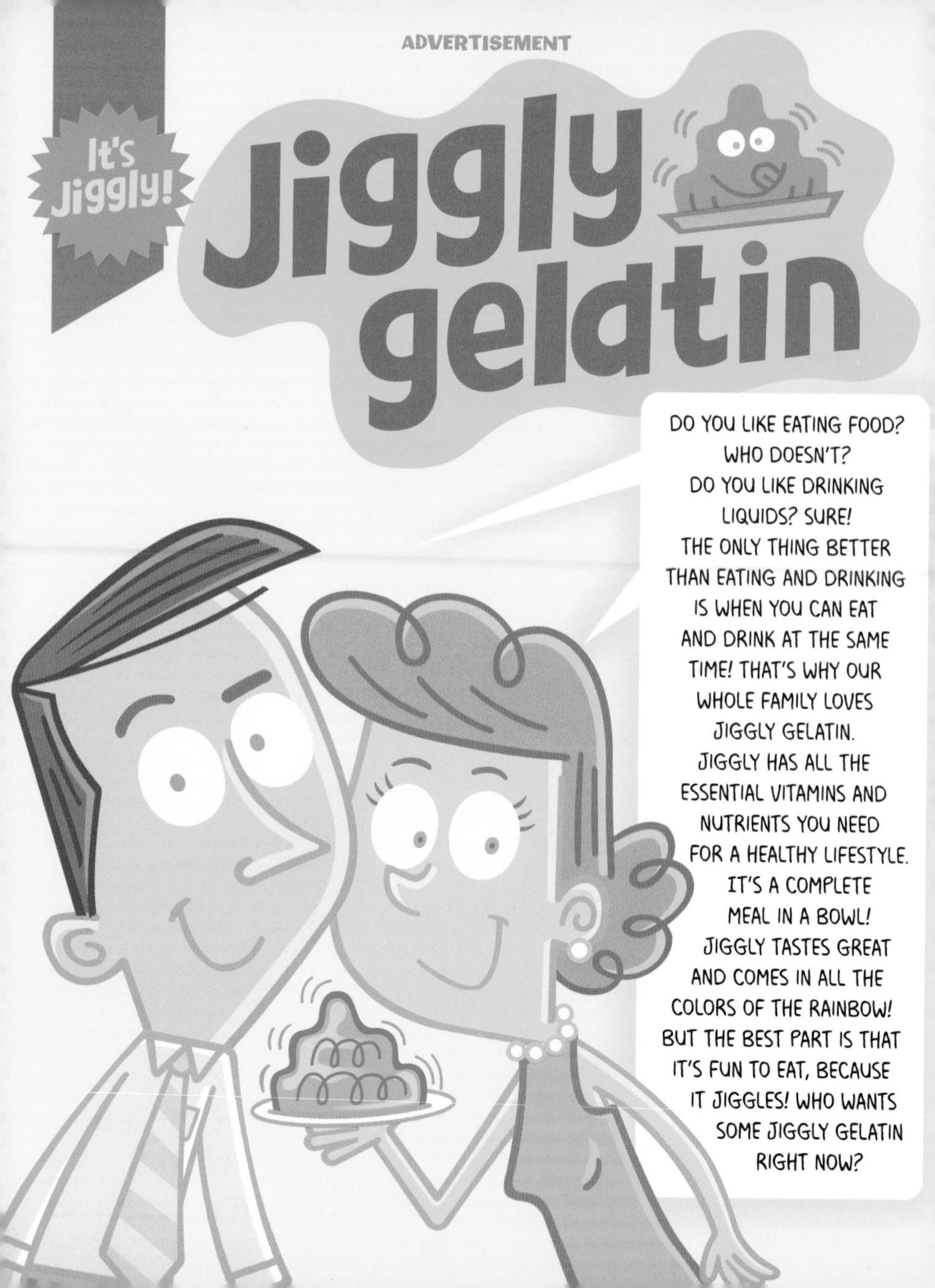
ADVERTISEMENT
It's Jiggly!
Jiggly gelatin
DO YOU LIKE EATING FOOD? WHO DOESN'T? DO YOU LIKE DRINKING LIQUIDS? SURE! THE ONLY THING BETTER THAN EATING AND DRINKING IS WHEN YOU CAN EAT AND DRINK AT THE SAME TIME! THAT'S WHY OUR WHOLE FAMILY LOVES JIGGLY GELATIN. JIGGLY HAS ALL THE ESSENTIAL VITAMINS AND NUTRIENTS YOU NEED FOR A HEALTHY LIFESTYLE. IT'S A COMPLETE MEAL IN A BOWL! JIGGLY TASTES GREAT AND COMES IN ALL THE COLORS OF THE RAINBOW! BUT THE BEST PART IS THAT IT'S FUN TO EAT, BECAUSE IT JIGGLES! WHO WANTS SOME JIGGLY GELATIN RIGHT NOW?

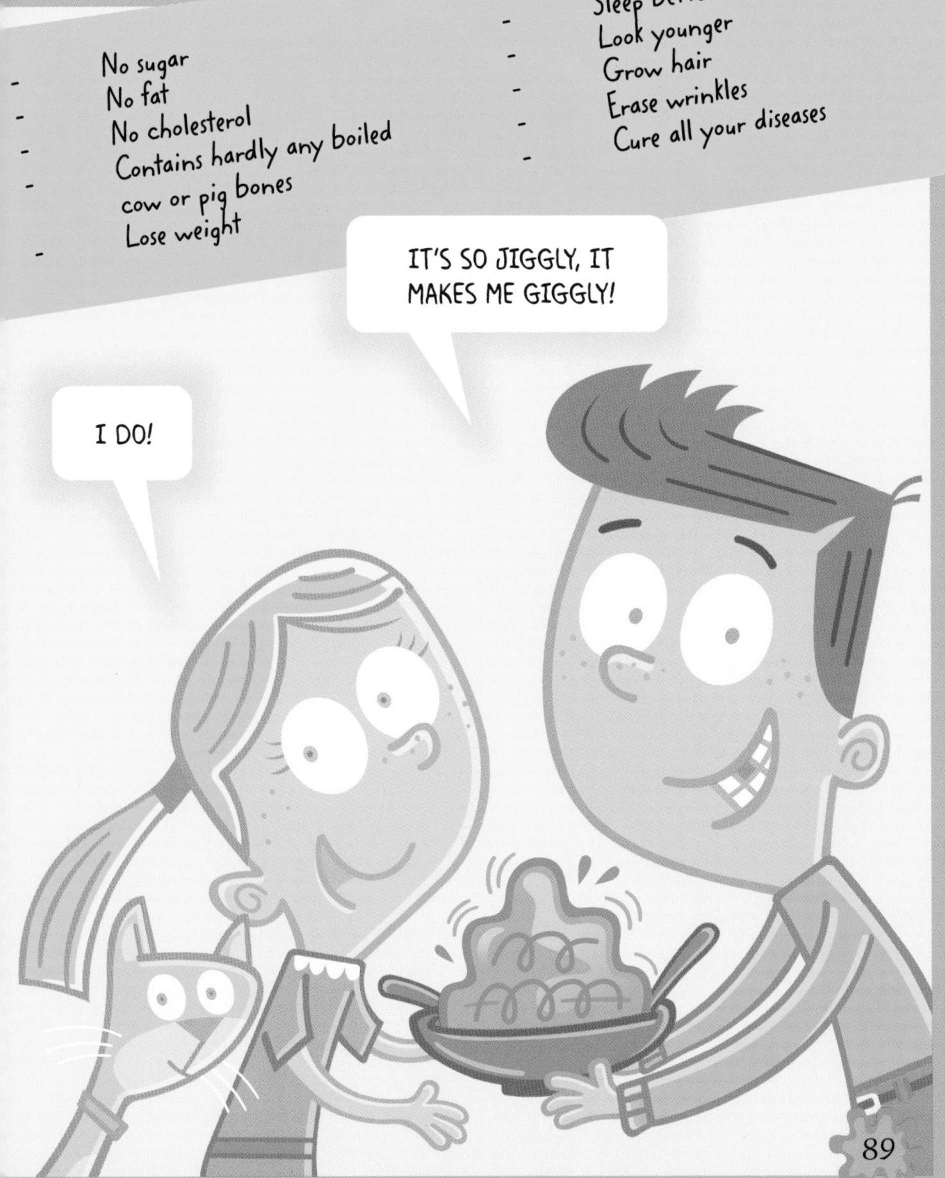
- No sugar
- No fat
- No cholesterol
- Contains hardly any boiled cow or pig bones
- Lose weight
- Sleep better
- Look younger
- Grow hair
- Erase wrinkles
- Cure all your diseases
IT'S SO JIGGLY, IT MAKES ME GIGGLY!
I DO!

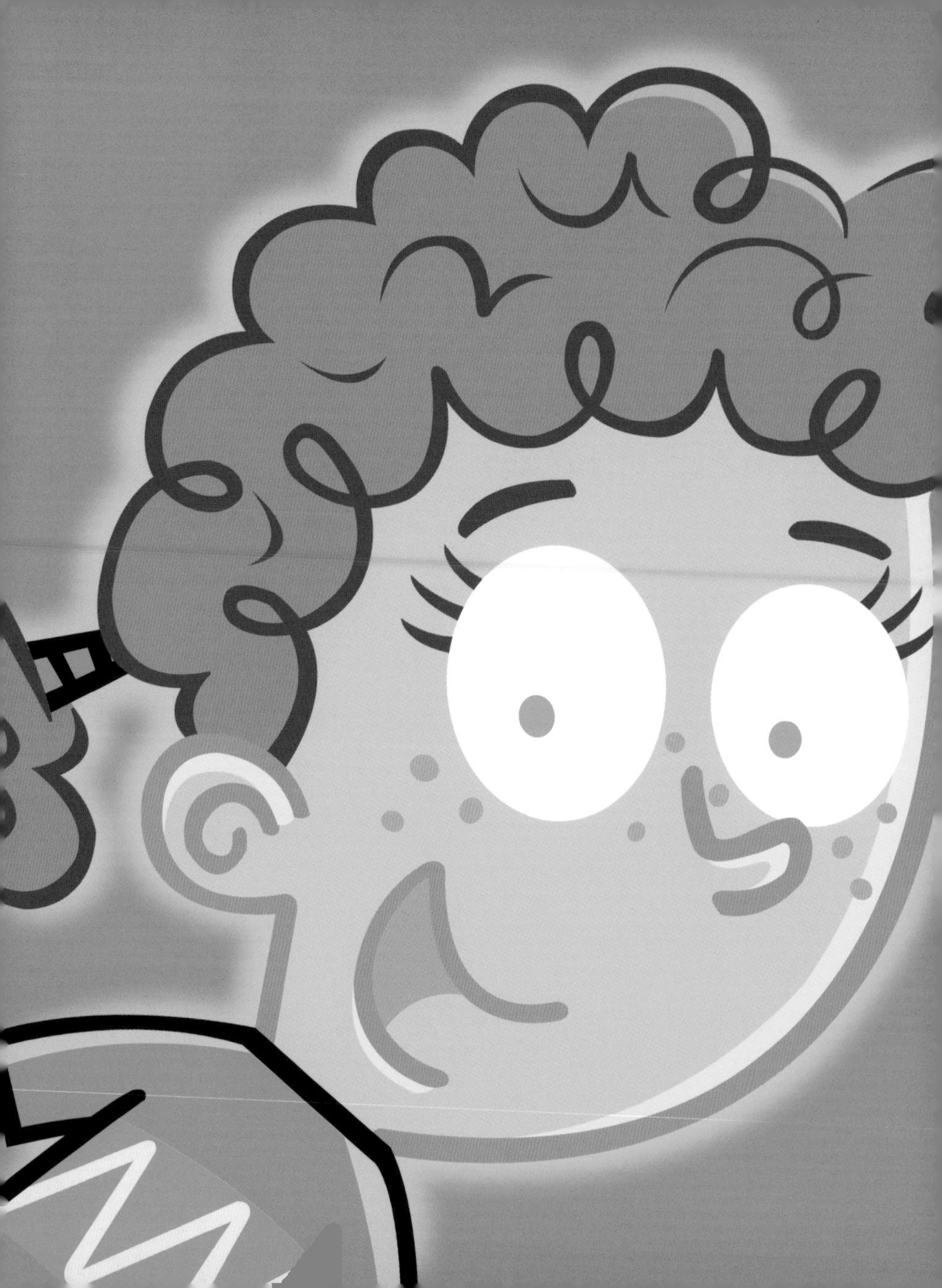

CHAPTER 6

We Should Really Get Rid of Some of This Stuff!

I LOVE SURPRISE ENDINGS!

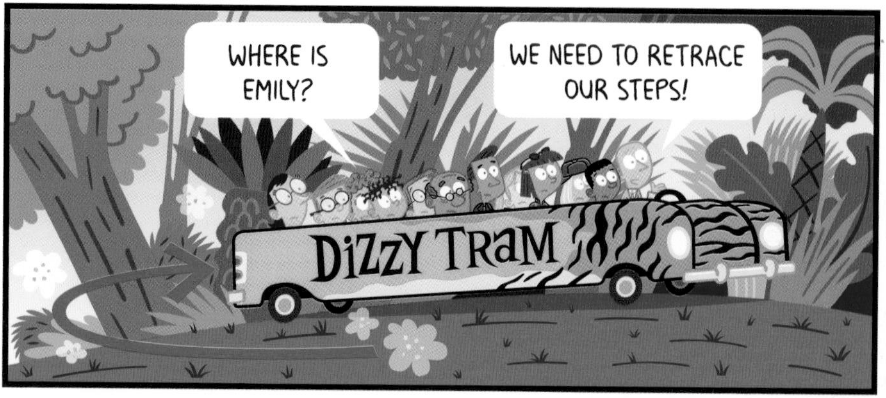
WHERE IS EMILY?
WE NEED TO RETRACE OUR STEPS!
DIZZY TRAM

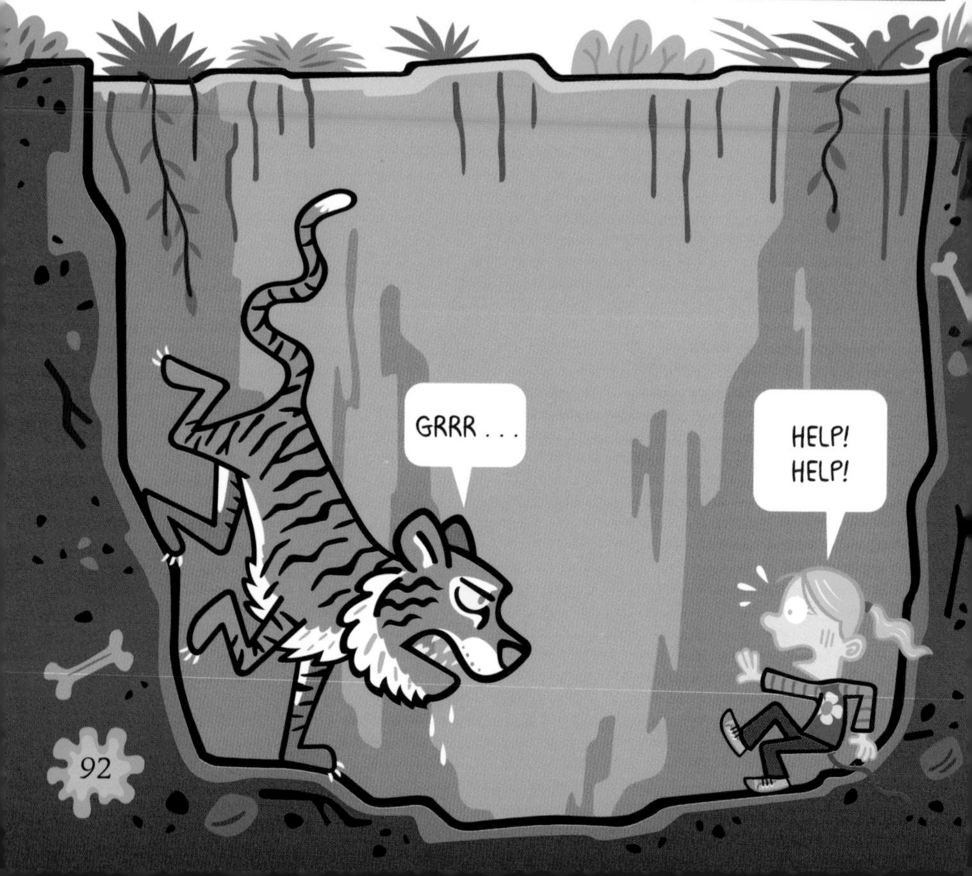
GRRR . . .
HELP! HELP!

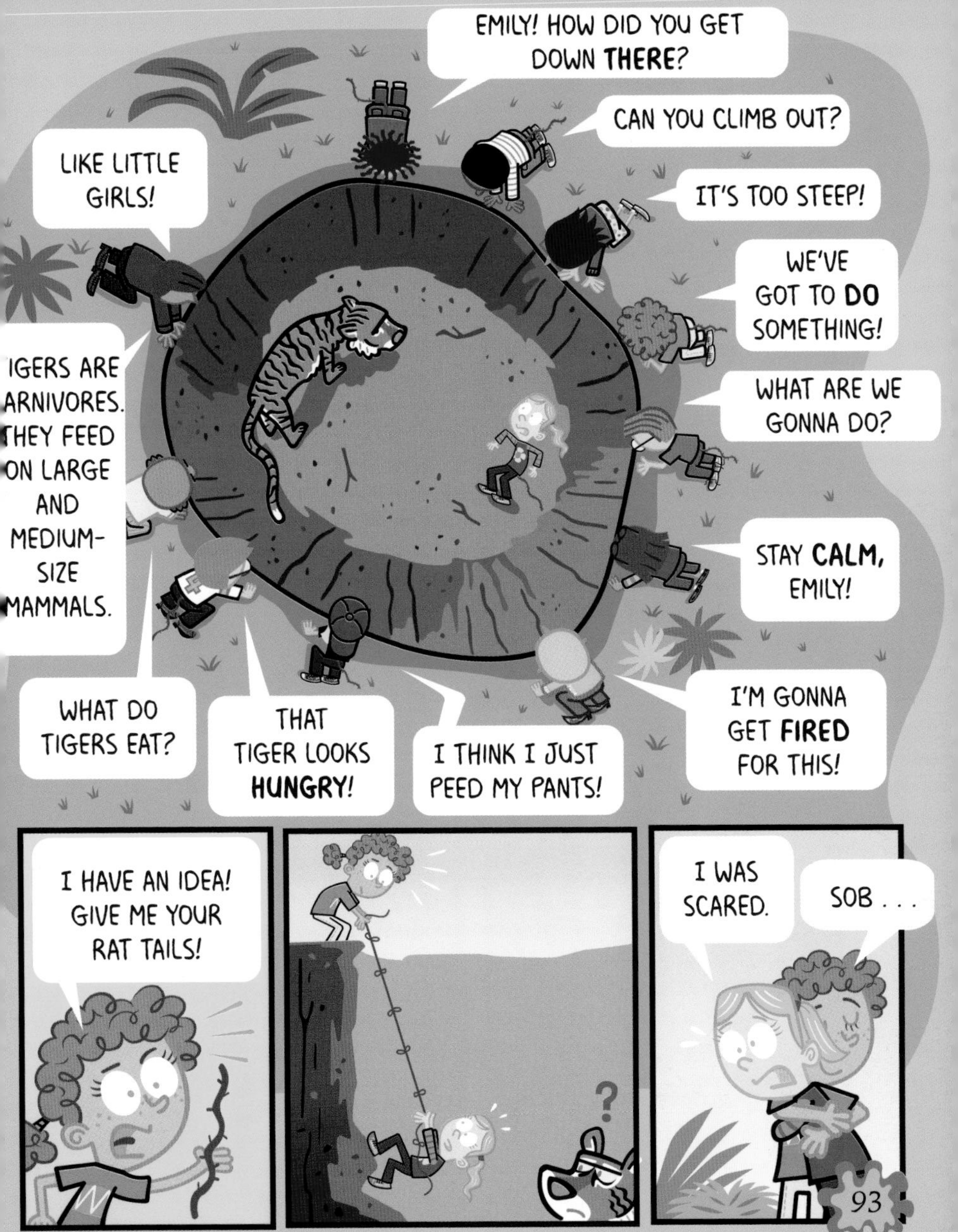

EMILY! HOW DID YOU GET DOWN THERE?
CAN YOU CLIMB OUT?
IT'S TOO STEEP!
WE'VE GOT TO DO SOMETHING!
WHAT ARE WE GONNA DO?
STAY CALM, EMILY!
I'M GONNA GET FIRED FOR THIS!
I THINK I JUST PEED MY PANTS!
THAT TIGER LOOKS HUNGRY!
WHAT DO TIGERS EAT?
IGERS ARE ARNIVORES. THEY FEED ON LARGE AND MEDIUM-SIZE MAMMALS.
LIKE LITTLE GIRLS!
I HAVE AN IDEA! GIVE ME YOUR RAT TAILS!
?
I WAS SCARED.
SOB . . .

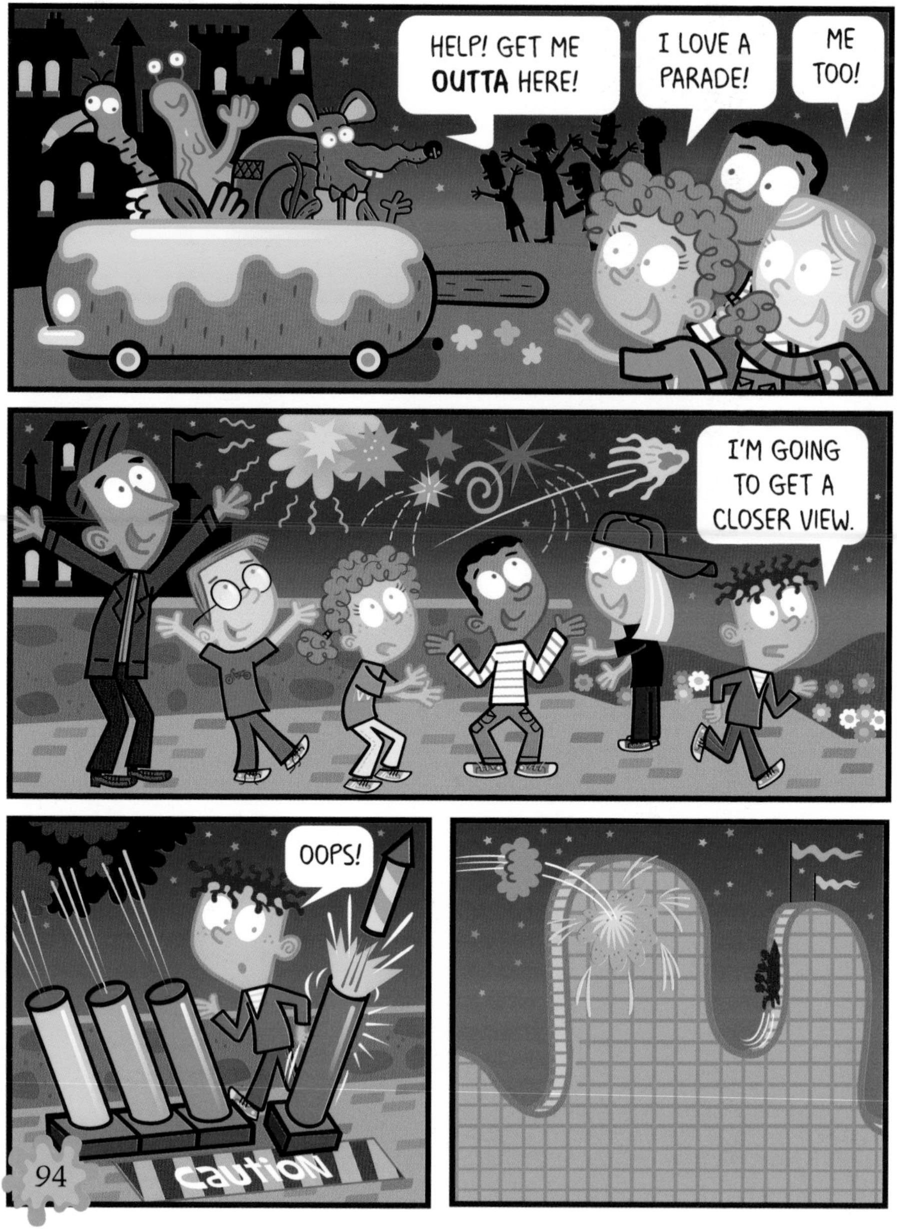
HELP! GET ME **OUTTA** HERE!
I LOVE A PARADE!
ME TOO!
I'M GOING TO GET A CLOSER VIEW.
OOPS!
CAUTION

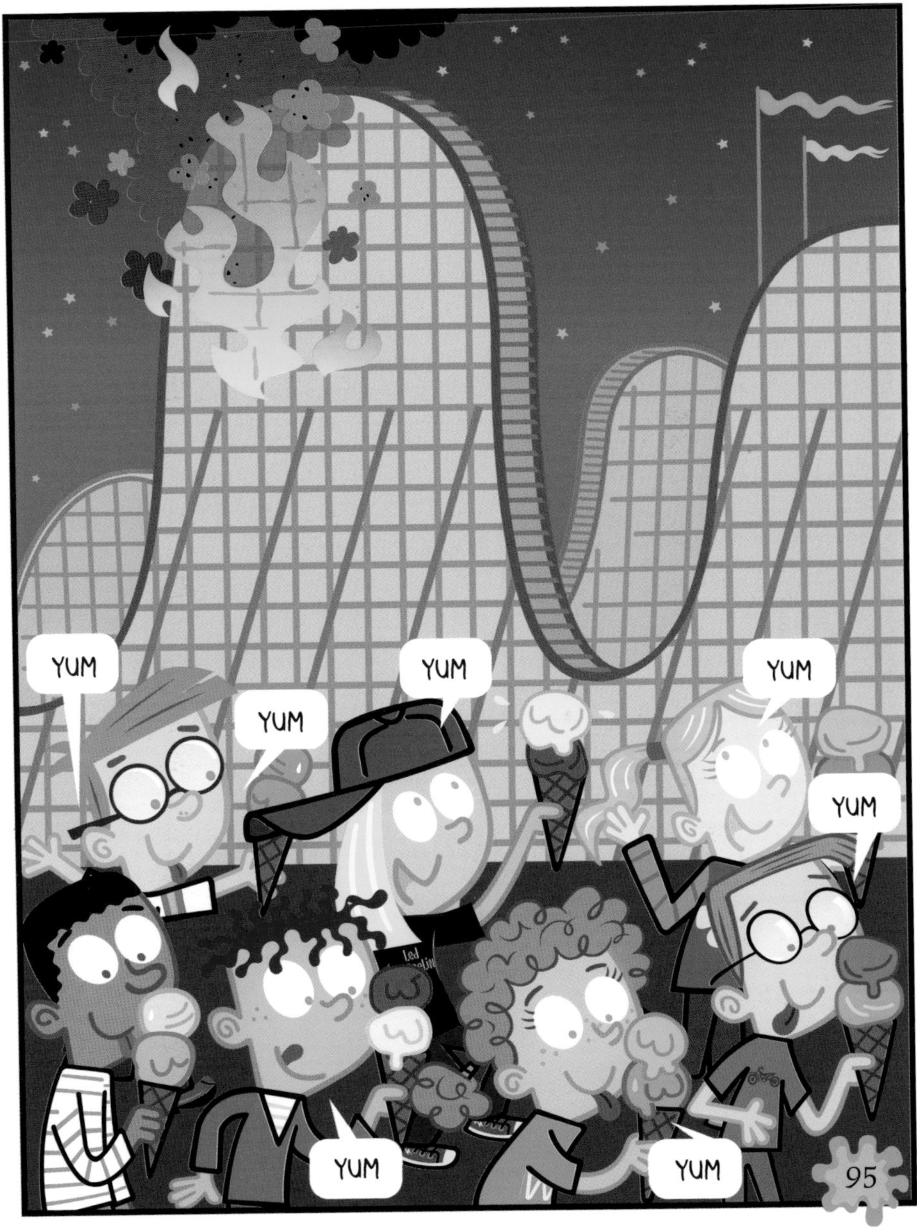
YUM
YUM
YUM
YUM
YUM
YUM
YUM

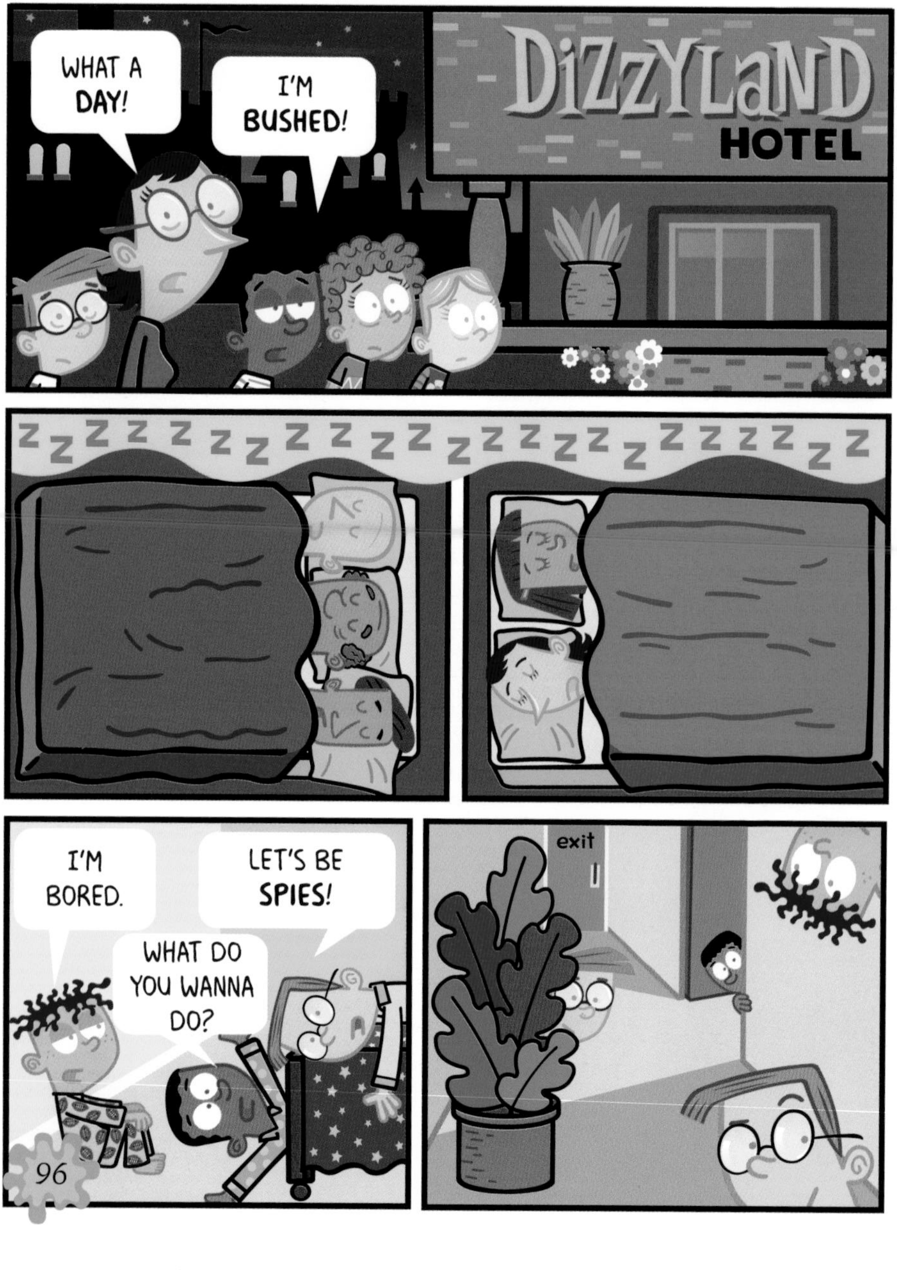
WHAT A DAY!
I'M BUSHED!
DIZZYLAND HOTEL
Z Z Z Z Z Z Z Z Z Z Z Z Z Z Z Z Z Z Z Z Z Z Z Z
I'M BORED.
WHAT DO YOU WANNA DO?
LET'S BE SPIES!
exit

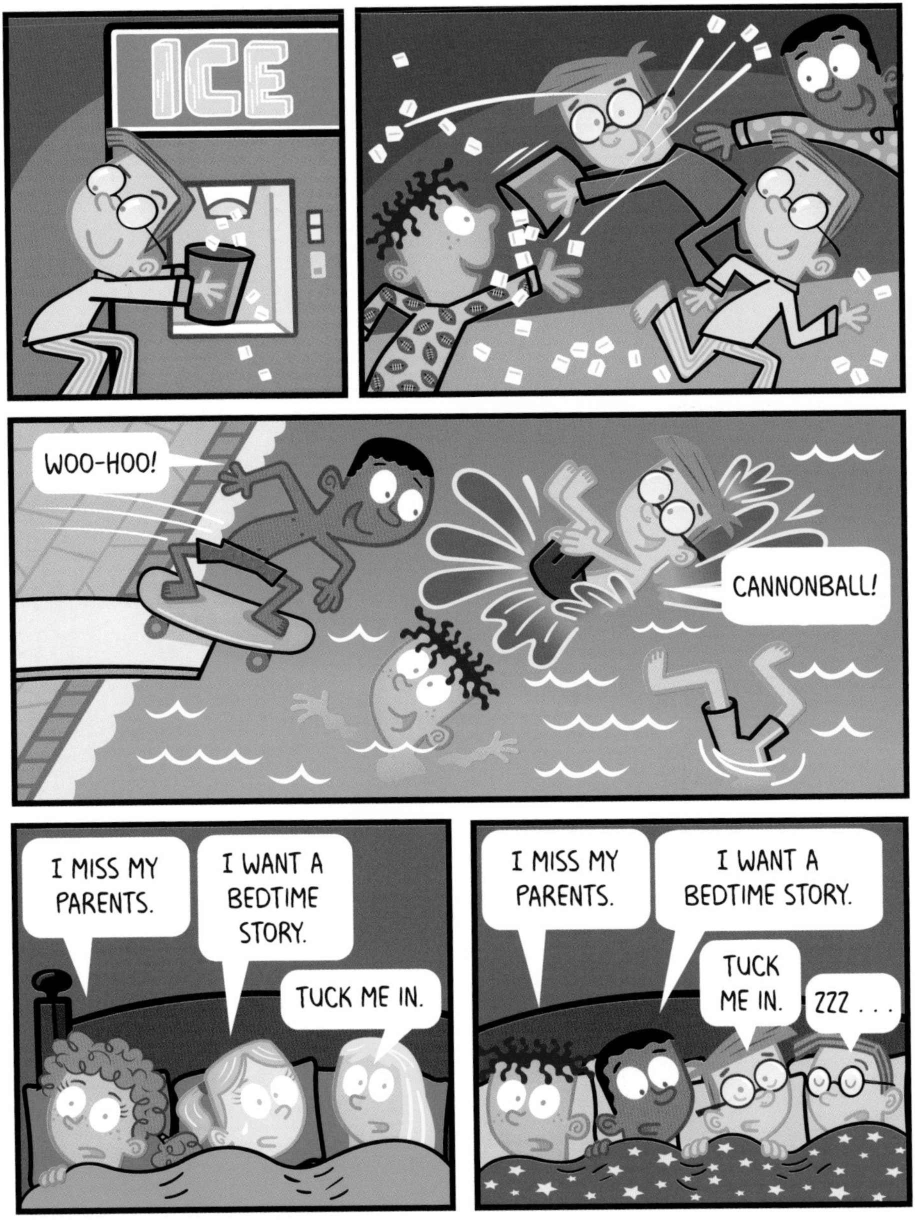
ICE
WOO-HOO!
CANNONBALL!
I MISS MY PARENTS.
I WANT A BEDTIME STORY.
TUCK ME IN.
I MISS MY PARENTS.
I WANT A BEDTIME STORY.
TUCK ME IN.
ZZZ . . .

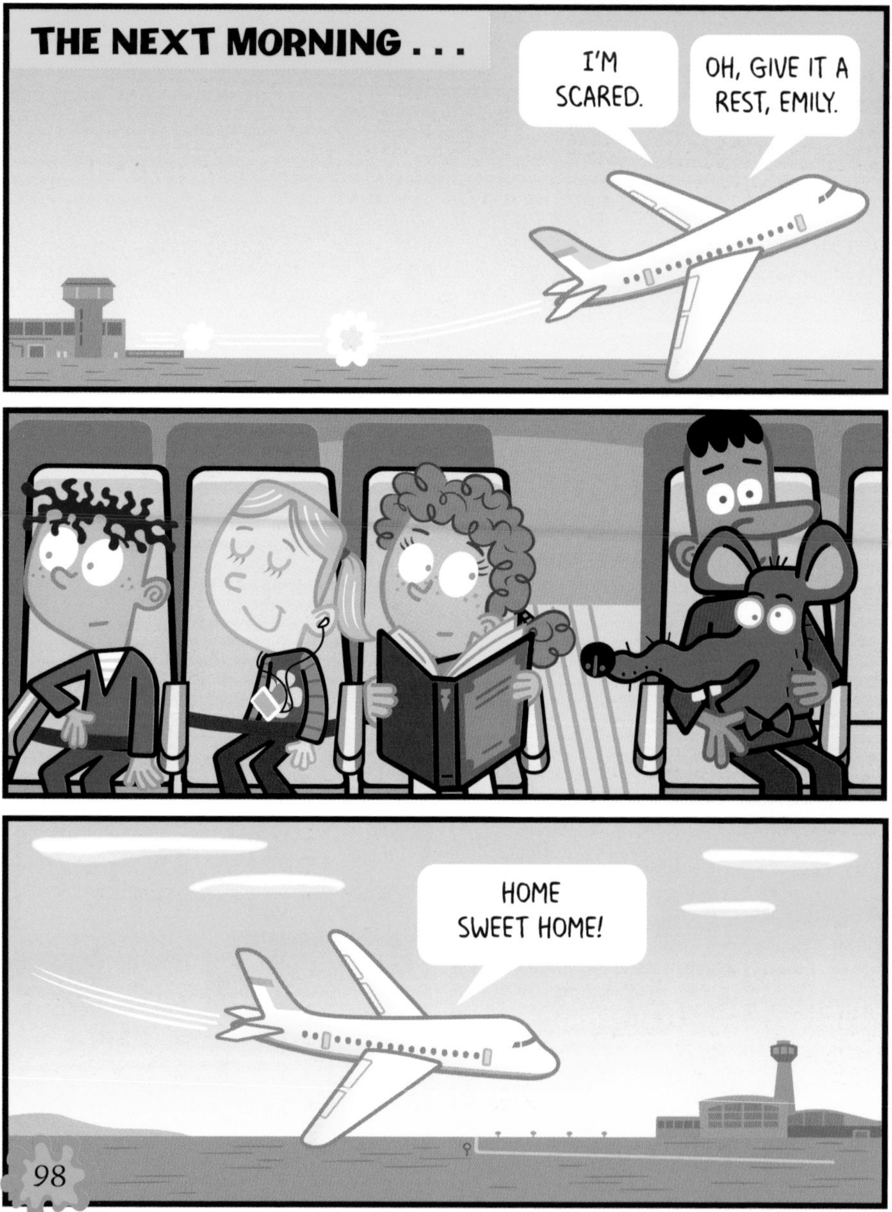
THE NEXT MORNING . . .
I'M SCARED.
OH, GIVE IT A REST, EMILY.
HOME SWEET HOME!

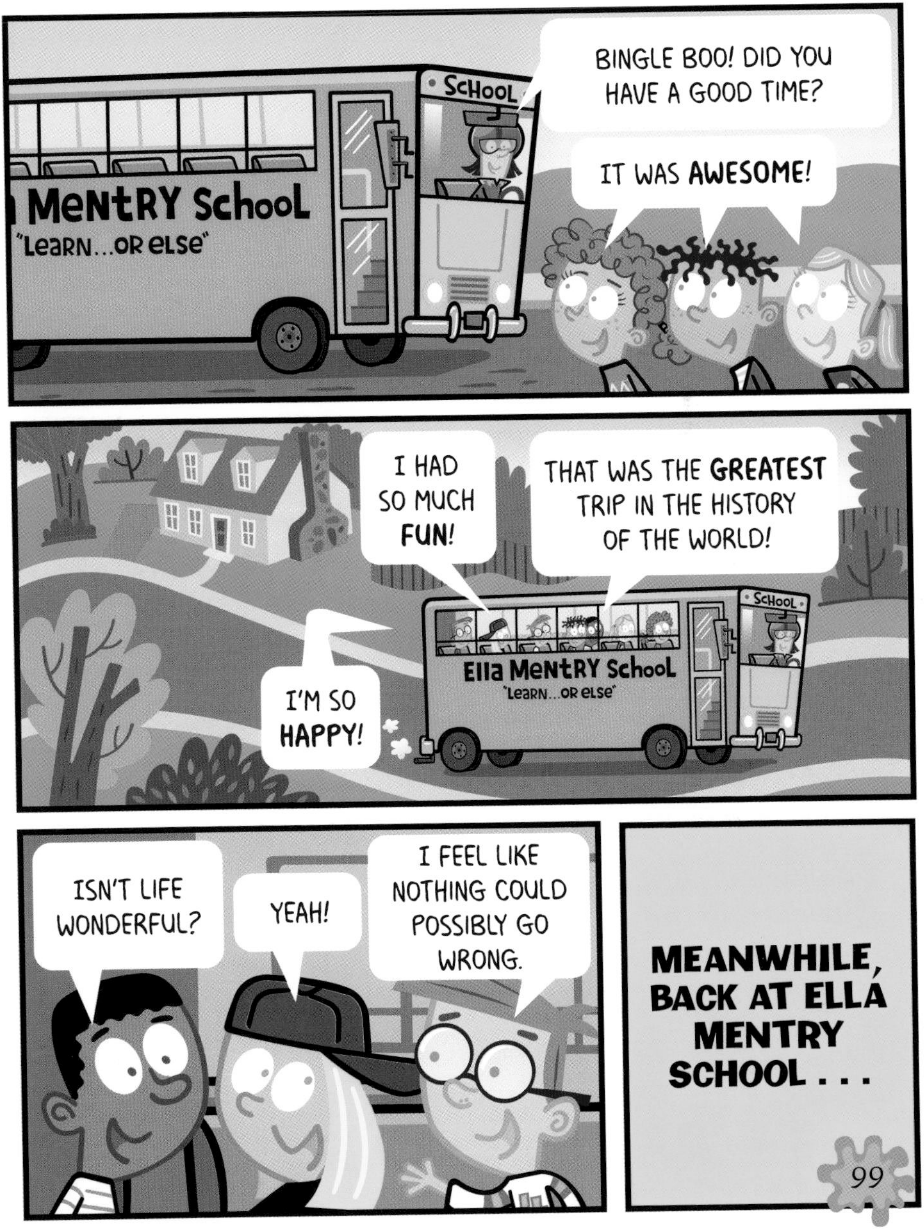
SCHOOL
Ella MENTRY School
"LEARN...OR ELSE"
BINGLE BOO! DID YOU HAVE A GOOD TIME?
IT WAS **AWESOME**!
I HAD SO MUCH **FUN**!
THAT WAS THE **GREATEST** TRIP IN THE HISTORY OF THE WORLD!
SCHOOL
Ella MENTRY School
"LEARN...OR ELSE"
I'M SO **HAPPY**!
ISN'T LIFE WONDERFUL?
YEAH!
I FEEL LIKE NOTHING COULD POSSIBLY GO WRONG.
MEANWHILE, BACK AT ELLA MENTRY SCHOOL . . .

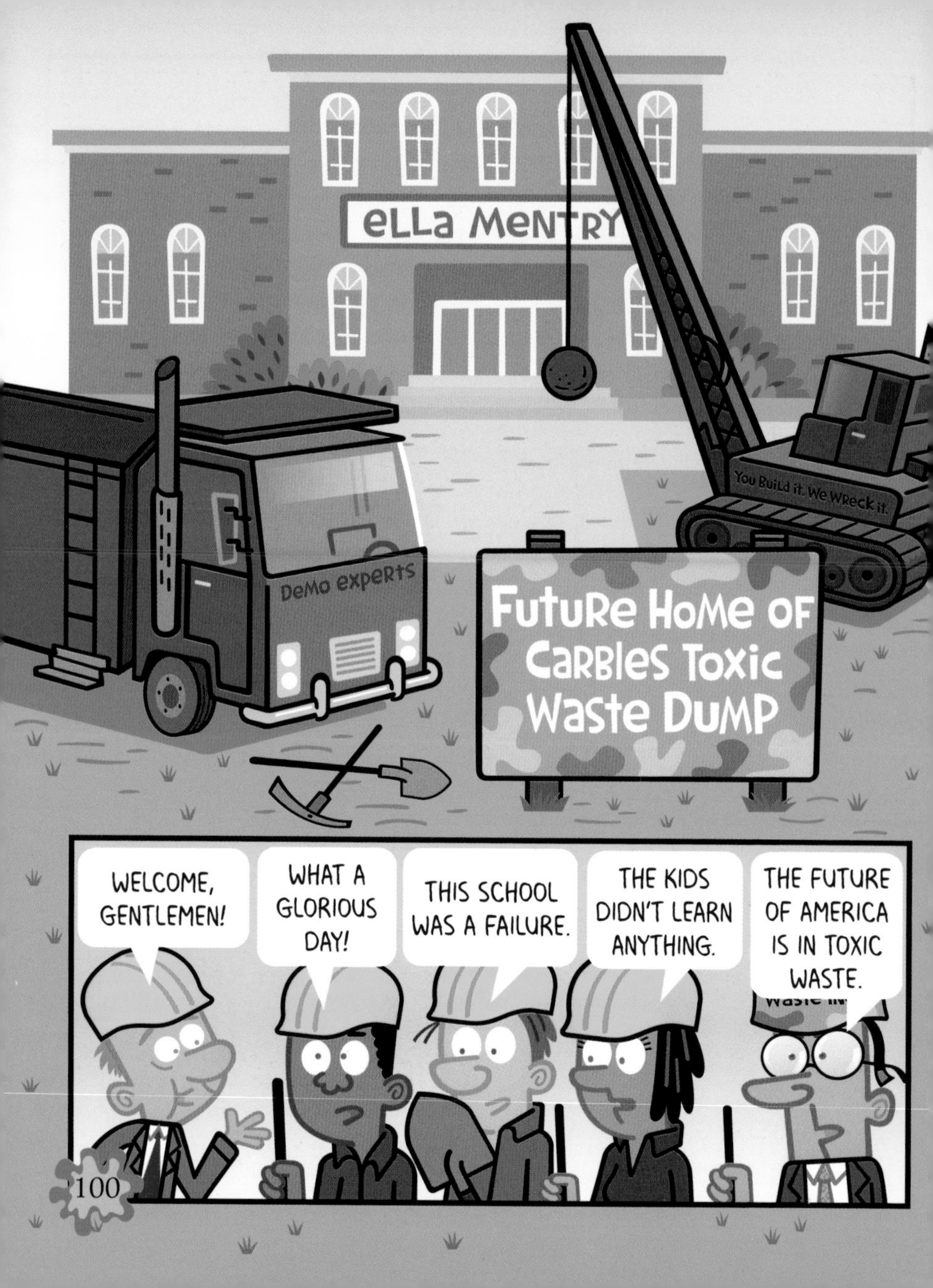
ELLA MENTRY
YOU BUILD IT. WE WRECK IT.
DEMO EXPERTS
FUTURE HOME OF CARBLES TOXIC WASTE DUMP
WELCOME, GENTLEMEN!
WHAT A GLORIOUS DAY!
THIS SCHOOL WAS A FAILURE.
THE KIDS DIDN'T LEARN ANYTHING.
THE FUTURE OF AMERICA IS IN TOXIC WASTE.

NO!
JUST IGNORE THAT OLD BAG. LET'S DO THIS! TEN . . . NINE . . . EIGHT . . . SEVEN . . .
Carbles Toxic Waste Inc.
BLOWING STUFF UP IS COOL!
TNT

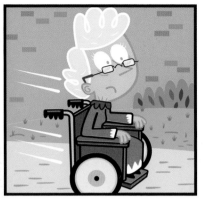

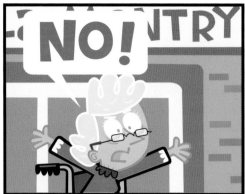

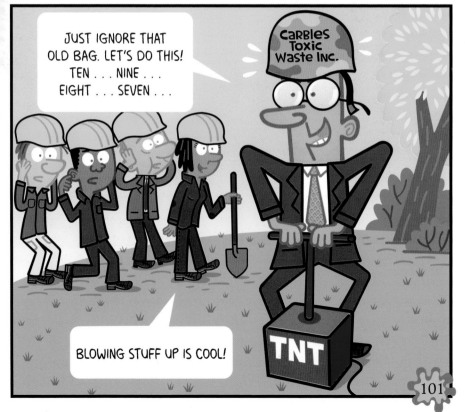

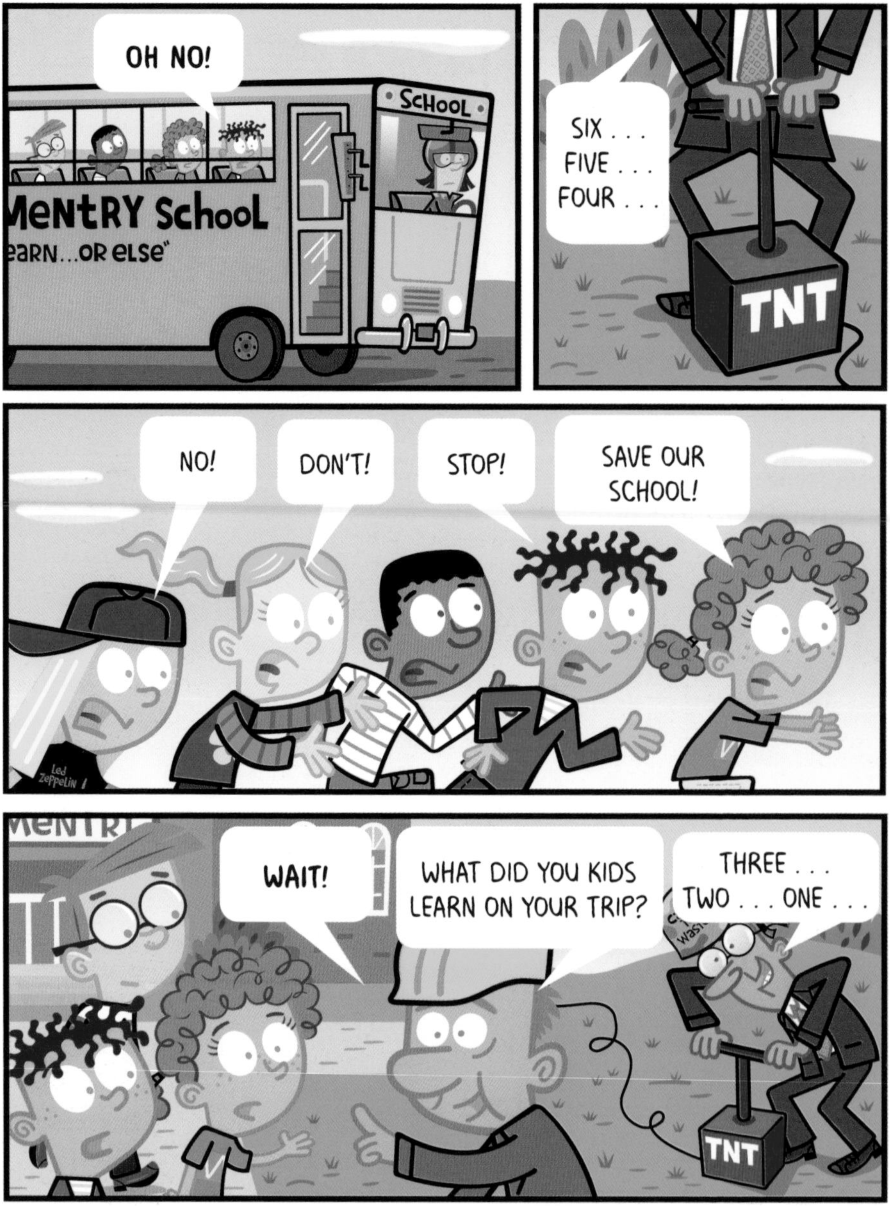
OH NO!
SCHOOL
MENTRY SCHOOL
EARN...OR ELSE"
SIX . . .
FIVE . . .
FOUR . . .
TNT
NO!
DON'T!
STOP!
SAVE OUR SCHOOL!
Led Zeppelin
WAIT!
WHAT DID YOU KIDS LEARN ON YOUR TRIP?
THREE . . . TWO . . . ONE . . .
TNT

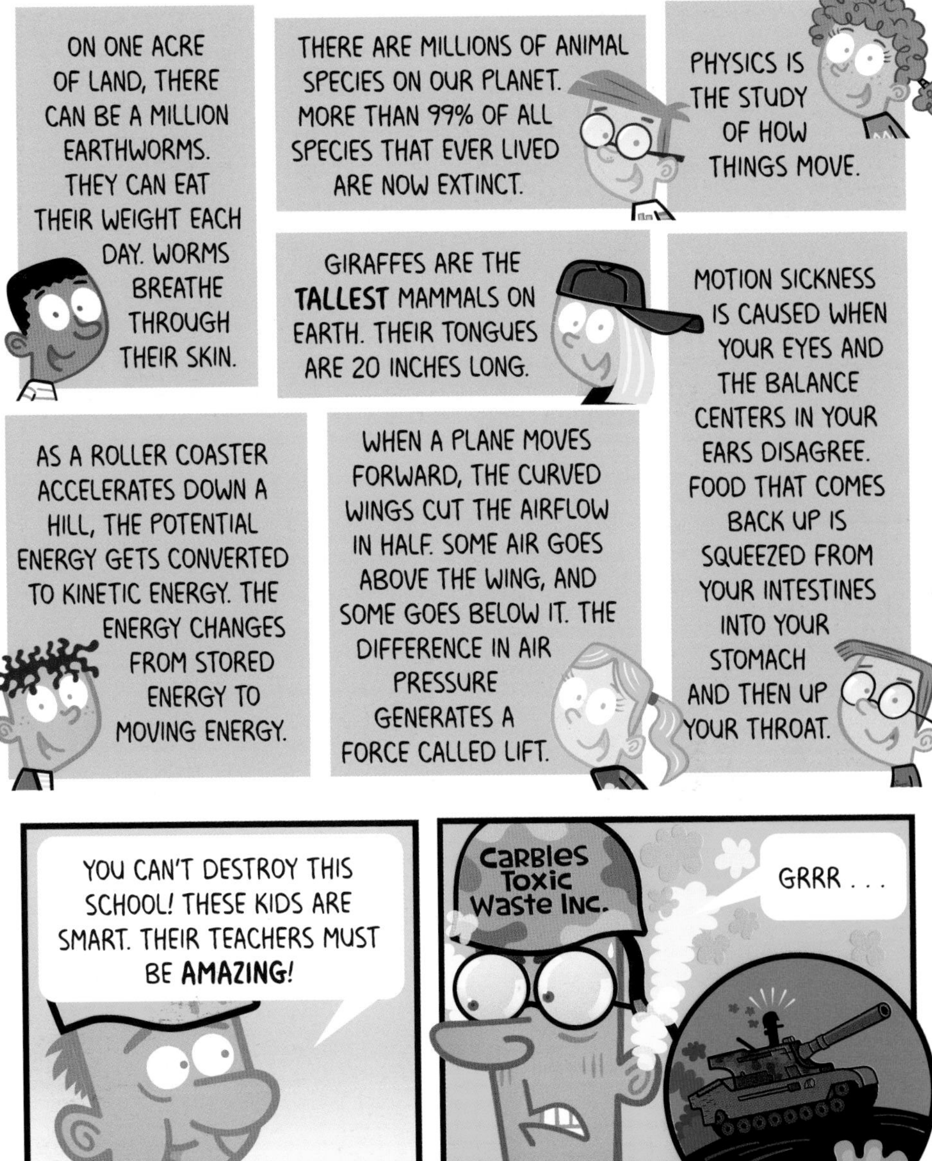
ON ONE ACRE OF LAND, THERE CAN BE A MILLION EARTHWORMS. THEY CAN EAT THEIR WEIGHT EACH DAY. WORMS BREATHE THROUGH THEIR SKIN.
THERE ARE MILLIONS OF ANIMAL SPECIES ON OUR PLANET. MORE THAN 99% OF ALL SPECIES THAT EVER LIVED ARE NOW EXTINCT.
PHYSICS IS THE STUDY OF HOW THINGS MOVE.
GIRAFFES ARE THE **TALLEST** MAMMALS ON EARTH. THEIR TONGUES ARE 20 INCHES LONG.
MOTION SICKNESS IS CAUSED WHEN YOUR EYES AND THE BALANCE CENTERS IN YOUR EARS DISAGREE. FOOD THAT COMES BACK UP IS SQUEEZED FROM YOUR INTESTINES INTO YOUR STOMACH AND THEN UP YOUR THROAT.
AS A ROLLER COASTER ACCELERATES DOWN A HILL, THE POTENTIAL ENERGY GETS CONVERTED TO KINETIC ENERGY. THE ENERGY CHANGES FROM STORED ENERGY TO MOVING ENERGY.
WHEN A PLANE MOVES FORWARD, THE CURVED WINGS CUT THE AIRFLOW IN HALF. SOME AIR GOES ABOVE THE WING, AND SOME GOES BELOW IT. THE DIFFERENCE IN AIR PRESSURE GENERATES A FORCE CALLED LIFT.
YOU CAN'T DESTROY THIS SCHOOL! THESE KIDS ARE SMART. THEIR TEACHERS MUST BE **AMAZING**!
Carbles Toxic Waste Inc.
GRRR . . .

AND SO THE CONFLICT IS OVER . . . FOR NOW. THANKS TO THE BRAVE LEADERSHIP OF MR. KLUTZ AND HIS SMALL BAND OF REBEL EDUCATORS AND STUDENTS, PEACE AND ORDER HAVE BEEN RESTORED. THE GREEDY AND RUTHLESS DR. CARBLES HAS BEEN EXILED TO THE FARTHEST CORNERS OF THE SCHOOL SYSTEM. HIS OBSESSION WITH DESTROYING ELLA MENTRY SCHOOL MAY HAVE BEEN TEMPORARILY INTERRUPTED, BUT THE MERCILESS DR. CARBLES LIVES ON TO FIGHT ANOTHER DAY. WHO KNOWS WHEN HE MIGHT RISE FROM THE ASHES, MORE DESPERATE THAN EVER, AND RETURN TO INFLICT PAIN AND TYRANNY ON ALL THOSE WHO STAND IN HIS WAY? HOW LONG WILL THE FORCES OF GOOD-NESS AND NICENESS BE ABLE TO RESIST THIS RELENTLESS ONSLAUGHT OF EVIL?

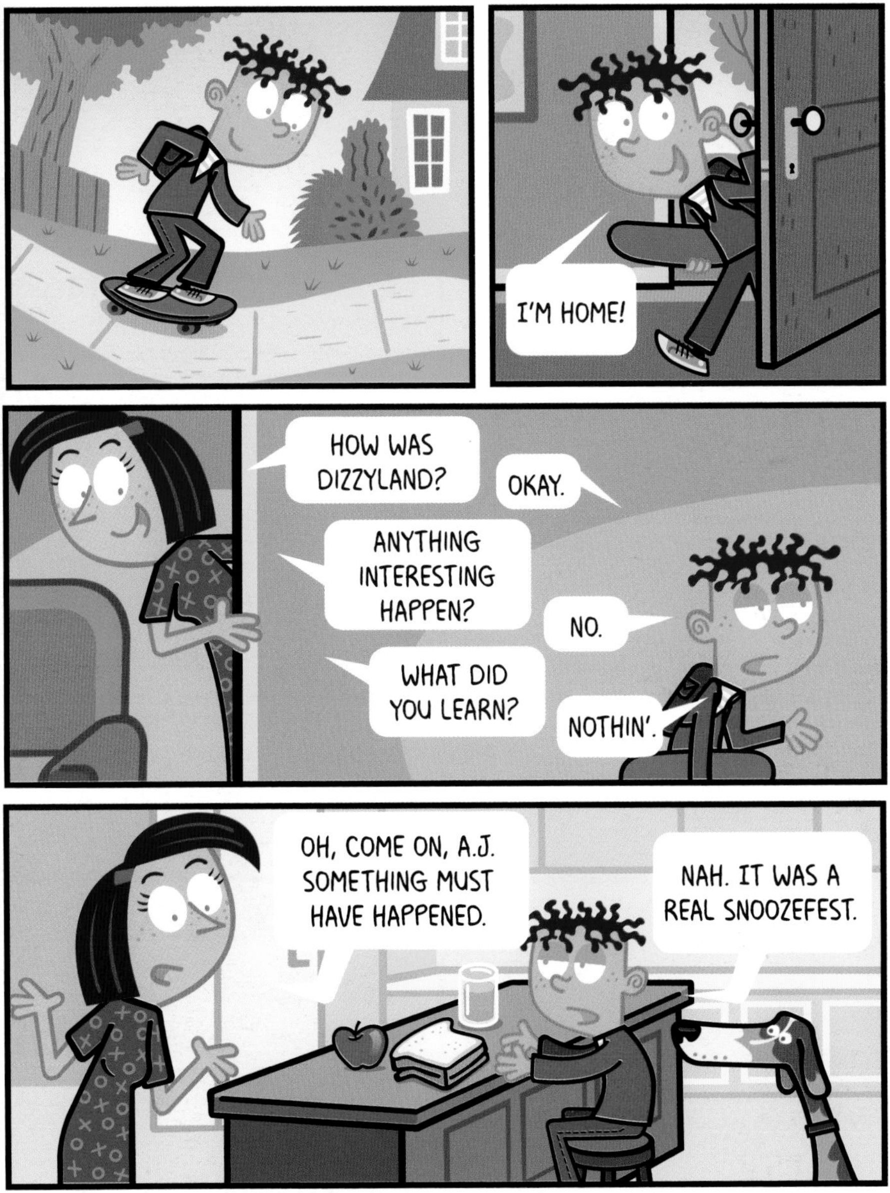
I'M HOME!
HOW WAS DIZZYLAND?
OKAY.
ANYTHING INTERESTING HAPPEN?
NO.
WHAT DID YOU LEARN?
NOTHIN'.
OH, COME ON, A.J. SOMETHING MUST HAVE HAPPENED.
NAH. IT WAS A REAL SNOOZEFEST.

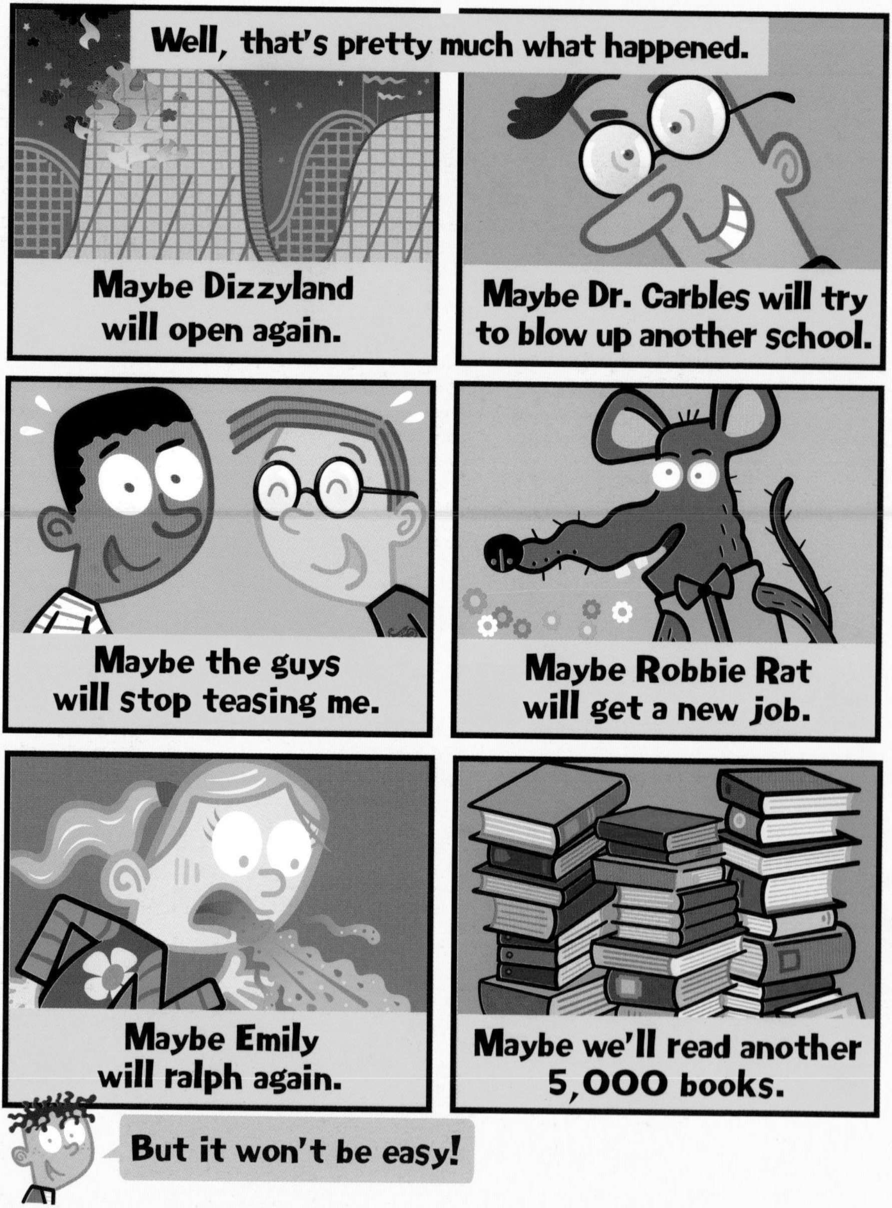
Well, that's pretty much what happened.
Maybe Dizzyland will open again.
Maybe Dr. Carbles will try to blow up another school.
Maybe the guys will stop teasing me.
Maybe Robbie Rat will get a new job.
Maybe Emily will ralph again.
Maybe we'll read another 5,000 books.
But it won't be easy!